SEPARATED BY TIME

BOOK THREE
OF THE THISTLE & HIVE SERIES

BY
JENNAE VALE

Acknowledgments

Thank you to my editor, Deb Williams - The Pedantic Punctuator, for all your help and for making the editing process a fun learning experience.

A big thank you also goes to Sheri McGathy, Covers by Sheri, for the beautiful cover design for Separated By Time.

I'd also like to thank Hannah Schwartz for helping me plot this story, it made the writing process so much easier.

Thanks to my family and friends for your support and encouragement throughout this process.

Chapter 1

A beautiful woman alone in the woods was the last thing he'd expected to find on his morning walk. The fact that he knew the woman, and she was hundreds of years away from where he'd last left her, was almost unbelievable. Almost, but not completely. Because as crazy as it seemed, he knew better than to doubt the possibility that Maggie MacKinnon stood before him looking as beautiful as he remembered.

"Hello, Dylan." Her voice sounded sweet to his ears. A coy smile danced across her lips.

"Is it really you?" He had to be sure he wasn't hallucinating. Maggie had become an obsession for him. He hadn't been able to get her out of his thoughts, not since he'd last seen her, five hundred years in the future. The day he left, he had kissed her soft, warm lips and vowed to himself that he'd be back for her. He'd regretted leaving her, every moment since. The fact that he'd only known Maggie for a few short days didn't matter. He'd known from the first moment he laid eyes on her, that this was the woman who he wanted to spend the rest of his life with. It would come as a shock to anyone who knew Dylan, and it was an even greater shock to himself, to discover he wanted to leave his perpetually uncommitted status behind - especially since he'd never truly been in love before. And now here he was, ready to give it all up for a woman he'd met only briefly at The Thistle & Hive Inn in Glendaloch.

"Of course 'tis me, you silly man. There arenae two of me," she teased. Her sweet Scottish accent danced in his ears.

The last person he'd expected to see on his daily walk was Maggie, and the impact of her sudden appearance found Dylan staring at her with a dumbfounded expression.

"Well, are ye going to greet me properly, or are ye going to stand there all starry-eyed?" she asked.

"I'm sorry. I'm just so surprised to see you." Dylan closed the distance between them and leaned in to kiss her cheek. She smelled of honeysuckle and roses, and her silky red hair caressed his face softly as he lingered there for just a moment, his hand resting gently on her arm. He took her hand and smiling brightly, tried to clear his head of the cobwebs making it hard to think. "Did you walk here on your own?" he asked, looking around to see if anyone had accompanied her. He couldn't believe her aunt and uncle would allow her to travel here alone.

"No, of course not. I mean, I came on my own, but I certainly didnae walk here." She made a funny face and rolled her eyes at him.

"Oh, I see. Witchcraft?" he asked. She *was* a witch, so it only made sense.

"You could say that." Maggie seemed quite pleased with herself, a satisfied smile on her face.

"Well it doesn't matter, because I'm excited to see you." Dylan wasn't certain he should let her know just how happy he really was. Would that scare her away? He didn't know her particularly well and he wasn't very good at this kind of thing. He was more of a 'love 'em and leave 'em kind of guy. Maggie was the first woman he'd met who piqued his curiosity enough that he had actually cared about seeing her again. A redheaded beauty with sparkling green eyes, she was dressed in a simple green gown and wore a brown velvet cape and hood. She truly was a sight for sore eyes. "We should get you back to the castle," he said, his eyes never leaving hers. "Chester," he called to his dog. The big black Rottweiler came charging through the trees, tongue lolling from the side of his mouth, and stopped right in front of Dylan. "Look who I found, boy," Dylan announced.

"Hello, Chester," Maggie said.

The dog turned and approached Maggie cautiously. He appeared confused, which Dylan found surprising. Chester generally displayed one of two reactions to people - he knocked them over in excitement, or he growled with his hackles raised. There really wasn't any middle ground. At least there hadn't been, not until this very moment. Chester sniffed Maggie's outstretched hand and whimpered slightly, backing away.

"That's strange," Dylan observed. "I've never seen him do that before."

"Mayhap he doesnae recognize me," Maggie offered.

"Yeah, that's probably it. You're out of context." The last time Chester had seen Maggie was back in twenty-first century Glendaloch, where Dylan and his cousin Jenna had arrived to speak with Edna about sending them both back to the sixteenth century so that Jenna could be reunited with Cormac, the love of her life. Upon arriving at the inn, they met Maggie, and Dylan was smitten right from the start. Much to his surprise, Chester was practically hiding behind Dylan now. "Come on, Chester. It's just Maggie. Nothing to be afraid of." Dylan had to admit, he was concerned by the dog's reaction.

"Maybe it's the magick," Maggie offered. "Perhaps he can smell it."

"Oh, yeah. I didn't think of that. Of course, that must be it." Dylan was still smiling brightly. "Shall we?" Maggie took his arm and he led her along the path, back through the woods. It wasn't a long walk, but they had been sheltered by the trees and once they were out in the open, the castle became visible, looming large over the valley. They passed the small crofts that dotted the landscape leading to the gates and Dylan and Chester exchanged greetings with those who were outside, tending their plots.

"This is lovely," Maggie observed. "Have ye been enjoying yer stay here, Dylan?"

Dylan stopped and surveyed the castle and the area around them. "I have. I wasn't sure what to expect at first, but everyone has been so welcoming and I feel right at home here."

"I suppose you've been learning to be a fine warrior," Maggie stated, blatantly admiring his muscular physique. She ran a hand up his arm, settling her fingers on a flexed bicep.

"Learning… yes, but I'm a long way from being a fine warrior."

"I doubt that. A big, braw man like yerself is sure to be good at everything he does." He didn't remember Maggie being such a flirt, but then again, he was certain there were plenty of things he didn't know about her.

"Thanks," Dylan said. He was feeling awkward with Maggie, which surprised him and had him off-kilter. When he had spent time with her in Glendaloch, it had been anything but awkward. On the contrary, their relationship had been easy and natural. They'd enjoyed an instant connection and gotten along like kindred spirits. That was one of the reasons she'd been on his mind so much. They had talked for hours and even in their silent moments, he had felt a deep bond with her. Where was that feeling? Had he been wrong about her? Maybe it wasn't as he remembered it at all. Maybe he was romanticizing the whole thing. Dylan was disappointed and mentally shook himself. Of course it was going to be odd to meet up with Maggie again. *You haven't seen her in weeks. Give it time,* he told himself.

They walked through the gates and into the hustle and bustle of the inner courtyard. Out of the corner of his eye, Dylan watched carefully for Maggie's reaction, but she showed no response. She didn't seem in the least bit fazed by the medieval surroundings. She certainly wasn't behaving like someone who'd just found themselves in a different century. Instead, she looked very comfortable. *Odd,* he thought. "Maggie, have you been here before?" he asked.

Before she could respond, Cormac's voice boomed from the stables. "Dylan, there ye be! I've been searching for ye everywhere."

"I was out walking with Chester and I came across an old friend." Dylan gestured towards Maggie.

"Good day to ye, lass," Cormac said. "Where have ye come to us from?"

"This is Maggie. She's Edna's niece," Dylan said, by way of introduction.

"Edna's niece! Well 'tis pleased I am to meet ye," Cormac said. If Cormac thought it odd that Maggie had arrived from twenty first century Glendaloch, he certainly didn't reveal it.

"My pleasure," Maggie said.

"This is Jenna's husband, Cormac," Dylan explained.

Maggie simply nodded her head and smiled, looking bored and uninterested.

"Did you need me for something, Cormac?" Dylan asked.

"'Tis not important, I can see that yer busy. I'll find Cailin," Cormac said. "I'll see ye later, then." Cormac walked away and left Dylan and Maggie in the middle of the courtyard.

"Shall we go in?" Dylan headed for the large wooden castle doors and Maggie followed along behind. Chester ran off after Cormac.

"Chester loves him. He never misses an opportunity to spend time with Cormac. I'm a little jealous," Dylan joked. Maggie didn't reply and Dylan frowned. He didn't remember her being this quiet. On the contrary, she had been quite talkative back at the inn.

As they walked towards the castle doors, Dylan smiled and nodded at a number of women who eyed him as they passed. He had been a big hit with the women of Breaghacraig, who not only found him attractive, but also considered him interesting because he was so different from the men they usually met. Dylan took it all in stride and while he was happy to flirt with them, in the back of his mind he always knew Maggie was the only woman he wanted.

Entering the silent castle, no one seemed to be in the great hall and Dylan wasn't sure where everyone might be. Under normal circumstances, he would have been happy to be alone with Maggie, but he was uncomfortable and uncertain with her.

"I'm sure someone will be along shortly. Let's sit here for a while and catch up with each other," Dylan said, as he led Maggie towards the chairs near the fireplace.

Maggie sat and glanced around the room. "So, this is the home of the MacKenzies," she observed.

"Yes. It is. Robert is the Laird of the clan and his wife, Irene is sister to Cormac, who you just met. They have another brother, Cailin. I'm sure Edna told you all about them."

"Hmmm…"

Dylan wasn't sure what that response was all about, but Maggie seemed more intent on memorizing the layout of the hall and uninterested in him or what he was saying. He was disappointed by her reaction and disappointed that the spark he had experienced in Glendaloch seemed to be missing. In fact, it bothered him a great deal. There was definitely something different about Maggie now, but what was it?

The doors opened and Jenna and Irene made their way into the hall. Jenna hesitated just a moment, doing a double take as she looked at Maggie. "Maggie, is that really you?"

"That seems to be the question of the day," Maggie replied.

"I can't believe it. Where did you come from?" Jenna asked.

"And that is the other question of the day," Maggie teased. "I'm here to see Dylan."

"I'll bet he's happy to see you," Jenna said. She reached Maggie and pulled her into a hug, raising an eyebrow in Dylan's direction. Maggie appeared stiff and ill at ease with the show of affection, and didn't respond to Jenna's embrace.

After spending some awkward moments with Maggie, Dylan was relieved to see his cousin, but he was almost certain that Maggie didn't recognize Jenna. Something about her demeanor was definitely off. By the look in Jenna's eyes, she seemed to be aware of it, too.

"You do remember me, don't you," Jenna asked.

"Of course I do. I'm just nae verra good with names," Maggie replied. Dylan got the distinct impression she was lying, but maybe he was jumping to conclusions. Since he hadn't known her very long, it was completely possible that she really wasn't good with names.

"Jenna. I'm Jenna," she said, sounding confused. "Oh, and this is Irene."

"I'm pleased to meet ye, Maggie. Welcome to Breaghacraig," Irene said, and by the slight frown on her brow, she was picking up on Jenna's confusion.

"Thank you and it's nice to meet ye as well," Maggie replied.

The atmosphere in the Great Hall was a little icy as the women eyed each other warily. After a moment, Maggie's dismissive attitude became apparent and she very clearly began to ignore Jenna and Irene. She behaved as if nothing unusual was happening, and appeared completely unfazed by her interaction with them. In fact, she didn't seem affected by much at all, to this point. It was as if she was physically in the room with them, but mentally somewhere else. Dylan noted her facial expression hadn't changed at all. Not out in the courtyard and not here in the great hall. This definitely wasn't the Maggie Dylan had remembered. That Maggie had been warm and engaging back in Glendaloch, but here she was standoffish and cool, based on her reaction to Jenna's hug. The Maggie he had known had been full of questions - a naturally curious person. Dylan liked that about her, because he had a similar personality. He was a geeky surfer to his friends back home, but not everyone thought of him that way. He had that laid-back California attitude, sun-streaked golden locks and a ready smile. Those were all things the ladies loved and up until this point, he had loved every lady he'd had a chance to be with. He'd never really cared too much about whether he was compatible with them or not. When he met Maggie, everything had changed and Dylan knew he'd found the girl he didn't know he'd been searching for.

"How long will ye be staying with us, Maggie?" Irene asked.

"Oh, I'm nae sure. I thought I'd just see how things go, if that's alright?"

Another odd response, Dylan thought. They were gradually adding up, but unfortunately, he didn't know what the answer to the equation might be.

"Our home is yer home. Stay as long as ye like," Irene responded. "I hope ye won't mind sleeping in the women's solar, Maggie. All of the bed chambers in the castle have been spoken for."

Dylan exchanged a questioning look with Jenna, who shrugged her shoulders in response. Obviously, she couldn't figure out this new and unusual Maggie either. "Irene, she can have my room. I'll sleep in the soldier's quarters," Dylan announced.

"Well, if yer sure ye dinnae mind, would ye show Maggie to her chambers?" Irene smiled sweetly at Dylan. She had become like a big sister to him, since his arrival at the castle. She was a lot like Jenna in many ways and Dylan had been comfortable with her right from the very beginning. She ran the castle like a well-oiled machine, which was saying a lot considering the size of the place and the number of people employed in feeding, clothing and protecting Breaghacraig. Irene had a hand in it all and she commanded the respect of everyone with whom she came in contact. Her partnership with her husband was based on love, mutual understanding and respect. Their children were very well behaved and even though they could be seen getting into mischief occasionally, Dylan knew that the mere sound of their mother's voice set them back on the right track immediately.

"Irene, we should get going," Jenna said. "Mary's waiting for us in the kitchen."

"Yer right, Jenna. Dylan, Maggie, we'll see ye at the evening meal." Irene hooked arms with Jenna and the two women departed, heads close in whispered conversation, leaving Dylan alone once again with Maggie.

"Well, I guess I should show you to your room, and then I'll take you on a tour of the castle, if you'd like." Dylan took Maggie's hand and led her from the great hall and upstairs to the bedchambers, all the while waiting for her to do or say something which would remind him of the girl he'd left behind in Glendaloch.

Chapter 2

"Auntie Edna, is everything okay?" Maggie asked.

Edna seemed to be in one of her trances as she stared into the flames of the fireplace.

"She's seeing something," Angus offered, concern in his voice. "Edna?"

"Aye. I'm fine, but there's trouble brewing at Breaghacraig. Maggie, my girl, you'll be needed there." She turned away from the fire and faced Maggie.

"Me? You want *me* to go to Breaghacraig?" Maggie asked incredulously. "You want me to time travel?" She wondered if she'd heard that correctly. Wasn't Edna the one that was needed there?

"This is something that only you can fix, my dear."

"Edna, you can't really be thinking of sending Maggie back in time by herself," Angus stated.

"Aye. That is exactly what I'm thinking. Let me explain my vision." Edna slumped heavily into a nearby chair, as if she had the weight of the world on her shoulders. "It seems that our friend, Sir Richard is up to his old tricks once again. Every time I think we're rid of him for good, he reappears. He's much like a bad penny that way. This time he's in league with a very powerful witch back in his own time. They, of course, are plotting and planning to take down the MacKenzies and this time he plans to use magick, not men, to accomplish his goals. The problem, my dear Maggie, is that this particular witch has worked her magick and is pretending to be you."

Maggie gasped. "Are you sure, Auntie? How does she know what I look like and what I sound like?"

"Aye, I'm sure. I'm not the only one with the sight. She's been watching you and learning all about you." Maggie shuddered at the thought. "She has her sights set on Dylan and is using your relationship with him to gain his trust and the trust of the MacKenzies."

"Oh, my. What can I possibly do to stop her? There's still so much that I don't know. How can I be expected to go up against a powerful witch?" Maggie fidgeted nervously, alternately wringing her hands and twirling anxious fingers through her hair.

"We'll do our best to prepare ye, but I have no doubt that ye can do this. I wouldnae send ye otherwise." Edna took hold of Maggie's hands. "You're going to knot that hair up good, my dear. Ye'd best stop."

Maggie couldn't believe she was the only one who could stop this witch, but she certainly didn't want anything bad to happen to Dylan. She had been hoping Edna would allow her to go back in time at some point soon, so she could see Dylan again. There had been a spark between them and she wanted to explore it. She had never imagined her visit would be anything more than for the fun of it. Now she was expected to hone her skills as a witch and save Breaghacraig, the MacKenzies *and* Dylan? Her stomach was doing somersaults as she thought of all the things that could go wrong if she failed. "I'm not so sure I'm the best person to send. What if I can't do it? What if she's too powerful for me?"

"She's right, Edna. I think ye go too far this time. Ye cannae send Maggie." Angus looked quite angry as he paced in front of the fire.

"I understand how ye feel, Angus. And ye as well, Maggie, but I know what I saw and I also know Maggie is the only one who can stop this." Edna took hold of Maggie's chin. "Maggie, yer a much more powerful witch than ye ken. Ye're even more powerful than me. I have every faith in yer abilities. You can do this."

Maggie found that hard to believe, and hesitating for just a moment she gathered what little confidence she felt and said, "I'll go."

"I'm going with her then," Angus announced firmly.

Fear had rendered Maggie speechless. Her brain conjured images of the evil witches she recalled from fairy tales. *This can't be happening. But Dylan needs me. I can't let any harm come to him, or to any of the others. If Auntie thinks I must go, then I don't see that I have a choice.*

"Maggie, would ye feel better about this if I sent Angus along with you?" Edna asked.

"I don't know. I imagine it would help, but do ye really want to come with me Uncle?" Maggie asked, holding her breath as she waited for his answer.

"Aye, love, I most certainly do wish to accompany ye. 'Tis been a long time since I've seen me own century and I'm thinking now is as good a time as any to do so. It's been ages since I've had to fight for anything. I believe I'll enjoy meself. And I'll get to see me little girl, Arlena, once again." Angus glanced lovingly at Edna, who as always, appeared to be a little melancholy at the mention of her daughter's name.

"Okay, then, I'll do it." Maggie said. *I only hope I won't regret this,* she thought.

"That's my girl," Edna said, rubbing Maggie's back soothingly. "We've a lot of work to do before ye can leave, but I think ye're up to the challenge. I'll teach ye some spells that will come in handy and we'll disguise yer appearance, so ye'll have that little trick up yer sleeve. Angus will work with ye on using weapons and before ye know it, ye'll not only be a skilled warrior, but ye'll be a powerful witch. A powerful good witch who can repel the dark magic of this evil harridan."

"When do we start?" Maggie asked, thinking there couldn't possibly be enough time for her to master everything Edna needed to teach her.

"I think first thing in the morning will be soon enough," Edna answered.

"What's her name, Auntie?" Maggie questioned.

"It's Brielle," Edna said.

"Do ye know her?" Angus asked.

"Aye, I do. I've met her once, a long, long time ago. I've not seen her since."

"Is she from this time, or does she belong in the past?" Maggie had so many questions, she didn't really know where to start.

"She is from the past, but she has her own relationship with our bridge and the time travel. That is how we met. Many years ago she tried to cross the bridge and I wouldnae allow it. She has held a grudge against me ever since. She does not normally seek out trouble, but she has a mischievous side that enjoys creating it. Richard has taken advantage of that and has asked her to help him in his quest to rid the world of the MacKenzie clan."

Maggie didn't understand the whole 'Richard vs. the MacKenzie clan' dynamic. She had heard all the stories about Lady Irene and what happened to Ashley, but why did he persist in wanting to destroy them? Why didn't he just move on with his life and forget about them?

"Until Richard finds someone new to love, he'll continue down this path," Edna explained, apparently reading Maggie's mind.

"If he would just open his eyes and see that the world is full of possibilities to find love, maybe he'd give up this nonsensical vendetta." Maggie responded, thinking about Dylan. She was positive he was her possibility. She wouldn't let anything come in the way of that, especially not a conniving witch.

"I'd have to agree with ye. But Richard has to come to that conclusion on his own, my dear."

"Couldn't Brielle make him love her?" Maggie hoped that if Brielle and Richard had a love connection, Brielle would leave Dylan alone.

Edna laughed out loud. "Brielle is not interested in love and believe me if Richard has seen the real Brielle, he's not interested either.

No, she gets immense satisfaction out of creating a whirlwind of trouble and then walking away and into the lives of her next victims."

"I don't like the sounds of that," Maggie uttered. "I have to fix this."

Edna smiled softly at Maggie. "That's my girl. Ye work on Brielle and I'll work on Richard. I believe with a little magical intervention, I can make him see the error of his ways."

"Are ye sure yer telling us all of it," Angus asked. He sounded skeptical.

"Of course not, love. I've told ye all ye need to know." Putting her arm around Maggie's waist, Edna walked with her to the dining room to set up for their evening diners. As they left, Maggie glanced back to see Angus shaking his head in apparent disbelief as he prepared to man the front desk.

* * *

The next morning Maggie began her training, bright and early. She started with Edna, who taught her the basics - or Witchcraft 101, as Edna liked to call it. Maggie learned how to create fire out of thin air. Of course, she already knew how to create a fire in the hearth, but she always had fuel to work with in those instances. This fire was definitely different, but she could see it would be useful to understand how and when to use it. She also learned how to levitate items and move them from one spot to the other. She was a quick study and Edna seemed pleased with her progress. It only took a few tries for her to master the magick Edna was showing her. They worked well past lunch, which Maggie's grumbling stomach could attest to, but knowing how important it was for her to be armed with a thorough knowledge of witchcraft, she ignored it.

Maggie had known she was a witch from an early age. Her mother had tried to steer her away from it, but Aunt Edna insisted it was her duty, as a member of the MacKinnon family, to learn to use her skills for the good of those around her. Ellen, Maggie's mother, had not been verra happy about this pronouncement and she had moved her family to a nearby village and opened a teashop, in the hopes of keeping Maggie away from any witchcraft. Try as she might, Ellen couldn't dissuade Maggie from what she had begun to see as her destiny. Any chance she got, Maggie would visit with Edna, wanting more than anything, to follow in her footsteps.

In deference to her sister, Edna hadn't given Maggie any training during that time. She hadn't wanted to upset Ellen, so instead, she had merely given Maggie a glimpse into her world, showing her what she could do, but not how to do it.

When Maggie had tired of working at her parents' teashop, she had come to live at the inn, with the hopes of becoming a full-fledged witch like her aunt. Up until today, she had only learned how to run the inn, not how to cast a spell. She was excited; finally, she was learning the one thing that had fascinated her for as long as she could remember.

"Now, Maggie, I'd like to teach ye some things that will help protect yerself and those around ye from any spells Brielle may cast."

Maggie thought that would be most useful, although she secretly hoped she would never need it. Maybe Brielle would go away and leave everyone be, before she even got there. Then she could spend all her time with Dylan. That sounded a whole lot better than fighting Brielle.

"Maggie, are ye paying attention?" Edna raised her voice and woke Maggie from her daydream about Dylan.

"Aye. I am. Yer about to teach me a spell of protection."

The lessons went on for the rest of that day and into the next. Edna gave Maggie a book of spells, to read and memorize. Maggie was exhausted both mentally and physically, and she still had her lessons with Angus coming up, but she had progressed way beyond Witchcraft 101. Maggie liked to think of it as a college course, one that she was passing with flying colors. One thing was definite, she was going to need a good night's sleep before tomorrow's lessons with Angus.

* * *

"Alright, my dear, I've set up a course, which we will work our way through. Once ye've mastered one thing, we'll move on to the next. How does that sound?" Angus seemed quite excited to get started. He had prepared the back garden with hay bales, scarecrows, used tires and wooden poles. "Edna has provided ye with a sword, a dirk and a bow - charmed fer yer protection, but we'll start off with practice equipment, so that neither one of us ends up being injured."

Maggie was overwhelmed at the thought of learning to fight. It must have shown on her face because Angus commented, "Don't be frightened, Maggie. I'm a good teacher and when we're done, I'll be able to trust ye with me life. Now let's get started."

Angus started with the basics. He showed her the correct stance and position, how to hold the sword and a lot of things she should not do. Maggie's head was full to bursting, but she wanted to learn and that was half the battle.

"Very good, Maggie. I think yer ready for yer first practice fight." Angus smiled reassuringly as he took his stance opposite her. "Remember, keep yer distance. Ye dinnae wish to be too close to yer opponent. Yer not strong enough to get into a wrestling match just yet."

Maggie waited in her stance, holding the sword the way Angus had shown her. "'Tis important to aim fer the weapon, not yer opponent. Ye leave yerself open to their sword if ye do so." She took a few practice swings with the sword, which felt incredibly awkward in her hands. In fact, everything she did seemed off. "Keep at it, Maggie. Ye'll get more comfortable the longer we do this." Maggie took a wide swing and the sword went flying out of her grasp. Angus ducked just in time, and the sword flew over his head, landing in one of Edna's prize rose bushes.

"Sorry, Uncle Angus," Maggie said, feeling about two inches tall for making such a rookie mistake.

"Well, 'tis one way to decapitate yer opponent, but not the best way. When ye swing wide like that, ye leave yerself an open target. What I'd like ye to do is concentrate on deflecting my assault. If yer focus is solely on attacking, ye fall prey to injury, or worse. Always keep the correct distance. When I come at ye - ye need to back up. Think of it like a dance. Follow my steps while backing away, do ye ken?"

Maggie nodded her head and they practiced for a while. At first, she found herself stumbling over her own two feet, but eventually her confidence began to build and her feet no longer got in the way.

"I think ye've got it. Now we need to work on yer speed and once ye've mastered the art of stopping yer opponent, we'll work on stopping them and striking at the same time."

Maggie was panting from her efforts. This was hard work and she wasn't sure she'd ever be good at it. "Uncle, could we take a break for now?"

"Of course, Maggie. Go see yer Auntie. She'll feed ye and give ye something to drink. I'll be along shortly." With a reassuring pat on her shoulder, Angus sent Maggie on her way.

* * *

Lunch had been prepared and set out in the dining room. "Ah, there ye be, Maggie. Pour yerself some tea." Maggie began to lift the pot with her hand, but Edna shook her head. "Not that way, dear. Use yer magick." Maggie concentrated and levitated the pot, pouring herself a perfect cup of tea, every drop going into the cup.

Edna applauded. "I'm so proud of ye, Maggie. How did your lesson go with Uncle Angus?"

"I feel like a fish out of water, Auntie." Maggie took a sip of her tea and then bit into her sandwich, swallowing down a mouthful. "Do ye really believe I can do this?"

"Aye. I do. I believe yer the only one who can." Edna sat opposite Maggie, watching her eat.

"Why are ye nae going to Breaghacraig yerself?" Maggie wondered aloud.

"As ye ken, I must stay here and see that ye have safe passage across the bridge and then back again."

"True. I guess I forgot about that," Maggie said with a smile. She finished her food and then settled back in her seat for a few minutes of rest. She desperately wanted to go upstairs and take a nap, but knew that wouldn't be possible. She had far too much to learn and no doubt, Uncle Angus awaited her outside for another round.

Chapter 3

After days of preparation and practice, the time had finally arrived for Maggie and Angus to begin their journey. To suggest Maggie was nervous would be an understatement. She was anxious, apprehensive and terrified of what might lie ahead. The one bright spot in all of this, was that she'd have an opportunity to be with Dylan again and she couldn't wait to see him. She smiled as she remembered his curly blonde locks, always in disarray, how soft they'd been entwined around her fingers. He had been so easy to talk to and so much fun, not to mention the most handsome man she'd ever set eyes on. Maggie had never met anyone like him and she'd known instantly he was the man for her. As she stood in the lobby waiting for Angus, she released an audible sigh.

"Are ye alright, Maggie?" Edna asked, concern in her voice.

"Aye, Auntie. The thought of what awaits me on the other side of the bridge is a bit overwhelming, but I'm prepared. Both ye and Uncle have seen to it." Maggie fidgeted with her hair, something she always did when she was nervous.

Edna grabbed her hand. "Enough, my darlin' girl. Leave yer hair be."

Maggie laughed at herself. "Bad habit," she replied clasping her hands together.

"We've one last thing to do before ye go, lass," Edna explained. "As I mentioned to ye before, ye cannot go as yerself, so ye need a disguise."

"Disguise!" Maggie had been imagining herself dressed in a beautiful medieval gown, with a hooded cape, which she'd draw forward to cover her face. She would be very mysterious, like the heroines in the books she loved to read. "But Auntie, how will Dylan know it's me?"

"It will be for the best if he doesnae know it's you, initially." Maggie began to protest, but Edna held up a finger to stop her. "When the time comes, Dylan will look into yer eyes and know the truth, but until then you shall be Alec, a companion to yer Uncle Angus. Now stand still, while I work on yer appearance."

Maggie did as her Aunt requested and while she couldn't see anything happening, she could certainly feel it. Edna was waving her arms to and fro, almost as if she was conducting an orchestra, and with each movement of Edna's hands, Maggie was pulled and tugged, as little gusts of air blew past her and around her. "'Tis finished," Edna finally announced. "And I've done a fine job of transforming ye into a lad. Look fer yerself."

Maggie hurried across to the mirror behind the front desk. She gasped when she saw her dirt-covered face and less than flattering clothes. She turned her astonishment on Edna, not entirely certain whether she wanted to laugh or cry. She was so shocked she couldn't speak. This was most definitely not what she wanted to look like, not to see Dylan again. "Auntie, I don't know…"

"Don't worry, dear, I've cast a spell that will cause those who see ye to believe ye are a lad and a stranger to them." Edna made a few small adjustments to Maggie's new look and then stood back to admire her work.

Maggie turned back to the mirror. She was wearing brown trewes and a saffron liene. Over the shirt and pants was a voluminous brown cape, the hood of which, along with a cap hid her lustrous red locks.

"If I didn't know it was me I was looking at, I'd wonder who this lad was," Maggie giggled, finally coming to terms with her new *look*. "'Tis a fine costume."

"I've equipped ye with the very best sword, knives and bow. I feel confident ye'll know how to use them, should the need arise. Yer uncle will look after ye and protect ye to the best of his ability. There will be some things, though, that he'll not be able to defend against."

"Ye mean the witch, Brielle," Maggie stated.

"Aye. Brielle." Edna seemed especially sober as she repeated the witch's name, which gave Maggie a distinctly uneasy feeling.

The sound of horses' hooves approaching and coming to a halt in front of the inn caught their attention.

"Shall we?" Edna escorted Maggie outside where Angus sat astride an enormous bay horse with a black mane and tail. Alongside him stood a petite blue roan mare, perfectly sized for Maggie to ride.

"Look at ye lass. I mean lad," Angus chuckled. "I hardly recognize ye."

Maggie rolled her eyes at Angus and followed the uncharacteristic reaction with a bright smile, to let him know she wasn't offended by his comment. "Goodbye, Auntie," Maggie said, turning to Edna.

Edna gathered Maggie in her arms and hugged her tightly. "All will be well, Maggie. Dinnae fear. I love ye."

"And I love ye," Maggie responded, kissing Edna's cheek.

"Do ye need help mounting yer horse, *Alec*?" Angus questioned. It was obvious he was having far too much fun teasing her and Maggie wondered how long it would continue before he tired of the game.

"Nae, Uncle. I can do it meself. How would it look if ye had to assist me every time I needed to do some manly thing?" Maggie questioned, with a touch of sarcasm. She turned to Edna, gave her aunt one last big hug and another kiss goodbye and then mounted her horse. She glanced towards Angus with a 'see-I-told-you-I-didn't-need-any-help' look of triumph on her face. "What's her name?" Maggie asked.

"Blue, of course," Angus responded, as he effortlessly dismounted and wrapped Edna in a warm embrace. "I love ye, my sweet," he said as he kissed her forehead. "We've nae been apart since we first met. 'Twill nae be an easy thing to do - leaving ye here."

"I ken it, my love. Come back to me safely. Protect each other and if ye need me, I am here." Tears formed in both Edna's and Angus' eyes and Maggie herself choked up as she watched. Angus bent low and lifting Edna's chin with his fingertips, placed a gentle kiss on her lips. It seemed neither of them wanted it to end. Maggie couldn't help but think of Dylan and hoped she'd found a love like the one her aunt and uncle shared. She'd know soon enough and the anticipation of seeing Dylan had her anxious to get started.

Angus reluctantly let go of Edna and remounted his horse. "Shall we go, Archie?" he said to his equine companion. They both turned their horses and headed away from the village and towards the bridge that would take them back to the year 1514 - and a less than certain outcome to the confrontation they were heading towards.

* * *

Approaching the bridge, Angus and Maggie noticed a thick, swirling fog bank which had descended over the bridge, leaving it barely visible to them.

"I believe we're to go through the fog," Angus stated. He nodded to Maggie and she nudged her horse, forward into the grey abyss. "Hold onto me hand, Maggie, and don't let go until we reach the other side."

Maggie inched Blue closer to Angus and held out her hand, which Angus grasped. They slowly made their way into the fog, unable to see even each other. Maggie could feel her horse shaking and quivering with fear beneath her. She laid a comforting hand along Blue's neck. Bright lights flashed around them as they moved further into the mass of grey. And then, in a flash, it was completely gone and they were being greeted by a handsome, dark-haired man astride a horse that looked very much like the one Angus rode.

"Ye must be Angus. Welcome! I be Ewan, yer son-in-law, sir." Ewan extended his arm towards Angus.

"Thank ye for awaiting our arrival," Angus said. "I'm verra happy to finally meet ye." He pulled his horse up alongside Ewan's and reached out to clasp his hand. "And where is my daughter, Ewan?" Angus asked as he glanced around searching for Lena.

"Lena is back at home with the boys. We'll all join ye at Breaghac-raig once this business with Sir Richard and the witch is taken care of. I'm here to travel with ye to yer campsite for the night."

Maggie noted the look of disappointment on Angus' face. He had been looking forward to seeing Lena and his grandsons sooner rather than later.

"When ye return home, tell them that I'm anxious to see them." Angus sat a little taller in his saddle, obviously putting on a brave face.

Maggie searched her surroundings for any sign that they were ac-tually in a different time period, but nothing about the forested area they stood in gave even a hint of the past, present or future. She found herself looking forward to seeing the castle with her own eyes and meeting the people she'd heard so much about.

"And who is this lad ye've brought with ye?" Ewan questioned with a knowing grin. "I was expecting ye to be travelling with anoth-er."

"This be Alec. He's along to give me assistance." Angus winked at Maggie and she nodded in acknowledgement.

"If Edna hadnae told us who ye be," Ewan stated, "I'd truly take ye to be a lad. Maggie, isn't it?"

"Aye. Maggie it was, but from now on I'm Alec." Maggie experi-mented with deepening her voice to complete her disguise. The two men chuckled at her awkward attempt.

"Well, Alec and Angus, shall we get started? I will camp with ye tonight and I'll see ye on yer way in the morn, before I head back home." Ewan turned his horse to lead them away from the bridge.

"Camp?" Maggie repeated. She'd never been camping before. This was truly going to be an adventure.

'Aye. We'll nae want to travel in the dark, so ye'll have nae choice. We'll make it quite far before the sun sets," Ewan explained.

"Alright. We should get going then." Maggie took one last look back at the bridge they had crossed only moments before, and taking a deep breath, nudged Blue into a trot beside her uncle and Ewan.

Maggie did her best to relax and enjoy the scenery, but the weather was getting colder and the dampness was seeping into her bones. The end of October was near and with the change of months, would come even colder temperatures. She didn't know how she was going to stay warm in this strange world. Her toes were already numb from the cold and she wasn't certain she'd be able to uncurl her fingers from the reins she held so tightly.

After hours of riding, they arrived in a small clearing, hidden amidst the trees. This was to be their campsite, Ewan explained. Angus and Ewan set about making a fire and once it was blazing, Maggie sat as close to it as she safely could manage. Once her teeth stopped chattering and her toes were no longer tiny ice cubes, she asked, "Can I help ye with anything?"

"Nae," both men answered in unison. Angus was preparing their bedding and Ewan was busily unpacking food from his saddlebags for their evening meal. With her offer of help unnecessary Maggie sat watching the flames as they danced in the evening breeze. She was mesmerized by the colors, the sounds and the way the fire flickered high in one spot and then another. Maggie was surprised when she realized she was watching herself in a scene that was unfolding in front of her eyes. This was a first for her. She'd never experienced a vision before and had never imagined she could. This was Edna's territory and Maggie mimicked what she had seen Edna do on countless occasions when she was experiencing a vision. She steadied her breathing and cleared her mind of all doubt as she allowed herself to be immersed in her first experience with the sight. She quickly concluded that she wasn't seeing herself in the vision, but rather this was Brielle, doing an incredible job of impersonating her. Maggie saw a man enter the vision and she smiled warmly when she realized it was Dylan who approached Brielle. Her smile soon faded when she watched him take Brielle's hand, gazing lovingly into her face. Brielle reached up, ran her fingers through Dylan's hair and cupped his cheek against her palm. Abruptly, she turned her head and looking right into Maggie's eyes from within the vision, sneered at her before she let loose with a wicked laugh. Anger bubbled up in Maggie, breaking the trance. How dare Brielle touch Dylan? How dare he let her? And most disturbing of all to her, how could Dylan be fooled by Brielle? He was looking right into her eyes, not Maggie's. He should have known the difference.

"Steady, my girl." Edna's voice floated to Maggie on the soft evening breeze. She quickly scanned the area searching for the location of her aunt. Ewan and Angus were still busy, and obviously unaware of Maggie's vision or the sound of Edna's voice. "Things aren't always as they appear." Silence followed and Maggie let go of her anger. Edna was a wise woman and was far more experienced than she was. Maggie was also happy to know that Edna was keeping an eye on things, even though she wasn't physically present.

* * *

"Shall we eat?" Ewan asked. Maggie, still recovering from the strange vision, noticed that the men had finished setting up camp and were staring at her expectantly.

"I'm sorry, I guess I got lost in thought."

"I can see a family resemblance between ye and Lena," Ewan said. "The same fiery red hair and emerald green eyes."

"Aye. The women of the family all share those features. Edna as well, when we were younger. Now her hair is completely white, with streaks of blue, of all things." Angus chuckled and winked at Maggie.

"Are ye excited to be here, Maggie?" Ewan asked.

"Excited probably isn't the word I'd use. If the circumstances were different, then I would definitely be excited, but as it stands, I'm more anxious, you could say." Maggie watched Ewan as he nodded his understanding. She could see why Lena had decided to stay here. He certainly was handsome with his dark hair and eyes. It all seemed so romantic to Maggie - Arlena crossing the bridge and meeting the love of her life when Ewan found her, and brought her back home with him. Now they were married and had a family together. If all went well, she hoped she'd get the chance to see her cousin while she was visiting this century. Things had to be much more serious than she'd assumed, for Lena, Ewan and the boys to stay away from Breaghacraig. Maggie wished she could shake the sense of dread that had settled on her, ever since she'd seen Brielle in the vision.

The three of them sat around the fire, Ewan and Angus getting to know each other better, while Maggie remained quiet and introspective. The men certainly seemed to be enjoying each other's company. This meeting had been a long time coming and it was nice they hit it off so well.

"I'm tired," Maggie said, yawning deeply as if to prove her point. "I'm going to get some sleep."

"Alright, love," Angus replied. "We'll get an early start tomorrow morn."

"Good night, Ewan," Maggie said.

"Good night, Alec," Ewan responded, with a teasing tone in his voice.

Maggie curled up with a blanket and closed her eyes, listening to the comforting sounds of Ewan and Angus quietly talking and laughing. It was all she needed to drift off to sleep.

* * *

The practice field was the place Dylan always chose to rid himself of his frustrations and today's target was Cormac. The two men circled each other, looking for an opportunity to strike. Cormac and Cailin had both been working with him since his arrival in Breaghacraig and Dylan was confident that he had made much progress since his first days of holding a sword in hand. He now hefted it easily and with precise control. If his football buddies back home could see him now, they'd be amazed. They'd make fun of him for sure, but that was to be expected. His body had gone through some changes as well. He wasn't big and bulkily muscled anymore - instead, he was lean and chiseled. He assumed he must look good, based on the way the women around the castle stared at him when he passed by. He had to admit, it did his ego good, but he wasn't interested in any of them. He wanted Maggie - the Maggie he'd known from Glendaloch.

Cormac struck first and Dylan blocked him with his guard. He shoved Cormac away from him and then attacked immediately. Cormac was fast, parrying with a countermove of his own. This went on for a good long time, neither man besting the other before they were both completely winded, Cormac calling a halt to their practice first.

"Were ye fighting me or someone else, my friend?" Cormac asked, holding his hands on his knees as he tried to catch his breath.

Dylan was in a similar state and he shrugged in response.

"I think that lass, Maggie, is getting under yer skin."

"How did you know?" Dylan asked.

"Just a good guess," Cormac answered.

"Yeah, she is, and not in a good way. I don't know what happened to her, Cormac. She was sweet and funny and I felt such a connection with her back in Glendaloch. Now she's anything but sweet and funny. She's more like a pesky fly."

"I wish I could disagree with ye, but she hasnae done anything to endear herself to anyone while she's been here. Jenna has done nothing but complain about her since her arrival. At first, I thought it was just that she was concerned fer yer welfare, but as the week has gone on, I can see that she truly doesnae care for Maggie. Cailin tells me Ashley feels the same. And as for Irene, well, let's just say she's ready to cast her out on her ear."

"I don't know what to do and I'm not sure why she's so different. It's as if she's someone else." Dylan stood to his full height and waited for Cormac to do the same. "What would you do?"

"Me? Well, ye ken yer cousin was a might bit prickly when I first met her, but I remained patient, showing Jenna that I was the right man for her. It took a while, but she came around and now look at us."

"Yeah. You're both nauseatingly in love," Dylan joked. "Maybe you're right. I'll try to be patient with her and we'll see if she comes around. I just don't know why she bothered to come here, if not to see me."

"Mayhap ye should talk to her about it. It might help, especially if things are as bad as they seem to be."

"I think I will. You're right, it can't hurt." Dylan made up his mind he would confront Maggie about her behavior. Maybe she'd open up to him and explain why she was acting so badly.

* * *

Dylan found Maggie up on the battlements, staring off into the distance. "Maggie, I want to talk to you about something."

"Talk to me? About what?" Brielle questioned sharply, looking suspicious.

"About us. I'm not sure why you're here. I thought it was to see me, but you don't really seem that interested in spending any time with me. I'm always having to search for you and you've been rude and unfriendly to everyone here at Breaghacraig and well, I'm not sure I want you to stay any longer." There he'd said it. He didn't want to hurt her feelings, but she needed to know what he was thinking. Tears welled up in her eyes and Dylan immediately felt terrible. "I'm sorry, Maggie. I didn't mean to hurt your feelings, but I don't know what's happened to you. You seem so distant and different from the girl I left in Glendaloch. I'm feeling really confused about us."

"I'm so sorry, Dylan," Brielle said. "I didnae mean to behave so badly. It's just been a difficult time for me."

"What's wrong? You can tell me." Dylan wrapped her in a hug. She was apparently having some sort of problems and he'd made her feel bad. Now he felt like a complete ass.

"I don't want to talk about it just yet." Brielle snuggled a little closer to him and tentatively put an arm around his waist. "Can ye forgive me? I'll behave better. I promise."

"Everyone deserves a second chance. Of course you're forgiven."

"Will ye tell me when I'm being rude or unfriendly, so I'll know?" she sniffled. "Everyone must hate me."

"No one hates you. They don't know you, that's all. Whatever you've been going through, I hope you know that I'm here for you." Dylan knew the others didn't hate her, but he was reasonably positive that they didn't like her. Hopefully, with his help, she would show them the real Maggie and they could be convinced to change their minds.

Chapter 4

Maggie and Angus approached Breaghacraig around midday. They bid goodbye to Ewan soon after sun up and they'd all agreed once again that Ewan and the family would come to Breaghacraig once the danger had passed. Maggie was happy Angus would finally get to meet his grandsons and reunite with his long absent daughter. She only wished Edna could visit with them, as well.

"Uncle, will they know who we are?" Maggie asked as they reached the gates. Her fingers instinctively went in search of her hair, for a bout of anxious twirling, but much to her frustration 'twas out of reach, neatly tucked beneath her cap.

"Ye'll need to call me sir, Maggie, and I'll need to call ye Alec, if we're to make this work."

"Yes, sir," Maggie snapped a salute in his direction and they both laughed.

"To answer yer question, even though this is my time, Robert & Irene willnae ken who I am as I've never had the pleasure of meeting them, even though I did know their fathers. I've not met Cormac either. Jenna, Ashley and Cailin, however, have all met me at The Thistle and Hive, so they will no doubt recognize me."

They drew their horses up at the gates and Maggie admired the completely intact castle. There were hundreds of castles dotted around Scotland, but not many looked as fresh and new as this one did. She realized, of course, that 'new' was a relative term, because even in 1514, this castle was more than likely already a few hundred years old. Still, it was a thrill to see it in daily use and occupied by the MacKenzie clan - instead of operating as a museum, open to the public and manned by employees who sold tickets and souvenirs.

"State yer business," the guard called down from the barbican.

"Me name is Angus Campbell - an old friend of the laird's father and this be me companion, Alec," Angus called back.

The guard continued staring at them for a moment longer, before giving the signal to open the gates. Angus and Alec passed through and into the very busy courtyard, where they were met by boys from the stable who waited for them to dismount and then took their horses.

Maggie was fascinated by it all. She'd heard so much about this castle and she'd been excited about being able to see it firsthand. It was pleasing to discover it was everything she had expected and more, and she was not disappointed in the slightest. Everything about it seemed larger than life and it met all her expectations. Maggie couldn't believe she was actually in medieval Scotland, and that in her time, these people were all long dead. Or were they? She'd have to ask Edna about this question, wondering whether it could be possible that they were all living at the same time, just on different planes of existence? She was going to give herself a headache if she kept thinking along those lines, but for some reason, it was easier to believe that, than to believe she'd actually travelled back in time five hundred years.

"Try not to seem as if this is all brand new to ye lad," Angus cautioned quietly, as they headed towards the heavy wooden doors to the castle. "Not everyone here knows about the bridge."

"Right." The word 'lad' got Maggie's attention and she knew that from this point forward she had a job to do and that meant she could not let her guard down - ever.

Angus was just about to reach for the doors, when they practically flew open, knocking them back a pace. His facial expression changed from serious to delight in a split second. "Jenna! Ashley!" he crowed.

"Angus?" Both women spoke at once and then ran into his waiting arms. He kissed the tops of their heads, first one and then the other, and held on to them tightly. "What are you doing here?" Ashley asked. "Did you bring Edna?" She peeked around him, searching for Edna and her gaze landed briefly on Maggie.

"Nae. I'm afraid not." Angus reluctantly released the two women. "I'm sure ye both ken that my niece, Maggie, is here. I've come to escort her home. Edna has need of her at the inn."

Maggie noted that at the mention of her name, the women exchanged a troubled look. She wondered what that was all about. What had Brielle been doing while she'd been at Breaghacraig? Maggie wasn't certain she wanted to know, but she hoped Brielle hadn't done anything to ruin Maggie's good name.

"You can stay for a while though, can't you?" Jenna asked.

"Aye. I've much to catch up on with ye both." Angus twirled Ashley and whistled. "Look at ye lass. When is the babe due?"

Ashley giggled at this big teddy bear of a man. "April. Thank you so much for the baby gift you sent back with Jenna. You made it, didn't you?"

"Aye, that I did. Whether the babe be a lad or a lassie, a wee wooden sword will come in handy. They can start to practice with it almost as soon as they can walk. I made it especially for a wee little hand. Of course, they'll outgrow it quickly, but I can always fashion another when that happens."

"I hope you'll come back and visit after the baby is born. Then you can give the little one the benefit of your knowledge and teach them how to use it."

"It would be my pleasure, Ashley. I'm a lucky man to have so many wonderful women in me life. Ye ken yer both like daughters to me."

"We're the lucky ones," Ashley said. She put her fingers to his lips to quiet his protest. "Cailin will be so excited to see you. Come on, let's go find him."

Maggie cleared her throat to remind them that there was someone else present.

"I'm sorry. We didnae mean to ignore ye lad," Angus announced. "Ladies, let me introduce ye to Alec. He accompanied me from Glendaloch, he's a local lad and Edna wanted to give him the experience of time travel. She thought I could use his help while I'm here."

"Nice to meet you," Jenna stuck out her hand and Maggie did her best to shake it with a suitably manly grip. "You look really familiar," Jenna added, examining Alec's face curiously.

"You're right, Jenna. He does look familiar. Did we meet you in Glendaloch?" Ashley asked.

"I dinnae think so," Maggie replied, averting her eyes and trying her best to sound more masculine. "Oftentimes people mistake me for someone they know. I must have one of those faces, I guess." This was harder than she had anticipated. Remembering to speak and act like a lad was going to be a constant struggle for her. She only hoped she didn't mess up.

Ashley shrugged and took hold of Angus' hand. Jenna went to his other side and wrapped her arm through his.

* * *

Lagging behind, Maggie watched the easy way Angus had of speaking with these two women. They obviously both adored him and the feeling seemed genuinely mutual.

"Cailin," Ashley called to two men, who were undoubtedly brothers, as they walked away from a larger group of men. She waved her arms frantically in the air and the two men exchanged glances and trotted towards their small group.

"Is that Angus I see?" Cailin asked. Not waiting for an answer, he pulled Angus into a bear hug that was returned in kind. Cailin then introduced Angus to the other man. "Angus, this is me brother, Cormac, husband to Jenna." Cormac offered Angus a hearty handshake and slapped him on the back.

"I've heard so much about ye," Cormac said. "I'm happy to finally meet ye, but where is yer wee wife?"

Angus explained that she hadn't been able to come along and that he was visiting Breaghacraig to collect Maggie.

"This be my companion, Alec," Angus explained. Both Cailin and Cormac nodded in greeting.

"'Tis good to meet ye," Maggie responded, again deepening her voice as much as possible. She was grateful that there was no back-slapping where she was concerned. She would surely have ended up on the ground in a heap if either one of these strapping men had attempted it. She was also thankful that neither of them had met the real Maggie before now. Ashley and Jenna moved to stand beside their respective spouses and Maggie suffered a twinge of jealousy when she saw how in love they appeared. She could hardly wait to see Dylan, although she would be forced to continue the pretense of being Alec for the foreseeable future. She would have to accept that fact, and that she might see some things here that she didnae want to see. As the others talked, Maggie cast her gaze towards the group of men Cormac and Cailin had just left. Her breath caught in her throat when she recognized Dylan standing amongst them. He looked even more amazing than she remembered. Of course, here he was shirtless and wearing a kilt, which only made him more attractive. He seemed very comfortable with the other men as they all laughed and joked with one another. She couldn't seem to take her eyes off of him.

"Is everything alright?" Ashley asked, seeming to notice Maggie's keen interest in the men.

"Oh, aye, it is," Maggie said, casting her gaze down towards the ground and scuffing at the dirt with her boots. She was going to have to be more careful. She tuned her ears back in to the conversation at hand.

"I hope ye two lads are taking good care of these precious gems." Angus had donned his protective father face and raised a questioning eyebrow at Cailin and Cormac.

"Of course," Cailin said, squeezing Ashley around the waist.

"Aye. We are," Cormac agreed.

"Ladies? Any complaints?" Angus asked.

Ashley and Jenna acted as if they were giving it some serious thought and then burst into laughter. Cailin and Cormac both shook their heads at their wives antics.

"We were just heading in for the noon meal. Come, join us and we can introduce you to Robert and Irene." Cailin took Ashley's hand and they led the way towards the great hall. Maggie wandered along behind, scarcely able to keep her mouth from dropping open at the wonder of finding herself in a real medieval castle.

* * *

"My father spoke of ye often," Robert said, after Angus and Alec had been introduced to him, Irene and their children.

"As did mine," Irene added.

"They told of your unmatched bravery in battle and of how the three of ye fought side-by-side, on more than one occasion. They were heartbroken when ye disappeared," Robert said.

"Yer fathers were good men," Angus said. "I'm sorry I caused them such heartache. I had no way to let anyone know what had happened and that I was alright."

Robert nodded his acceptance and understanding, as did Irene.

"I met the woman I'd always hoped to meet, my Edna, and there was no way I could leave her behind to return. I wanted to spend the rest of my days with her and I haven't regretted my decision for a moment." Angus glanced around at the other men, who were all holding their wives just a wee bit tighter.

Maggie was once again reminded of the one thing lacking in her life. Love. It's what she wanted, what she dreamed of and what she hoped to have with Dylan, if she wasn't already too late.

"There she is!" Robert suddenly shouted. "Maggie, yer Uncle Angus has arrived."

Everyone turned to the doors and watched as an obviously startled Brielle recovered her cool demeanor and reaching behind her pulled Dylan into the room. She made sure to cozy right up next to him, which had the real Maggie seeing red. Brielle scanned the faces in the room and settled her gaze on Maggie, in her disguise as Alec. She offered Maggie a withering stare before she focused her attention on Angus. With a bright smile, she spoke. "Uncle Angus, what brings ye here to Breaghacraig? I hope all is well at home." She came forward to hug Angus, looking extremely uncomfortable in the process.

"Aye. 'Tis indeed, my dear niece, but yer Auntie Edna would like ye to come home with me. She is in need of yer help."

"Cannae it wait, Uncle? I've come to see Dylan and I wish to spend more time with him." Brielle had a temperamental pout on her lips, which was very uncharacteristic for the real Maggie, as she snuggled closer to Dylan.

"We dinnae need to leave in a hurry. We can stay for a bit longer if ye like," Angus said. Maggie could tell he was carefully wording his responses. There was no way that Brielle could not know that Angus was on to her, but she kept up the pretense of being Maggie without batting an eye. An awkward silence followed his answer and the others in the room watched this exchange with curiosity.

"Angus, it's good to see you again," Dylan chimed in, breaking the quiet filling the room. He left Brielle's side and reached out a hand in greeting.

"It's good to see ye again, lad," Angus said. "How have you fared since yer arrival?"

"Great. I love it here. I've been enjoying it more than I would have imagined." Dylan glanced at the others and then his eyes landed on Alec.

This is it. He's going to recognize me now. Maggie smiled brightly at Dylan, forgetting for a moment that she was in disguise. Her stomach was doing flip-flops and her heart was racing as she waited for him to say something.

"Hi, I'm Dylan." He reached out his hand to shake Maggie's and she visibly deflated. He didn't recognize her. Shouldn't he? How could he look her in the eyes and not know who she was?

"I be Alec," Maggie replied, grasping his hand. She didn't know if he could feel it, but when she touched Dylan she began to shake. *This would not be a good time to lose it, Maggie.* She made an effort to stand up taller and look as unaffected by their encounter as possible. For his part, Dylan simply turned away from her and went back to Brielle's side. *Damn it all,* Maggie thought. She glared at Brielle and there was a palpable tension in the air. Energy shifted back and forth between them, causing Maggie to feel nauseous and wobbly. She grasped the back of a nearby chair to steady herself and with a good deal of effort broke contact with Brielle's eyes. *She's a strong one. This will not be easy.*

"Alec," Angus sounded concerned. "Are ye alright, lad? Mayhap ye need to sit for a moment."

"Ye must be hungry," Irene said. "It's time for the noon meal. Why dinnae we all sit and eat?" Irene showed Angus and Alec to their seats and everyone else sat down as well. Soon servants carrying trays filled with food were streaming from the kitchen to the tables and everyone was helping themselves.

Maggie was a bit hesitant, but Angus handed her a platter and said, "Alec, put some food on yer trencher. I ken ye be hungry."

"Aye," Maggie said. "I am." She started plucking things off the platter and onto her trencher, not caring what it might be that she was grabbing. Brielle caught Maggie gazing in Dylan's direction and gave her the evil eye. *I'm going to need to protect myself from that witch.* She no sooner had the thought than her throat began to tighten and she was having a hard time breathing. She immediately started running through the list of spells she'd been taught. Surely, Edna had given her one to protect herself? She was panicking now and that was never a good thing. She could feel her thoughts running in a million different directions. *Deep breaths, calm yerself.* After a moment or two, the spell came to her and she quietly recited it in her head. When she was done, the panic had left her and Brielle was left looking disappointed and angry. Maggie avoided looking in her direction for the remainder of the meal. She noticed that Angus had spoken more today than she had ever heard him do so before. He was usually the strong silent type, but for some reason, he was babbling on about life in Glendaloch, The Thistle & Hive and Edna. No one else seemed to notice, and Maggie knew that he was trying to distract their attention from what had been happening between her and Brielle. The meal couldn't be over soon enough for her taste. She had been uncomfortably aware of Dylan at the other end of the table and acutely aware of her enemy, Brielle, at his side. As soon as it was polite, Maggie excused herself and practically bolted from the room. Once outside, she gulped in a huge lung full of the crisp, fresh air. She leaned against the stone walls of the castle, which were warm from the sun shining directly upon them. It felt good to Maggie and calmed her frazzled nerves. *What a mess! How am I going to succeed? She's so much stronger and better at this than I am.* Maggie shielded her eyes with her hands. No one in the courtyard had noticed her. Apparently, there was nothing remarkable about her for anyone to take note of. That was a good thing, she imagined. That way she could go about undetected by the others. She still wasn't sure what she was supposed to do to defeat Brielle, she just hoped she wasn't going to die trying.

Angus walked out the doors with Dylan at his side. She hardened her heart just a little in order to dull the pain she felt at the sight of him.

"There ye are, Alec. Come along. Dylan is going to show us to our room. We'll be staying in the soldier's barracks, but we'll have our own private room," Angus said, motioning towards the other side of the courtyard.

Maggie didn't respond, instead falling into step behind the two men. And silently plotting her revenge against Dylan, for forgetting her so quickly. Who was she kidding? As much as she might like to see him fall flat on his face, she could never do anything to hurt him, no matter how angry she might be.

They entered the soldiers' barracks and Maggie was relieved to find they were empty. "Where is everyone?" she asked.

"They're all out tending to their daily duties, or they may even be out on the practice field." Dylan shrugged his broad shoulders and Maggie found him absolutely adorable. To her eyes, he looked very fit and his body appeared more sculpted than she remembered. His muscular chest was straining against the fabric of his shirt and Maggie had to look away before he noticed the effect he was having on her. "Your chamber is right in here. I'm staying in the room right next to you while Maggie's here, so if you need anything, just give a holler."

"Thank ye, Dylan, ye've been ever so kind," Angus said.

Maggie made a weird grunting noise in response and escaped into their chamber, where she tried to melt into the corner. *At least he's not staying in the same room with Brielle,* she thought.

"I'll see you around," Dylan said as he walked away.

"Are ye alright, lass?" Angus asked, after it seemed he had looked up and down the corridor one hundred times to be sure no one would hear him.

"I'm fine, Uncle," Maggie's head was pounding, her heart was racing and she was definitely hyperventilating, but she wasn't about to let Angus know that. He was already stressed out enough over their situation.

* * *

"What did she do to ye in there?" Angus raked his big hands through his salt and pepper hair, leaving it standing on end in the process.

"I'm nae sure. She was staring me down and the next thing I knew, I couldn't breathe. I used one of the spells Auntie taught me, and it worked, but it made her verra angry."

"I don't like this one bit. Edna shouldnae have sent ye. Yer just a wee slip of a thing and much too kind hearted for this kind of work."

Angus paced back and forth across the small bedchamber. He was so angry Maggie could practically see the steam coming off him.

"Uncle, dinnae worry about me. Auntie wouldnae have sent me if she didnae think I could do it. I must try." Maggie knew she needed to calm things down in her own mind if she were going to be successful against Brielle. "She knows who I am and she thinks I'm afraid of her, so in her mind, she's already won. I know that now and I won't let her get the best of me again."

"If she hurts even one hair on yer head..." Angus started.

"Don't, Uncle. She'll not harm me. I'm a grown woman. I *can* handle this and I will." Maggie had made up her mind. She would not cower in front of that witch again. She'd fight her with everything she had. Edna had taught her well and she *could* do this. She had to do this - for the MacKenzies and for Dylan. "I just wish I understood exactly what it is that I am supposed to do."

"It will reveal itself, lass. I'm here for ye and I will protect ye as best I can." Angus reached out and pulled her to him, hugging her tight to his chest. "Dinnae fear, all will be well." Maggie didn't think he sounded very convincing.

Chapter 5

Doubts were still whirling through Dylan's mind. He was having a hard time locating the strong connection he had felt when he met Maggie for the first time back in Glendaloch. Never having been in a committed relationship, he was at a loss as to how the Maggie he remembered had changed so much. He wasn't a quitter though, he was still crazily attracted to her, and he was determined to figure out the problems between them and make her his. *Where is she?* Dylan had been searching for Maggie for the past hour and hadn't found her anywhere. Not much had changed in her behavior since his last conversation with her, but he could see that she was trying to make an effort, so he decided to give it more time.

His next area to search was the kitchen, where he found his cousin, Jenna, Mary, the castle cook, and Sophia - a girl from twenty first century San Francisco, who found herself unwillingly brought back to medieval Breaghacraig by Jenna's crazy ex-husband. Mary was teaching Sophia how to heat up the bread oven, by starting a fire inside it first with small pieces of kindling, and then adding bigger pieces of firewood.

"Once the bread oven is good and hot, ye'll sweep the burning embers out into the hearth and then place the bread inside to bake," he heard Mary explaining.

Cooking in medieval times was a challenge and since marrying Cormac, Jenna had made it her mission to try and help Mary find ways to make her job easier. She also wanted to try to replicate some of the dishes they all missed from the twenty first century. Mary had been skeptical at first, but eventually she had warmed to Jenna and they had developed a friendship of sorts. Dylan had been surprised at how well Jenna fit in at Breaghacraig. She had always been a take-charge kind of girl when they lived in San Francisco, which tended to rub some people the wrong way. She had been quite the accomplished chef herself - not a professional, but Dylan had always suspected she could have been if she'd wanted. Jenna had been responsible for running her parents charitable foundation, arranging for the collection of excess food from local restaurants, which was then distributed to the homeless shelter. Consequently, Jenna was generally busy all of the time and had been searching for things to keep her equally busy in medieval Scotland.

"Hey, Jenna… Sophia," Dylan greeted them as he entered the kitchen. "How are you today, Mary?"

"I be fine, Sir. Jenna is trying to teach me to make *pasta*." Mary screwed up her face and pronounced the word with something close to disgust.

"Mary, we have to try. Cormac loves it and I want to make it for him," Jenna said.

Dylan laughed at Mary's comical expression. "It's very good, Mary. I think you'd like it. Of course, I'm not sure Jenna will be able to get all the ingredients she needs to make it."

"I'm improvising," Jenna said. "We'll work with what we've got here." She examined the ingredients she had set out on the table and he could see her calculating in her head just how she was going to manage this task.

"Have any of you seen Maggie?" Dylan asked.

Three heads bobbed up to stare at him and Mary spoke. "Have ye looked behind ye?"

Dylan turned to find Maggie standing there, smiling at him. "How long have you been there?"

"Not long," Maggie replied.

"I've been looking all over for you. Where were you?" Dylan couldn't seem to read Maggie's mood. She was smiling at him, but he didn't think it was a genuine smile.

"Oh, wandering about. No place special. I just needed some breathing room." Maggie surveyed the room and its occupants. "Do ye mind if I sit down for a bit?"

"Nae. Of course not, lass. Please join us." Mary said, as she began kneading some bread dough. She had several loaves set out and waiting to go in the oven. "Sophia, is the oven ready yet?"

"I'll check for you," Sophia responded.

"Sophia," Maggie said, and she sounded as if she were testing the sound of the name on her lips. "You arrived here around the same time as Jenna and Dylan, didn't you?"

"That's right." Sophia was bent over the bread oven and nodded, seeming satisfied with the heat. "Mary, I think it might be ready now. Do you want to check it to be sure?"

"Aye. Let me look," Mary said. She stepped closer and put her hands near the opening of the bread oven. "Very good, Sophia. You're learning, lass." Mary patted Sophia on the back and handed her a small shovel, which was kept by the stove for this very purpose. "Be careful now. We dinnae want to set the place afire." Mary returned to her kneading and Sophia began carefully clearing out the oven.

Dylan stood behind Maggie, placing his hands on her shoulders. When he had touched her in Glendaloch he'd experienced a rush of heat, but here, he didn't feel anything. Maggie didn't seemed impressed by his touch either. If anything, her posture had grown more rigid, as if she was uncomfortable with his attention. Dylan removed his hands and sat down in a nearby chair. Strangely, now that he was in the same room with Maggie, all he could think about was getting as far away from her as possible. He took a deep breath and forced himself to stay put.

Mary and Jenna had their heads together over the pasta dough and Maggie seemed mesmerized by Sophia's actions as she carefully brushed the burning embers out of the oven and into the hearth. She had a very strange expression on her face and Dylan was just about to ask her what was wrong, when Sophia screamed. All eyes turned towards her in horror as they realized her gown had caught fire. Jenna and Dylan sprang into action, pushing Sophia down onto the floor and rolling her back and forth, until the fire was out.

"Oh my God," Jenna cried. "Are you alright, Sophia?"

It was apparent Sophia was in shock - her eyes were wide and her body shook uncontrollably.

"Fire! Fire!" Mary yelled. Everyone's attention was immediately drawn to the hearth. The fire seemed much larger than it should be, and was leaping dangerously towards the wooden furniture and beams in the kitchen.

"Hurry! We need to get out of here," Dylan called. Mary was trying unsuccessfully to put the fire out, even as she continued to shout for assistance.

Mary's shouting drew Latharn, Cormac and Angus's young companion, Alec, to the kitchen; they appeared in the doorway and surveyed the situation swiftly, concern visible in their faces. The room was quickly filling with smoke and it was apparent everyone needed to get out before it was too late. Latharn ran to Sophia, picking her up in his arms, and battled his way through the thickening smoke and fire. Cormac grabbed Jenna under one arm and hurried her to the doorway before he turned and headed back for Mary, who was still trying to extinguish the fire single-handedly. "Mary, we must leave," Cormac shouted, picking her up and sprinting out of the kitchen.

"My kitchen!" Mary cried, trying to wriggle out of Cormac's firm grasp.

Dylan couldn't believe his eyes. Everything had been fine and then out of nowhere, they found themselves in the middle of a huge blaze. There was something strange about the way the fire had jumped out of the hearth and it had him concerned. To his shock, Maggie was still sitting in exactly the same spot. The fire seemed to be dancing around her as if she were cocooned inside a protective bubble.

"Maggie, come on! We've got to get out of here." Dylan put his hand out to take hers and was confused when his fingers seemed to hit something solid, as if there was an invisible wall between him and Maggie. He tried a second time and Maggie reached for his hand and took it. He dragged her out of the chair and ran toward the doorway, shocked to see Alec standing just inside the entrance of the kitchen, completely immobile. While Cormac and Latharn had immediately sprung into action to rescue the women, Alec seemed dazed and he stared at the fire, as though in a trance. "Alec, let's go!" Dylan shouted, but Alec remained focused on the fire.

In the split second that Dylan and Maggie stood waiting for Alec to react, the fire disappeared. Without any warning, it was completely gone. The kitchen was damaged, but there was not one lick of flame to be seen. "What just happened?" Dylan demanded.

"I dinnae ken," Alec replied, and the strange trance he seemed to have been held in disappeared as abruptly as the flames had. "'Tis odd. The fire's gone." Alec turned to Dylan. "We should all get outside in the fresh air. We've breathed in much smoke."

As if on cue, Maggie began coughing and Dylan gently guided her outside into the fresh air. 'Alec' followed along behind them, filled with annoyance because she knew Brielle had started the fire on purpose.

* * *

"I told ye to be careful, Sophia, didnae I?" Mary was saying. Despite the fact she was yelling, it was obvious that she was very concerned about Sophia's welfare.

"I don't know what happened. I did everything the way you showed me and it all looked fine and then next thing I knew, my dress had caught fire." Sophia sat cradled in Latharn's arms.

"Ye scared me good, Sophia," Latharn said as he stroked her cheek and planted a kiss on her forehead.

"I'm sorry, I didn't mean to. It all happened so fast," Sophia said.

The real Maggie knew exactly what had happened and she knew Brielle was to blame. She had rushed into the room with Cormac and Latharn when they heard Mary screaming and there sat Brielle, as calm as could be and not worried in the slightest that the fire would touch her. Thank God, Maggie'd been able to put the blaze out. If this was an example of the kind of magic Brielle was capable of, Maggie was going to have her hands full. And now, to add insult to injury, Brielle was sitting all wrapped up in Dylan's arms, seeming as innocent as a newborn babe. Maggie was seething with anger and jealousy. How dare Brielle steal her man? Maggie was typically a mild-mannered lass, but she did have a fiery temper when it was needed - one matching her flaming red locks, and seeing her rival with Dylan was enough to cause an explosion.

Angus approached the group from the Great Hall. "What happened, Alec?" he asked quietly.

"Brielle," was Maggie's one word response.

"I dinnae like this. We're lucky there wasnae any loss of life."

"Aye. Luckily I was able to put it out before it spread." Maggie was staring at the back of Brielle's head as Dylan hugged her close. Latharn and Cormac had risked their lives to save the women they loved. And so had Dylan.. Knowing how much he actually cared for Maggie should have warmed her heart, but the knowledge that he was being tricked by Brielle pretending to be herself was a horrible thing to endure. Maggie didn't think she could take much more of this. Watching him with Brielle every day was almost too much to bear.

Angus seemed to read her mind. "Come, Alec. Let's take a walk. Clear yer head."

With a sullen nod, Maggie agreed and they headed through the gates to the outer bailey and as they walked, Angus kept up the conversation.

"I ken ye feel betrayed by Dylan, but ye must ken that he is under Brielle's spell. He believes her to be ye."

"But it's not me," Maggie protested. "How can he look into her eyes and not know that?"

"I dinnae ken how it's possible, Maggie. But I'm asking you to be patient with him. We have much work to do here to rid the MacKenzie's of Brielle and until we do, ye cannae let anyone here know who ye be, just as ye cannae allow them to distract ye from yer task."

"I don't understand why. Wouldn't it be better for them to know who Brielle truly is and who I really am?" Maggie was confused by the whole situation. She stopped in her tracks and stared up at Angus. "It's just not fair!"

"I'm sure ye've heard it before, lass, but life isnae fair. We all have to learn to deal with it. And until yer Aunt Edna gives us clearance to tell everyone what's really happening, we must do as she asks and keep your business here a secret. We must trust that Edna knows what she's doing."

Maggie nodded grudgingly. "Okay. I don't like it, but I'll do as she said."

"And dinnae worry yerself, yer time to find love will come. I promise ye." Angus patted her on the back. She guessed he had gone with that more manly gesture, because he couldn't hug her without drawing suspicion to them. He had to treat her as if she was a lad, but Maggie needed a hug more than anything else right now.

"I dinnae think so, Uncle. I dinnae believe love is possible in the twenty first century." She knew she sounded pathetic, but it was how she really felt.

"Why on earth would ye say a thing like that?" Angus appeared completely bewildered by her statement.

"Look around ye. Jenna and Ashley had to come to the sixteenth century to find love." That was a fact and it merely proved her point. "Everyone I know is in love with someone from the past."

"That pout yer wearing is most appealing," Angus teased. She thought it was sweet that he was trying to lighten her mood. "'Tis simply nae true. What of yer Mum and Da?"

"They arenae in love anymore. They're divorced, you know that."

"Aye. They are, but that doesnae mean they dinnae love each other. They still work together every day and I believe that if they stopped being so stubborn, they'd be back together again in no time."

"Do ye really think so?" Maggie looked hopefully at Angus. Her parents did work at the teashop together. She had always thought it was just because they both owned it and had to be there. Now that she thought on it though, they were always very sweet with each other, except for those times when they werenae and then they wouldnae speak with each other and aye, their stubborn ways kept them like that fer days.

"Aye. I do. So dinnae give up on love just yet. There may be some surprises in store for ye just around the corner."

Maggie loved Angus. He was one of the best men she knew and his words had weight to them. When he said something, it was good to listen, because he always knew exactly what he was talking about and when he chose to speak, it was usually important.

As they made their way back to the inner bailey, they saw workmen carrying charred pieces of furniture from the kitchen. Every available person seemed to be congregating in the area. Some were going inside to help and others stood around outside, speculating about what had happened. Maggie knew that she had put the fire out completely and before leaving the kitchen, she had done her best to fix the worst of the damage, leaving only a charred table and benches among the ashes.

"The damage doesnae appear to be too bad," Cormac was saying to his brother Cailin. "We should count ourselves lucky that it didnae spread outside of the kitchen itself."

"Aye. What do ye think caused it?" Cailin asked. He was surveying the charred remains of the kitchen table and other, unidentifiable wooden objects.

"From the sounds of it, I'd almost believe magick was involved. Jenna said that the flames seemed to be leaping out of the fireplace towards anything made of wood." Cormac shook his head as if he were trying to come to terms with the thought of it. "We have Maggie to thank for putting it out." The immediate family were well aware that Maggie was a witch and were not in the least surprised by this information, after all, her Aunt Edna was a witch.

Maggie, who was standing nearby with Angus got some satisfaction from knowing that they realized she had put the fire out and then just as quickly, she recalled that Brielle was the one they thought responsible for saving them from a disaster because they thought *she* was Maggie. The next words she heard set her teeth on edge and had her balling her hands into fists.

"Maggie thinks that young Alec is the one who made the fire go out of control." Cormac said.

"Alec... how would he do a thing like that?" Cailin asked.

Maggie looked up at her uncle, panic in her eyes. "They think I did it!"

"Calm yerself, lad. We'll straighten this out." Angus assured her. "Cormac, Cailin could I have a moment of yer time?"

"Aye. Of course, Angus," Cormac said. The brothers eyed Alec warily as they approached.

"I heard what ye had to say about Alec and I believe Maggie was mistaken. Alec arrived after the fire started. He was right behind you and Latharn. You recall that, dinnae ye, Cormac?"

"He was," Cormac pondered that information for a moment and then laughed. "I be sorry for accusing ye, Alec, I forgot ye were not even in the room at the time."

Maggie nodded her acceptance of his apology.

"I wonder was there a wind blowing at the time?" Angus questioned. "Mayhap it blew into the hearth and sent the flames flying through the kitchen."

"I don't recall," Cormac said. "But I wasnae paying attention to the weather. Ye could be right, Angus. Magick, for better or worse, is always the answer when one doesnae ken how something has happened. Maggie is the only one of us who is capable of magick and she's the one who put the fire out. She *was* very suspicious of Alec, though."

"I will speak with her. She doesnae know Alec and so I understand why she might suspect him. I will set her straight." Angus assured them. Cormac and Cailin went back to helping with the kitchen and Angus winked at Alec. "Ye see? We've averted their suspicion."

"Thank ye, Uncle." Maggie was grateful to have Angus with her. He was the voice of reason in this whole crazy mess.

"I believe it would be a good use of yer time to head out to the practice field and work on the things I've been teaching ye, so ye don't get rusty." Angus nodded towards the area where the men of Clan MacKenzie could be seen sparring with one another.

"Are ye sure, Uncle?" Maggie wasn't sure at all. "Won't they be able to tell that I'm not a lad? I'm not verra good."

"They won't be able to tell anything of the sort and ye *are* good. Mayhap not verra good, but that will come." Angus started walking and Maggie had no choice but to follow. She nervously cast her gaze around the field. Shirtless, well-muscled men were everywhere and she couldn't have felt more out of place. "Ye'll spar with me. Just like we did back home." Angus grabbed a practice sword and dirk and handed them to Maggie before arming himself. "Remember what I've taught ye. Try to anticipate my moves and counter them." He found a clear area where they'd have enough room to work, while Maggie was busy gawking at what was happening around her. "Alec... Alec!"

It took Maggie a moment to realize that Angus was talking to her. "Aye, Angus."

"Pay attention, lad," Angus demanded.

"I'm sorry. I'll pay attention." Maggie was embarrassed at her behavior. She knew she was going to have to work hard in order to better herself and she was determined she would.

They were just about to get started when Dylan arrived on the practice field. He threw his shirt off and stood there, looking utterly amazing to Maggie's eyes. She couldn't help staring as he sauntered up to them.

"I'd be happy to spar with you, Alec. Angus could give us both some pointers. I hear he's pretty good at this," Dylan teased.

"Aye. I am," Angus answered, sizing Dylan up. "I think that would be a fine idea. Don't ye agree, Alec?"

"What?" Maggie felt like she might vomit at the thought of sparring with Dylan. "I…"

"Don't worry, Alec. I won't hurt you, I promise," Dylan said, sounding quite sincere.

She could hardly speak, so Maggie took a stance opposite Dylan to let him know she was willing, all the while eyeing Angus in disbelief. Dylan stood opposite her and Angus checked their spacing and foot placement. After a few minor corrections and some direction on what he wanted them to do, Angus said, "Well, have at it, then."

They circled each other, keeping their distance. Maggie stumbled over a rock and almost fell, but she caught herself quickly, not allowing Dylan time to take advantage of her misstep. They continued, Maggie making a few tentative swipes with her sword and Dylan handily deflecting them. Next Dylan came at her, but Maggie had been calculating where his next move would come from and she was pleased to discover she'd read him like a book. He no sooner lunged her way than she blocked his move and used her momentum to spin away and place her sword at his throat.

"Excellent," Angus called. He then pointed out where Dylan had gone wrong and showed him what he could've done differently.

"Thanks," Dylan said, looking slightly embarrassed. "I'd like to try that again."

A sheen of sweat was causing Maggie's clothes to cling to her. She pulled the fabric away from her body hoping no one would notice her curves. Where the sweat was making her uncomfortable, on Dylan it was an added bonus. Maggie was determined to focus on Dylan's eyes, rather than his beautiful upper body. She was so busy thinking about how good he looked that she missed his next move and before she knew it, found herself flat on her back on the ground, the tip of Dylan's sword at her chest.

"That was good, Dylan," Angus remarked. "Explain to me why you think that worked."

"I was following Alec's eyes and could see he was no longer paying attention. I tried to take advantage of that moment."

"And it worked. It may not always. Ye should try to observe everything about yer opponent. Eyes, stance, where their sword is and then what will be their next move. Ye'll almost never find yerself up against an opponent who is simply not paying attention." Angus shook his head in disappointment at Maggie.

She was terribly embarrassed. Her cheeks were flaming. Both Angus and Dylan knew she had been distracted. She only hoped that at least Dylan had no idea what was distracting her.

"I'm sure ye'll do better next time, Alec," Angus said.

"I hope so," she responded.

"Shall we do some close work with yer dirks," Angus suggested.

"I could really use some help with that," Dylan said as he put his sword aside and took out his dirk.

Maggie turned to her uncle and rolled her eyes in exasperation.

"Is there a problem, Alec?" Angus asked.

"No, sir," she answered, even though she thought it was going to be a big problem.

"Hold yer dirk the way I showed ye. Ye'll have more flexibility if ye hold it underhand." Angus demonstrated with his own dirk clasped in his fist and pointed down away from his hand. Dylan and Maggie did as he instructed and then turning to each other began the same tentative dance that had started their sword lesson. "I'd like ye, Dylan, to be in defensive mode. Let Alec attack ye and show me how ye'd defend against him."

They got started and right from the beginning, Dylan was good at defending against Maggie's attacks. "Alec, how can ye overcome those defenses?" Angus questioned.

"I can use my free hand," Maggie said.

"Let's see ye do it then," Angus instructed. Maggie attacked Dylan with renewed energy and while he did his best to avoid her knife, Maggie made contact on more than one occasion.

"I'm glad we're using practice dirks," Dylan said. "I'm afraid I'd be dead by now."

"Or badly wounded," Angus agreed. "Let's do the opposite now. Dylan you attack and Maggie you defend." Maggie had learned a lot from the first go round and was quite good at defending. "Okay, now add yer dirk into it," Angus said, sounding pleased. They continued on, until they were both out of breath. "That was well done." Angus patted them both on the back. "Shall we work on our bows?"

"Can we have a minute to catch our breath?" Maggie asked.

"Aye. Why dinnae ye get some water and I'll meet ye over by the targets." Angus walked away, leaving Dylan and Maggie to rest a moment.

"You're pretty good," Dylan said.

"As are ye," Maggie answered.

"It must be nice to have Angus as your teacher. He's a great guy."

"Aye. He is and I am lucky." Maggie started walking towards the well and Dylan hurried to keep up.

"So, how do you know him? Angus, I mean." Dylan asked as he dipped his cup in the bucket of water by the well.

Maggie did the same and took a long drink before answering. "He's a friend of the family."

She was purposely keeping her answers short, because she was uncomfortable disguising her voice. To her it sounded fake, but no one had questioned it and Dylan certainly didn't seem to notice anything.

"You live in Glendaloch? I was wondering if ye knew Maggie." He took another drink of water.

"Nae. I dinnae. I live in Edinburgh. I've been staying with Edna and Angus since just after Maggie left, so, nae I dinnae know her."

"I don't know what it is about you, but she sure doesn't seem to like you," Dylan observed.

"I dinnae know either," Maggie said. Apparently, it was obvious to the others that there was some tension between her and Brielle. "Angus is waiting fer us." She headed off towards the targets, knowing that Dylan would follow.

Maggie felt confident about her skills with a bow, so she let her competitive nature come out. She had great aim and hit the target dead center nearly every time.

"Wow! You're pretty impressive with that bow, Alec." Dylan tried his hand at it and while he wasn't bad, he only hit the bull's eye a time or two. On one of those occasions, Maggie took the opportunity to split his arrow with hers, causing him to throw his arms in the air in concession.

"You win! I can't possibly compete with you," Dylan said, clapping Maggie on the back. She wasn't expecting it and it knocked her off balance.

Grabbing her and setting her back on her feet, Dylan said, "Sorry about that. Sometimes I don't know my own strength."

"How could ye not?" Maggie asked feeling flushed and barely recovering from the feel of Dylan's hands on her. *They're truly beautiful hands,* she thought, catching herself before he noticed her staring at them. Angus on the other hand, seemed completely aware of what was going on in his niece's head.

"Alec, why don't ye go rest up? Ye've worked hard today."

"Aye." Maggie walked away realizing that Angus had saved her from making a fool of herself.

* * *

Dylan watched Alec walk away. He was experiencing the same, uneasy feeling that he'd met him somewhere before.

"Dylan?" Angus asked.

"Yeah, I'm sorry did you say something to me?" Dylan responded.

"I was wondering how ye were enjoying yer stay here and how ye were getting on with my niece," Angus said.

"I love it here. This has been the best experience of my life. I've learned so much from Cormac and Cailin. They're great guys."

"And Maggie?" Angus asked.

Dylan realized he wasn't going to get away without answering. But what could he tell Angus that wouldn't sound insulting? "We're getting to know each other. It's been different here... different than it was in Glendaloch."

"I see," Angus said, smiling.

Dylan was surprised by that. He'd expected him to be... well he wasn't quite sure what he expected. Would Angus mind if his feelings for Maggie had changed? He had to know that they'd made a connection back in Glendaloch. Maybe he was happy that things had slowed down between them, because he seemed absolutely elated by Dylan's vague answers.

"Thanks for the help today, Angus. I've been working with Cormac and his brother almost every day, but it's nice to get a different perspective. I learned a lot."

"Yer quite welcome, lad. I'll see ye later on then."

Angus walked off with the same huge grin on his face. "I thought he liked me," Dylan muttered to himself.

Chapter 6

Over the next few days, Maggie found herself fighting off Brielle's attempts to harm her more and more regularly. She had to keep her guard up and remember to use the spell of protection whenever she was in Brielle's presence. Not always an easy task, as Brielle had a habit of sneaking up on Maggie at the oddest moments. So far, she was aiming the majority of her magick at Maggie and she had, for the most part, left the others alone while she focused her attention on getting Maggie out of the way. That's not to say that she wasn't causing problems throughout the castle. In the grand scheme of things, they were just small problems, but to the residents of Breaghacraig, they were as annoying as the midges that pestered them when they ventured outdoors.

"Alec, would ye mind helping the boys mop up the water pouring down from Ashley and Cailin's chambers, please?" Irene looked completely flummoxed as she came storming through the great hall. "I'm not sure where all that water is coming from!"

"Aye. I'd be happy to help," Maggie said. Making her way to the stairs, she saw an unbelievable amount of water cascading down and several young boys with mops trying in vain to wipe it up. As fast as they were mopping, the faster the water was falling. Maggie ran up the stairs to the source of the flood and found a bathtub filled with water. Upon further examination, she noted a good size hole in the side and while water was pouring out through it, the water level in the tub had not diminished. She focused her intention on the tub and with a minimal amount of effort, she was able to plug the hole as if it had never even been there. Next, she used her magick to dry up the water in the bedchamber and the passageway leading to the stairs. When she was satisfied that the water had been stopped, she headed to the stairs where she found the boys looking extremely relieved that the waterfall that had been pouring down the stairs had stopped and they were finally able to make some headway in their efforts to clean up the mess. Maggie made it to the bottom of the steps and discovered Brielle staring at her, a malicious grin on her face, but before Maggie could open her mouth to speak she heard Mary caterwauling from the kitchen.

"Och! What have ye done here, Jenna?" Mary cried. "I've nae seen anythin' like this."

Maggie headed towards the source of the shouting and found Mary and Jenna surrounded by loaves of bread that had been set to rise. The only problem was, they had risen to ten times the size they should have and were slowly making their way across every surface in the kitchen.

"I cannae believe this," Mary said in exasperation. "Ye are truly bad luck, lass. Ye always seem to be about whenever something goes wrong in me kitchen."

"Mary, I don't know what happened! You can ask Sophia. We made the bread the same way we always do. There was nothing in the bread that would have caused this to happen."

"Dinnae speak to me of Sophia. She's as cursed as ye are. I dinnae believe I want ye in me kitchen again!" Mary ran from the room with Jenna in hot pursuit.

Maggie took the opportunity to fix the mess that Brielle had undoubtedly created and when she left the kitchen, the loaves were back to normal and ready to be placed in the oven. Mary and Jenna passed her in the hallway, on their way back to the kitchen. Mary was waving her arms and going on and on about the bread and the mess in her kitchen. Jenna followed behind her, trying to get a word in edgewise. Maggie waited nearby, to hear the two women's reactions as they entered the kitchen and saw the bread and kitchen looking as if nothing out of the ordinary had happened. Mary abruptly stopped speaking and from the sounds of it, Jenna ran straight into her back as she entered the kitchen and came to a standstill.

"I cannae believe me eyes," Mary said. "Jenna, were the loaves not overflowing all over the kitchen when we left?"

"They were," Jenna sounded just as confused. "This is weird. They shouldn't have been overflowing in the first place and now it's like nothing happened."

"Strange things be happenin' here in Breaghacraig, Jenna. I dinnae ken why, but someone is using magick. I feel it in me bones."

Maggie listened as the two, obviously at a loss for words, began working together again in the kitchen.

"Well, let's get this bread in the oven and hope nothing else happens before it's baked," Jenna suggested.

Satisfied that all was well in the kitchen, Maggie went back to the great hall, where Irene was filling Robert in on all of the odd happenings occurring around the castle.

"Alec," Irene said. "Thank ye for helping the boys with the mopping. I see that ye got it under control a lot faster than I would have believed possible."

"Yer verra welcome. I am here to help in any way that I can," Maggie replied.

"Well, if I could ask one more thing of ye, lad," Robert said. "Dylan is out trying to round up the horses that escaped the barn earlier this day. He could use some help. The stable boys are out with him, but there are many to catch and I believe they could use another pair of hands."

"Of course. I'll go right away." Maggie wasn't sure she wanted to be anywhere near Dylan. She wasn't verra good at masking her feelings and she had to work extra hard at it when she was around him. It was a mixture of love, anger and jealousy, which overcame her whenever she saw him. Especially when Brielle was nearby.

* * *

It was apparent that every horse in the stables had gotten loose and they had all fled through the open gates into the pasture surrounding the castle. They were obviously happy to be out and were running like the wind, bucking and crow hopping everywhere she looked. Dylan and the boys were approaching individual horses, ropes in hand. Every time they would get close, the horses would bolt away. Without caring what the others would think, Maggie stood perfectly still with her hands out towards the horses. She settled her mind and called to them. The entire herd of horses trotted her way.

"Alec," Dylan called. "Be careful. They're heading right at you."

Maggie didn't respond. She was focused on getting the horses to come to her and she had no time to worry about what would happen when they reached her. She only hoped they'd stop before they trampled her and much to her relief, they did. She spoke to them softly as Dylan and the boys ran over to her.

"Don't frighten them," she ordered. "They've stopped and now, if you don't mind, I'll head back to the stables with them."

"That's impossible. How are you going to get them to follow you," Dylan questioned.

"You'll see." Maggie turned her back on the horses and speaking softly to them coaxed them into following her. She looked like the pied piper as the horses fell into line behind her and followed her back through the gate into the courtyard, where she turned and headed toward the stable. The doors were already open wide in anticipation of the return of the horses and Maggie walked down the center aisle, opening stall doors as she went. Each of the horses obediently entered their own stall as they came to them and Dylan and the stable boys closed and locked the doors behind them. Finally, the last horse was settled into his stall.

"Are you some kind of horse whisperer?" Dylan asked. He had one brow cocked over his beautiful, deep brown eyes.

"Let's just say I have a way with animals," Maggie answered, trying not to make eye contact with him. She got all fluttery in the belly when he spoke to her, which was not good. She turned to walk away, but Dylan grabbed her arm firmly. The feel of his warm skin through the light material of her shirt got her mind wandering to places it shouldn't.

"I'd say you have more than a way with animals, Alec. I've never seen anything like that. The boys and I were out there for more than an hour, trying to catch even a single horse with no luck and you walk out and stand perfectly still and they come to you. What's your trick?"

"I have nae trick," Maggie lied. It was her secret and she was not about to share it. "I must go. Irene may need me help." She wrestled her arm out of Dylan's grasp and attempted once again to walk away.

"Wait. I've been meaning to talk to you. I haven't had much chance since the other day, and I know you told me you don't know Maggie, but it sure seems like you do. I was wondering if there was anything you could tell me about her. Anything Edna or Angus might have mentioned to you?" Dylan was watching Maggie intently, and she quickly glanced down, rather than risk giving herself away by mooning over him.

As usual, whenever she was anywhere near him, her heart began to race and she found herself hyperventilating. She concentrated on getting that under control. "Why do ye continue to ask me?" she snapped. "I'm afraid I dinnae ken much about yer Maggie. I've only just met her." That wasn't a lie. She had just met Brielle, but she did know more about her than she could safely share. Maggie wished she could show Dylan that she was the real Maggie, but she had been sworn to secrecy. Why, she still didn't ken, but she hoped for Dylan's sake that soon he'd understand the truth. "Now if ye'll excuse me, I must go." Maggie raced off toward the great hall. She hadn't seen Brielle since the water incident and Maggie hoped that she was done causing trouble for the day. It was exhausting, continually trying to set things straight. At the last minute, she decided to change course and head to the soldier's barracks. Maggie needed to clear her head and take a few minutes to sort through everything.

* * *

"Ye look like ye've been to war," Angus announced to Maggie as she entered their chamber. Angus was relaxing on one of the beds and Maggie settled wearily on the other.

"I feel like it too," Maggie responded. "This is a lot harder than I thought it would be." She glanced over at Angus, who was giving her that fatherly look he saved for all *his lasses*. "Actually, that's not true. I had no idea what it would be like. One of the many things I don't understand is why the MacKenzies are putting up with Brielle."

"The MacKenzies are a very welcoming and hospitable clan. No matter how Brielle behaves and no matter what they think of her, they will be kind to her. Now, as for ye, yer doing an amazing job of keeping Brielle under control. Yer Aunt Edna would be so verra proud of ye. She had faith in ye and yer proving she was right to believe ye could do this."

"But what exactly am I doing? I know I'm putting out fires and stopping floods and a dozen other things, but what is the end goal? That's what I don't understand. I'm frustrated beyond belief, because no one here knows who I am! They all believe that *witch* is me, and I can't say I'm happy about it. She's rude and inconsiderate most of the time and yet smiling in their faces as she turns away to cause more trouble. I'd like to wipe that smile right off of her face." Maggie had built up quite a head of steam as she continued to vent her frustrations. "She could destroy them in a heartbeat, yet she doesn't. She's playing with them - like a cat with a mouse. What is she up to? Why is she even here? And why is she after my Dylan?"

"Are ye through with yer ranting, Maggie?" Angus shook his head. "I agree with ye. Brielle gives witches a bad name, but yer Aunt Edna is the only one who can answer those questions for ye and if she doesnae wish to, well, ye ken it's like requesting answers of a brick wall. A very lovely brick wall, but a brick wall, nonetheless." Angus chuckled at his own analogy.

"Well, that goes a long way towards *not* making me feel better." Maggie flopped back onto the bed with her arm covering her eyes.

"Rest awhile before we go in for the evening meal. I believe I'll take a nap as well," Angus yawned and closed his eyes.

Maggie ran through the day's events in her weary head and had to admit that despite her frustrations, she was pleased and proud of the way she had handled everything. When Edna had told Maggie she wanted her to take care of Brielle, Maggie had been terrified that she would fail, but so far everything had been relatively easy to fix. The one thing she had no control over, was what Brielle would do next and Maggie feared that this was just the beginning of her troubles with that one.

* * *

At the evening meal, everyone chatted about the unusual day it had been. Dylan was singing Alec's praises and telling how amazed he was, to see Alec gather all the horses and bring them back to the stables singlehandedly. Irene thanked Alec again for his help with the flooding and further down the table, Jenna was relating the story of the dough as she shared a piece of the bread, made from the same troublesome batch, with Cormac.

Maggie was sure to put up a protective barrier around herself and Angus. She wished she could cover all of the table's occupants, but Brielle was thwarting her efforts at every turn and casting a steely gaze her way, in an effort to intimidate her. As Dylan continued to sing Alec's praises, Brielle was getting more and more irritated and Maggie worried that she'd do something to hurt him. The thought no sooner came to Maggie, than Dylan's voice grew hoarse and he sounded like a croaking frog. He tried clearing his throat by coughing, but to no avail.

"Are ye alright, my love?" Brielle cooed. "Here, drink something, it should help." She handed Dylan his tankard of ale, which he drank from, but his voice did not come back to anything more than a whisper. "Don't speak, love. Rest yer voice for now." She smiled triumphantly towards Maggie. She couldn't have been any plainer regarding her intentions. Maggie got the message loud and clear.

Conversation picked up around them once again and Maggie gazed down the table, to see Brielle kissing Dylan's cheek and rubbing his back. Maggie ate the rest of her meal in silence and kept her eyes focused directly in front of her. She knew that if she saw Brielle touch Dylan one more time, she'd be tempted to break her arm and since that would be a verra bad idea, it was best to turn towards Angus and ignore the other end of the table.

"I believe tomorrow will be a day of celebration and feasting, Alec." Angus finished the last piece of food on his plate and poured himself another drink.

"Really. What are they celebrating?" Maggie asked distractedly.

"Samhuinn, of course. Where is your head at, lad?" Angus raised an eyebrow in disbelief.

"Oh, that's right. I forgot."

"It will be a good time. Ye'll see. First thing we'll do is go apple picking. And then we'll return here to a feast, music, dancing and end it all with a huge bonfire in the courtyard." From the gleam in Angus' eyes, Maggie could see how much he was looking forward to the next day's events.

"I don't know if a bonfire is a good idea. Not with you know who here," Maggie tipped her head in Brielle's direction.

"I see what ye mean, but we cannae ask them to ignore tradition without good cause." Angus took another sip of his cider. "Ye'll have to be extra vigilant."

Maggie was feeling overwhelmed. "It's exhausting keeping track of that witch," she muttered. "I wish she'd go away and leave us all in peace." Her anger and frustration were showing and she wasn't certain how to deal with it. Never in her life had she needed to deal with a situation like this. Up to this point, her life had been mundane. She had enjoyed a happy childhood, had good parents and the love and support of everyone around her. The only remotely difficult thing she'd had to deal with was her parents' divorce, and even that had been done in such a way that it caused little heartache in the family.

The MacKenzies were all finished with their meal and were slowly leaving the table, heading off towards their chambers or to seats in front of the fire. It had been a relatively quiet meal, Brielle had seen to that. Maggie had gotten her nerve up again and was about to peek down the table when Dylan walked right up to her. Casting a quick glance around, Maggie noted that Brielle wasn't with him and seemed to have already left the Great Hall. Dylan was trying to say something to her, but nothing was coming out of his mouth. Maggie couldn't stand to see him suffer from the effects of Brielle's magick, so she focused on his throat and with a few quick words spoken silently to herself and a wave of her hand, his voice was back. No one seemed to notice and Dylan, after clearing his throat a time or two, realized he could speak again.

"Looks like I finally got my voice back. I wanted to stop over here and thank you again for your help today. You were pretty amazing with the horses."

Maggie felt a blush creeping up her neck and suddenly felt extremely shy. "It was nothing."

"I wouldn't say that. The stable boys and I would have been out there all day, and long into the night, trying unsuccessfully to grab even one of them. They obviously responded to you."

She didn't answer him, instead turning to Angus. "Angus, I'm going to head off to bed."

"Alright then. I'll be up shortly," Angus rose from his chair and turned to Dylan. "I'm glad ye got yer voice back, lad."

"Thanks, me too. I don't know what happened. I was fine one minute and the next I couldn't make a sound." Dylan cleared his throat one more time, as if to confirm he could still speak.

"Allergies," Maggie offered.

"Maybe. Hey, I'm heading back to the soldier's quarters, too. I'll walk with you." Dylan smiled, nearly undoing her.

"Where's Maggie?" she asked, glancing around the hall.

"She was tired, so she went to her room. Are you going to this apple-picking thing tomorrow?"

"Aye. Everyone is, I think." Maggie was seeking some way to avoid walking with Dylan, but she didn't see how she could do it without appearing completely rude. She'd just have to keep acting as Alec and tried to guess how two guys would normally talk to each other. Maggie was definitely a girly-girl. Always had been, but even as a girl she didn't have a lot of experience talking to men, other than her Da and Uncle Angus. She decided the less said the better and let Dylan do all the talking, which he seemed happy to do.

"Your friend, Angus, he's a great guy. I met him back at Glendaloch and I wish I'd had more time there to get to know him. It's nice that he's here. I know Maggie is happy about it."

"Is she now?" Maggie queried lightly.

"Yeah. She's told me how much she loves him and her Aunt Edna. What they've meant to her, you know." They were approaching the stairs to the soldier's barracks and he stopped. Maggie was content to continue without him, but he caught her by the arm and stopped her.

"You know, you remind me of someone."

"I can't imagine who," Maggie said anxiously, getting nervous about where this conversation was going.

"Me either. I've been racking my brains since you got here, trying to figure it out. It'll come to me, but we've never met before, have we?"

"No, of course not. Where would we have met?" Maggie hated lying to him, but she had no choice. "I'm heading up. I'm really tired."

"Yeah, me too."

They climbed the stairs to their rooms and stopped in front of Alec's door. "Okay. Well, I'll see you tomorrow, Alec. Thanks again for your help." Dylan patted Maggie on the shoulder sending her flying forward. "You could use some muscle there, my friend, but don't worry, you'll get there. You're still growing, plenty of time for that."

Maggie stood there for a moment, feeling like a daft fool. How could she not? Here she was standing face-to-face with the most attractive man she'd ever met. Everything about him exuded masculinity. A sexual gravity was pulling her towards him and then, idiot that she was, she reached her hand out and tentatively placed it on his chest. The feel of the solid muscle beneath her fingers made her panic. "See you," Maggie darted into her room and closed the door in the face of Dylan's confusion. *That was close.* She'd had to bite her tongue to keep from telling him who she really was. Walking beside him from the great hall, she could feel the heat of his body next to hers and then standing so close to him outside her room and looking into his eyes, she'd wanted to reach up and kiss him and she almost had. Luckily she caught herself in time. It was bad enough she'd actually touched him and then she'd used what little control she had left, to turn away from him. Now here she stood, back against the door, fighting the urge to open it again and march down to his room and... *Stop it, Maggie! Don't be stupid! I've got to stop thinking about him that way, at least for the time being. I've got to let the thoughts I'm having go, for my own sanity. If Dylan is still interested in me when this is all over with, I'll be in a better place to pick up where we left off, but until then I have to focus on Brielle.*

* * *

As Dylan walked away from Alec's door, he was haunted by the continued suspicion that he knew the young guy. The idea would simply not leave his mind. Alec had told him they'd never met, but he didn't necessarily believe him. Dylan knew he had to figure it out. It would drive him crazy otherwise. He hummed to himself as he entered his room, happy that his voice had returned. It had been weird how he'd been fine one minute and the next he couldn't utter a sound. He had been talking about what a great job Alec had done rounding up the horses and then Maggie had given him a strange look. He was trying to read her, understand what she was trying to say to him with her eyes and next thing he knew he couldn't speak. *Did Maggie do that to me? What reason could she have, to want to stop me from talking about Alec?* Dylan shook his head, deciding he was letting his imagination get the better of him, but the more he thought about Maggie, the more he realized she had been acting very strangely, from the very first moment he saw her in the woods. Chester was scared to death of her, which was very unlike him, and now that Dylan thought about it, ever since Maggie had arrived, Chester had stayed as far away from Dylan as he could. He was spending almost all of his time with Cormac. Jenna and Ashley had also commented on Maggie's behavior. Jenna was having a hard time believing she was the same person they'd met in Glendaloch and Ashley thought the girl she'd met in the teashop had been much friendlier, with a bit of mischief hovering just beneath the surface. The Maggie currently residing in Breaghacraig definitely didn't fit that description at all. She was standoffish with everyone, seemed lacking in the personality department and as for mischief, there was something there, but it seemed a bit darker. Dylan could almost believe that she had been kidnapped and replaced with a physically exact replica, but was he being too cynical? He had always been a very easy-going guy, not letting things bother him, intent on enjoying life and up until this very moment, having a woman in his life for more than a day or two didn't seem to matter. *Maggie, Maggie, Maggie, where did you go?* Dylan decided he was going to have to dig deeper to find out what was going on with her. She had come all the way from Glendaloch to see him and while she was very attentive where he was concerned, she didn't seem sincere. He decided to play it by ear and see how things went in the next few days. Having briefly glimpsed love back in Glendaloch, Dylan wasn't about to give up on it now that he had the object of that glimpse here within reach, but he did have a few things to figure out. How could he have such strong feelings one day and then none. With any luck, whatever was going on with her would work itself out and he'd have the Maggie he longed for back in his life again.

Chapter 7

Sir Richard Jefford entered the great hall of his castle. Situated on the border between Northern England and Scotland, it was an expansive fortress, surrounded by lush green fields and forests. It was the type of castle any man would be happy to call home, but Richard rarely spent more than a few days there. Most of his time was spent plotting and planning ways to get back at Robert MacKenzie. Events of the past week had him questioning that need to seek revenge. After yet another sleepless night, Richard's normally handsome face revealed a haggard appearance.

"Richard, you look as though you've not slept a wink." The Lady Catherine stood before him with a disapproving scowl on her usually sweet, pretty face.

"That would be because I haven't, my dearest mother." Richard made his way wearily to the table where servants immediately set out food and drink for him to break his fast. "Will you join me, mother?"

Lady Catherine did not answer, silently seating herself by his side. "What troubles you, Richard?"

He ignored the food, staring off into a corner of the room. "I'm having terrible nightmares. I don't understand why. I normally sleep like a baby, but for some reason during this past week, every time I close my eyes I'm—" Richard dropped his head into his hands and lapsed into silence.

"Tell me what you are seeing. Mayhap I can help you," Lady Catherine suggested.

"It's those damn MacKenzies. Every time I close my eyes, I see them," he explained, sounding distressed. "I see all of the terrible things I've done to them, one after the other and the memories repeat themselves, over and over again. I feel so guilty and I don't know how to make it stop. Every night for the past week, I've been having horrible visions of my past." He lowered his voice to a whisper as he continued. "The young Lady Ashley, she haunts me more than the others. I struck her, mother. I feel I was possessed by a demon. Perhaps I am a demon." Richard searched his mother's shocked face for an answer. She had always been there for him and had been more than patient with Richard in the past, but she also never let him get away with anything without giving her opinion. Lady Catherine had been very unhappy with his behavior regarding the MacKenzies and she'd been quite vocal in her disapproval.

"Guilt can only be relieved by taking actions to correct the error in your ways, Richard."

"What do you mean? How can I possibly make anything I've done in the past right?" Richard pounded his fist on the table in frustration.

"Richard, you were such a good boy when you were young, but you have let your emotions rule you as you've gotten older. This vendetta you have against the MacKenzies is foolish. You need to stop it before it is too late, before you do something you will regret forever."

His mother was a wise woman, but he hadn't truly listened to her in years. She had always told him to forget about Irene and to go on and live his life. She had told him he would never find anyone to replace Irene in his heart, until he had truly let her go. Richard had turned a deaf ear to her all along. Instead, he'd spent all his time thinking of ways to exact revenge on Robert MacKenzie. He had begun to believe that he was losing his grasp on his sanity, but maybe the exact opposite was happening. Perhaps his mother had been right all along and perhaps these nightmares were the key to him reclaiming his future.

"What is it you have done this time, Richard? What is it that is giving you nightmares so horrible that you cannot sleep?" Lady Catherine seemed to see right through him. She stood and placed her hand on his shoulder. When he didn't respond to her questions, she said, "I love you so very much, my son. I want nothing more than your happiness, but you will never find happiness until you make your peace with the MacKenzies."

Richard was embarrassed to tell Lady Catherine what he had planned with the witch, Brielle, but she was the only person whom he could trust. The one person who would always love him. He wished he were a young lad again, so that he could seek solace in his mother's arms. He was too old for that though, or so he told himself. "Mother, I've..." he began to speak and then hesitated. Taking a deep breath, he forced himself to continue. "There's a witch named Brielle. I've sent her to Breaghacraig, disguised as someone they know, to destroy the MacKenzies. She's there as we speak and I don't believe I can stop her... not now."

"I don't understand," Lady Catherine said. "Why wouldn't you be able to stop her?"

Richard took a moment to gather his thoughts. "You see, Brielle has her own reasons for wanting to destroy the MacKenzies. She's not doing it solely for my objectives. She wants the bridge."

Lady Caroline frowned. "What bridge are you speaking of?"

"The bridge through time, mother. Have I not told you about it?" Richard suddenly remembered that he had never mentioned it to her. "It's a bridge that allows certain people to cross from one time period to another." Catching sight of his mother's incredulous expression, he explained further. "I did not believe it possible myself, to begin with, but I have travelled across it, mother, to a time far in the future." His mother was staring at him as if he had lost his mind. "It's true. I know it sounds absurd, but believe me, it is true."

Lady Catherine eyed her son sadly. "Richard, you are truly suffering from lack of sleep. That is all. There can be no such thing as a bridge that spans time, but if what you say is true about this witch, you must stop her."

Richard thought about this for a moment. He'd give anything to stop the nightmares. They played out continually in his mind, not only when he managed to snatch a few minutes of sleep, but also when he was awake. He couldn't seem to escape them. Perhaps his mother was right. He should ride to Breaghacraig and alert them to Brielle's presence, and beg their forgiveness at the same time. The thought of begging forgiveness from anyone galled him, but he knew in his heart that his mother was right, in fact, had been right all along. If he was ever to be happy again, he was going to have to humble himself in front of Irene and Robert. More than anything, he wished to apologize to Ashley. She undoubtedly hated him and Cailin would wish him dead. It mattered not if they were to forgive him, he would do it and if he lived through it, he would leave them alone and in peace from that moment forward.

"You are right, mother. I will take your advice and I will stop Brielle. It is the only way."

His mother seemed satisfied with this agreement and coaxing Richard to stand, she wrapped her arms around him, "I am proud of you, Richard." She held him close for a few minutes, and then slipped out of the room, leaving him alone with his thoughts.

Suddenly feeling lighter in mood, Richard found his appetite, eating and drinking like a starving man. In truth, he actually was starving. He hadn't eaten more than a few bites since the nightmares began, but it wasn't merely food he hungered for. He was hungry to unburden himself from the guilt, which over the years had become his constant companion. He was hungry for the love and approval of his mother; although he knew he had always had her love, he found that he also hankered for her approval. He decided there and then, he was going to be a changed man beginning immediately.

* * *

The inner courtyard was filled with people getting ready for the orchard visit. Carts were loaded down with baskets for the apples they would pick and filled barrels of honey, which would be brushed onto the trunks of the apple trees to feed the faeries. Three apples would be left on the branches of each tree for the Fae, in hopes that it would please them and ensure a good harvest the following year. It was an ancient custom and Maggie was fascinated by it all. Her love of ritual, myth and magick was being fed right along with the faeries today. She could hardly wait to get started.

"Do ye think we'll see any real faeries today?" Maggie looked up expectantly at Angus.

"Nae. They dinnae want to be seen. They'll be hiding and waiting for us to leave before they venture out. We can only hope they'll be pleased and bless the MacKenzies with another good harvest next year."

The procession to the orchards began. Robert and Irene struck off first, their children tagging along beside them. Next came Cailin, Ashley, Cormac and Jenna. Ashley and Jenna looked beautiful as always as they laughed and teased with their husbands. Dylan and Brielle were followed by Helene and Dougall, Sophia and Latharn. Watching all these happy couples was hard for Maggie to bear. She'd hoped to find her happily ever after in the arms of Dylan Sinclair and instead she was alone. Knowing that her self-pitying thoughts would not change anything, Maggie pulled herself together and followed Angus as he joined the others. After the last of the clan had fallen into line to begin the walk, the carts, filled to the brim with their cargo, followed behind. It was a lively, fun atmosphere and it couldn't have been a better day either. The sun was shining brightly and while the air was crisp, there wasn't a cloud in the sky. Luck was on their side - it didn't appear that it would rain and ruin their fun this day.

* * *

The group reached the first orchard and everyone joined in a song of praise for the apple trees. When they were done, baskets were retrieved from the carts and set at the base of each trunk. The couples paired off and found trees with plenty of apples they could gather. Cormac hoisted Jenna up onto his shoulders, so that she could reach high up into the branches. She handed the apples down to him and shrieked every time he dipped down to put them in the basket. Dylan chuckled as he watched them, amazed at the transformation Jenna had undergone since marrying Cormac. Before their marriage, she had been difficult at best and often prickly, as Cormac liked to say, but she had really settled in here and was obviously very much in love with her husband. She was much more relaxed and the prickly Jenna was no-where to be found. He smiled thinking about it. She had fought against her feelings for Cormac, tooth and nail, and when she'd finally given up the fight, she was the happiest he'd ever seen her. Her playful side came out whenever she was around Cormac. Dylan was happy for her and for his friend Ashley. She had also found love here at Breaghac-raig. Her husband, Cailin, doted on her and the expectant parents were excited about their future family. Even Sophia, who had unintentional-ly found herself here in medieval Scotland, had found her place among the MacKenzies. She worked in the kitchen every day and seemed to love learning about the way things were done here. She had a special relationship with Mary, the cook, who had taken Sophia under her wing and treated her as if she were her own daughter. Latharn was clearly smitten with Sophia and the feeling was obviously mutual. They spent as much time together as possible and Dylan was happy that de-spite the way she had arrived, Sophia was content. She wasn't even angry with Dylan anymore and the two had developed a nice friend-ship, which would never have been possible back in San Francisco. Now if he could only get his own love life straightened out. With a sigh, he glanced around the orchard. Maggie had disappeared on him again. He didn't know where she had gone off to this time, but it seemed as if he was always trying to find her. There were so many people wandering through the orchard that it made it difficult to see her through the crowds, but at last he found her, seated beneath one of the trees, staring up into the branches.

"Hey, there you are. I've been looking for you," Dylan said as he approached her. He sat down next to Maggie, searching her alluring face, hoping to see the old Maggie again and disappointed when he didn't.

"Have ye?" Maggie asked, continuing her perusal of the tree branches.

"Do you want to pick some apples? Looks like we've got this tree all to ourselves." Dylan waved his hand in front of her face to get her attention.

Maggie blinked and her eyes finally focused on him. "I'm sorry, what did ye say?"

"Let's pick some apples!" He stood and put his hand out for her, helping her up.

She gathered apples from the bottom branches and placed them in the basket. "This is fun," she said, sarcastically rolling her eyes.

Dylan sighed heavily and decided to broach the subject he'd been avoiding for days now. "Maggie, is something wrong? You seem so different from when we first met." She didn't respond, and Dylan tried again. "Have you changed your mind about me... lost interest?" he asked.

Seeming to wake from her trance, Maggie really looked at Dylan for the first time that day, "Lost interest? Don't be silly. I find ye verra attractive and I want nothing more than to be with ye." Her tongue darted out to wet her lips and before Dylan could question what was happening, she was in his arms and kissing him.

His first reaction was to push her away, but on second thoughts, Dylan decided that maybe if he hung in there, the kiss would get better. So far, it was doing nothing for him. It didn't improve in the next minute or so, but not for lack of trying. *I'm overthinking this.* He tried the kiss again and put everything he had into it. He could feel Maggie melting into him, but nothing was happening for him emotionally. He deepened the kiss, feeling Maggie's feet go right out from underneath her and she hung in his arms like a ragdoll. *At least I haven't lost my touch,* he thought to himself, even though at the same time he was thinking he couldn't remember not experiencing at least some reaction to a kiss. Opening his eyes, he noticed Alec staring daggers at him.

"I wonder what Alec's problem is? He must be jealous," Dylan murmured into Maggie's ear.

"But of which one of us?" was her strange response.

Dylan thought it an odd comment to make, but let it slip to the back of his mind. Releasing Maggie, they continued picking apples until the trees were almost bare. Robert was gathering everyone around him in the center of the orchard when Dylan and Maggie completed their own apple picking.

"Thank ye all for joining us today. I believe we've made the faeries happy with all our singing and playing. They will surely bless us with another good harvest next year. Now, let's all head back to the courtyard, where we will partake of cider made from the apples of these fine trees." Robert scooped Irene into his arms before he continued. "The celebration will continue long into the night. There will be plenty of food and drink, good music and, of course, our traditional bonfire."

The crowd cheered and began loading the apple-filled baskets back onto the carts. The sky was beginning to darken and the wind whipped fallen leaves in small flurries across the ground. Cloaks were gathered tighter to ward off the chill in the air and everyone moved quickly to finish loading the apples.

A clap of thunder rumbled loudly as the sky grew dark and ominous and a single bolt of lightning struck, too close for comfort, causing some of the group to shriek in fear. Striking a nearby tree, its shattered branches flew in every direction. The MacKenzies ran for cover as a second bolt flew from the sky, hitting another of the trees. A fireworks display of twigs and branches rained down on them as the tree exploded. Whole tree limbs were falling now and men and women dodged them, as they cried out to each other to avoid the heavy branches headed for the ground with such great velocity. Cormac grabbed Jenna and they ran towards the carts, followed by Ashley and Cailin. They huddled close to the wooden sides, Cormac and Cailin sheltering Jenna and Ashley with their large bodies. Robert and Irene, who had grabbed their children, were directing the rest of the clan to run. More lightning struck and more trees exploded around them. The sun, blotted from the sky, was unable to help them as they fled in almost total darkness. Latharn was hit by a sharp piece of tree branch that seemed to aim itself straight for him as he protected Sophia in his arms. Sophia screamed as he hit the ground, blood dripping from his head, where a jagged piece of wood had lodged itself in his skin.

Maggie knew this was not a random act of nature's majesty. This was an act of Brielle. She had to put a stop to this, before someone else was hurt or even killed by a falling branch. Eyes searching in the near darkness, Maggie spotted Brielle, who sported a gleeful expression. Dylan was trying to drag her away, but Brielle was standing firm, rooted to the spot. Maggie couldn't worry about her right now; instead, she concentrated her focus on the lightning and the exploding trees. She closed her eyes and took a calming inhalation, muttering beneath her breath. "Frozen in place, let these branches be. Lightning away from the apple trees. Calm once again, so mote it be." Opening her eyes, Maggie saw the fruits of her labor. The tree shrapnel was suspended in the air above their heads. The skies cleared and brightened and the lightning disappeared. Relieved, she glanced around and saw Sophia sobbing over an extremely still Latharn.

"Maggie," Dylan said to Brielle, as she stood with a knowing smile aimed at the real Maggie. "You did it! You stopped the trees from killing us all!"

"Aye. I did, Dylan. I couldnae let anything happen to you or the MacKenzies," Brielle lied, with obviously feigned sincerity.

The real Maggie ran across to Latharn and Sophia. "Help him, please," Sophia pleaded.

"I'll do my best, Sophia. Let me get a look at him." She guided Sophia out of the way and knelt beside Latharn. Maggie scanned the area surreptitiously, to make certain no one was watching. Fortunately, they all seemed to be preoccupied with other things. She passed her hand over Latharn's head and his eyes opened. She made another pass, this time removing the shard of wood, and all the while making it appear as if she were merely examining his head.

"Sophia," Latharn moaned. "Are ye safe?"

"Yes, Latharn. Is he okay?" Sophia asked Alec.

"Aye. It's just a slight wound, but ye ken head wounds bleed furiously. It looks much worse than it be."

"Oh, thank you, Alec. I was so worried when he wouldn't open his eyes." Sophia took hold of Latharn's hand and held on for dear life.

"Leave him rest there for a minute. I think he should ride back in one of the carts. I'll go see to it." Maggie got to her feet and headed over to the carts. Angus was waiting for her.

"Brielle?" was all he said.

"Aye. I heard Dylan speaking with her and he thinks *she's* the one who saved everyone and she agreed with him!" Maggie was fuming again. Brielle had gone too far this time. She had to find a way to get her away from Breaghacraig.

The MacKenzies, who had been enjoying the festivities so much all day had now become very subdued. All the joy had been sucked right out of them, which made Maggie both sad and infuriated. She would fix this. She had to, before someone ended up dead.

"Is Latharn going to be alright?" Angus asked.

"Aye. His wound was much more serious than it would appear now, but I used the healing spell Auntie taught me and it worked. I do think he should ride in one of the carts though."

Angus hurried off and spoke with one of the cart drivers, directing him to where Latharn was still laying on the ground with Sophia clutching his hand tightly to her chest. They loaded him up beside the driver and Sophia scooted in next to him, holding onto Latharn for all she was worth.

As Brielle passed, she whispered so only Maggie could hear, "A fine piece of work you did, lass. Ye ruined my fun. Yer auntie has taught ye well." She gave Maggie a challenging look and grabbed onto Dylan's arm for the walk back to Breaghacraig.

Angus caught the tail end of what had just happened. "I don't like this. I think we might be in over our heads."

"Nae, we arenae. Dinnae even think it," Maggie's confidence was building and she knew that no matter what Brielle threw her way, she would be able to counter it. She knew she needed to keep her guard up and keep a wary eye on Brielle though. One minor slip of concentration could be the end of her, Dylan and the MacKenzies.

* * *

The atmosphere at the evening's bonfire remained subdued, the day's events had seen to that. The clan gathered quietly around the bonfire and stared into the flames, some of them wondering aloud what type of omen the exploding trees could be. Would next year's harvest be lost? More than half of the trees in the orchard had been destroyed. People were whispering quietly to one another about the wrath of the faeries and the good witch Maggie, who had put a stop to their ire.

"How can I stop her?" the real Maggie whispered to herself.

"Stop who?" Dylan asked as he suddenly appeared behind her.

"Oh. The faeries. They'll want their revenge," Maggie said, surprised at being overheard and needing to think quickly to cover her thoughts.

"Why would that be your responsibility? Do you really believe in faeries?" Dylan was standing beside her now and once again, Maggie felt those familiar yearnings, tugging at her heartstrings.

"'Tis not my responsibility, of course. But I'd like to help though. If there were some way to put everyone at ease about what has happened, I'd like to do that." Maggie meant what she said. She hated that what had started out as a day of fun and tradition had ended in fear and sadness and it was all Brielle's fault.

"And the faeries?" Dylan wanted to know.

"Aye. I believe in faeries and witches, but I dinnae believe that the faeries were to blame for what happened today, though they willnae be happy that their trees were destroyed."

"Do you think it was a passing storm, or do you believe something else was at work here?" Dylan questioned seriously.

"Yer full of questions, arenae ye? I'm afraid I dinnae ken why it happened, but I'd like to find out."

"So would I. Maybe we could work together to figure it out." Dylan appeared to be very sincere in his willingness to help. He was watching Maggie with his heavenly brown eyes and Maggie had to swallow deeply.

Maggie straightened up and looked away from him, before she gave away her true feelings. "Maybe we could." She gathered all of her strength and walked away from him, melting into the crowd before he could follow.

Chapter 8

Dylan wasn't familiar with witches and faeries, but he was not one to discount their existence, especially since Edna Campbell had made him a believer by allowing him to cross the bridge into another time. He had also seen Maggie's handiwork yesterday, when she put a stop to the disaster that took place in the apple orchard. But what had caused it? It didn't add up. It had been a beautiful sunny day and then, without warning, the trees around them were exploding - there was no other way to describe it - and fiery branches rained down on them. It was a frightening spectacle and one he would never forget. Something, *or someone*, had caused it to happen and he was going to get to the bottom of it. He was going to ask Alec to join him today on a ride out to the orchard, to see if he could find any clues. Too many strange goings on here at Breaghacraig were being left without explanation. His natural curiosity had gotten the better of him and he wouldn't rest until he had the answers.

Dylan knocked on Alec's door. "Alec, are you in there?"

"Aye," came the reply. "Give me a minute."

"I was wondering if you'd like to ride out with me to the apple orchard. I want to look for clues." Dylan waited patiently. He could hear rustling on the other side of the door. He assumed he must have woken Alec. The door opened a crack and a sleepy-headed Alec peered out at him. "Do you sleep with that cap on?" Dylan questioned with a laugh.

"Of course I do. It keeps me head warm." Maggie answered a little testily.

"Well, what do you think? Do you want to go with me?"

"Aye. I'd be happy to join ye. I'll meet ye in the courtyard shortly." Maggie stifled a yawn. "Could ye bring some food? I'm quite hungry."

"Sure. I'll go get some from the kitchen and I'll have the stable boys bring our horses. See you in a bit." Dylan turned away and headed downstairs, first to the stables to speak to the stable boys, and next across the courtyard to the kitchen.

As he approached, he could hear the sounds of women talking. He knew it was Jenna, Sophia and Mary, already hard at work preparing food for the day ahead. "Good morning, ladies," Dylan said when he entered the kitchen.

"Good morning," they responded.

"You're up early," Jenna said, dusting the table with flour. The three women began kneading dough as they looked expectantly to Dylan.

"I had a lot on my mind. Sophia, how's Latharn? He took quite a blow to the head yesterday."

"He feels much better this morning. He had a nasty headache last night, but it's gone now. He's going to take it easy for a day or two, whether he likes it or not." Sophia spoke with a very determined expression on her face.

"He won't like it, but I have no doubt he'll follow orders." Dylan chuckled and Sophia's expression relaxed as she joined him. As a waitress in twenty first century San Francisco, Sophia had a crush on Dylan and he had behaved very badly after their first date by not calling her. She had been extremely angry with him, but thank goodness all was forgiven and he was once again in her good graces. He could now appreciate her for the special woman that she was. Latharn was a lucky man.

"What can we get fer ye?" Mary asked. Dylan knew the cook had taken a liking to him since his arrival. She didn't allow many people in her kitchen while she cooked, but she made an exception for him. "Come, love, sit down. Would ye like some bannocks?"

"That would be great. I was wondering if I could get them to go. I'm going riding this morning with Alec and he's hungry, too."

"Of course, of course." Mary grabbed a sack from a nearby rack and began filling it with bannocks, fruit and a flask of cider. "Will that be enough for ye?"

"That should do the trick." Dylan watched as Mary gave him an odd look. He realized she probably didn't understand the modern expression. "Thank you, Mary. You are too good to me." Dylan copied what he had seen the men of this time period do on many occasions and reached for Mary's hand to place a kiss on her fingers.

Mary blushed. "Och. Yer a charmer, ye are."

"Where are you off to?" Jenna asked, as she and Sophia expertly worked with the dough.

"We're heading back to the orchard."

"Do ye think that's safe now? I wouldnae want any harm to come to ye." Mary appeared concerned at his announcement.

"We'll be fine. Don't worry about me, Mary. I'll be very careful." He reassured her with a gentle squeeze of her shoulder. "I'll see you all later on."

Dylan couldn't help but laugh as he walked from the kitchen and overheard Mary speaking to Jenna and Sophia. "He's a handsome one, isnae he?" Mary, who was old enough to be his mother, apparently had a crush on him.

* * *

The courtyard was quiet this morning. Everyone had been up until the wee hours last night and they were probably catching up on some much-needed rest. Maggie stood waiting for Dylan to arrive, holding the horses that had been delivered by the stable boys a few moments before. She wasn't sure it was a good idea to do this, but she wanted to spend time with Dylan, even if she had to pretend to be someone else in order to do it.

"Alec," Dylan called.

Maggie watched as he strode towards her with a sack of food thrown over his shoulder. He couldn't look any better to her if he tried. She masked her obvious admiration by looking down at her feet. This was going to be a challenge. She hoped she didn't slip up.

"I've got some food, Mary packed plenty for both of us. I know you said you were hungry, so grab something and we'll get started." He held out the sack to Maggie and she reached in and took a bannock and a piece of fruit. She had been so preoccupied with Dylan that she didn't even look to see what she had picked, but saw now that it was a beautiful pear. Maggie placed the food in her pocket while she mounted her horse and watched as Dylan mounted his. Retrieving the pear, she bit into it and turned her horse towards the gate with Dylan following close behind. They were just about to pass through, when she heard Brielle calling out to Dylan. The sound of her voice resembled the sound of chalk on a blackboard, and it had the same effect on Maggie.

"Dylan, where are ye off to?" Brielle asked. She was mounted on her own horse and trotted up to them.

"We thought we'd head back out to the apple orchard and take a look around," Dylan answered. "I want to see if we can come up with any explanation for that sudden storm yesterday afternoon."

"Do ye mind if I join ye?" Brielle smiled sweetly at him.

"No. Not at all." Dylan replied.

"What about you, Alec, do ye mind?" Brielle was playing with her as far as Maggie could tell and she had all she could do to keep her voice under control, so she simply shook her head. "Good, I wouldnae want to interfere with yer outing," Brielle added.

Maggie was irritated beyond belief with Brielle, who had obviously intended to be coming with them, no matter what Dylan or she might have to say about it. She nudged her horse forward and rode in front of Dylan and Brielle, who rode side-by-side as they headed for the orchard. *I wonder what she's up to this time. It can't be anything good!*

* * *

"What made you decide to go riding this morning, Maggie?" Dylan was not happy to see her, but he hoped she didn't notice. He had wanted to examine the orchard with Alec alone. There was something strange about the whole situation and the thought had popped into his head that maybe Maggie had more to do with it than it appeared. But why would she do it? It didn't make any sense, and then there was the fact that she had stopped it. His hopes of getting answers, without her hovering around, had been dashed.

Maggie slowed her horse and they both fell back a good distance from Alec. "I was worried fer ye, Dylan," Maggie said quietly. "I believe yer little friend, Alec, may have been the one who caused the lightning strikes yesterday." She turned her sweet face to his.

"Alec? Why would he do something like that?" Dylan was baffled by her accusation. Alec was a young lad, sent by Edna to Breaghacraig along with Angus. What possible reason could he have to do something like that?

"I dinnae ken why, but just before the lightning struck for the first time, I was watching him. He stared into the sky, as if he was calling down the fiery bolts, and then once they began to rain down on us all, he stood there, smiling an evil smile." Rather than sounding concerned about what had happened, she seemed pleased with her recounting.

Dylan gave it some thought and while he didn't necessarily believe Maggie, he felt the need to watch his back on two fronts today. Could he trust either one of them?

"I believe Alec is a witch, Dylan, and I think she's a young woman - not a young lad as she would have everyone believe." Brielle sat atop her horse with a smug smile on her face. "She must have fooled my aunt and uncle into allowing her to come to Breaghacraig."

"I'm not sure what to think about that possibility." Could Alec conceivably be a woman? Admittedly, he was very slight of build and didn't have a lot of strength in his arms or shoulders - that much had been obvious when they'd sparred together a few days ago. Dylan ran everything through his head and had to admit, he was having a hard time believing what he'd just heard. He focused on Alec riding ahead of them and scrutinized the young lad very carefully. *Could he be a woman?* Anything was possible, he supposed. It was one more thing he would need to investigate. He had to get to the bottom of this. "Come on. Let's catch up with Alec."

He spurred his horse forward and Maggie followed along. They reached Alec as he was about to enter the orchard, where the damage was unbelievable. They had been in such a hurry to get away yesterday, that Dylan hadn't really taken notice of the destruction. More than half the trees in this particular orchard had been destroyed. Whole limbs, bits of tree bark, and broken branches were strewn everywhere. There was an eerie silence about the place as they dismounted and walked through the orchard. Dylan took note of each tree, examining the trunks for any sign that what had happened had not been a natural occurrence. Nothing was obvious to him. Alec and Maggie were conducting their own inspection, or at least he hoped they were. They all searched and searched, and yet there was nothing to suggest this was witchcraft and not merely a freak, natural occurrence.

They met in the middle of the orchard. While Alec appeared disappointed, Dylan noted that Maggie didn't look fazed in the least.

"Alec, would ye mind waiting fer us over by the horses?" Maggie asked.

Alec didn't respond, but his eyes flashed angrily at her and then Dylan before he turned to stomp away.

"Thank ye, yer a dear," Maggie called out to Alec's departing back.

"What was that all about?" Dylan wanted to know.

"'Tis nothing. I wanted to be alone with ye for a moment, 'tis all." She sidled closer to him and said, "Kiss me."

* * *

Maggie stood in the shadows and watched as Dylan kissed Brielle. To her eyes, it appeared to be a tender kiss, one that spoke of love and promise. *Her* love and promise, damn it! She fought hard against the urge to disrupt the couple's idyllic moment. *I should be the one he's kissing.* The thought of the sweet kisses she'd shared with Dylan back in Glendaloch assailed her, nearly shattering her fragile composure. Maggie should never have let Dylan leave. She had stupidly encouraged his sense of adventure. She'd let him go, expecting that when next she saw him she would run to his waiting arms and their love would bloom into the happily-ever-after she'd always dreamed of. Instead, she found herself at Breaghacraig, spying on him as he kissed the woman intent on destroying him and the entire clan. *He must be blind,* she thought. *How can he nae see that she isnae me? Surely one look in her eyes would be enough for him to recognize the truth.* Fists clenched and eyes tightly closed, Maggie was steaming mad. The tension was rolling off her body like waves crashing the seashore and the horses sensed her anger. They snorted and danced nervously around her. "Shhh… 'tis fine. Calm yerselves," she soothed. She purred to them like a kitten; a trick she knew would work to settle their harried nerves. "I'm so sorry," she whispered. "I didnae wish to upset ye." The horses visibly relaxed and that was Maggie's cue to do the same. "If this is what is meant to happen, then so be it. I will just have to accept that love may not be for me and perhaps neither is Dylan Sinclair."

* * *

Dylan found himself lowering his head and cradling Maggie's face in his large hands. He hadn't planned on kissing Maggie, but somehow he found himself doing so. He gently kissed her lips. Maggie kissed him back with great passion and intensity, wrapping her arms around his neck and leaning into him, but for Dylan, the kisses fell flat. There was no spark, no connection. Where had it gone? In Glendaloch, he had been so sure of it, but now it was all wrong. This appeared to be Maggie, but she was a really bad version of Maggie. The Maggie he met in Glendaloch had been sweet and engaging, smart and funny. Now she seemed distracted most of the time, and when she kissed him, her purpose wasn't clear. It was as if she was trying to prove something to him. But what? The sound of the horses, whinnying nervously made Dylan stop their kiss abruptly. "We should get back," he said, casting his gaze towards Alec and the horses.

Maggie's eyes grew wide with surprise. "Why? They'll not miss us yet. I dinnae wish to stop." She smiled coyly and traced his jawline with a soft finger.

"Maggie, this isn't the time or the place." He glanced back over his shoulder at Alec, who now stood perfectly still, holding the horses. What an odd expression he had on his face. It was a mixture of sadness and anger - or so it appeared.

"Don't worry about him," Maggie insisted. "The wee lad looks like he might need to sleep a bit." As if on cue, Alec yawned and rubbed his eyes. "See there, he *is* sleepy." She laughed, the sound sharp and cackling as she reached up and kissed Dylan again.

Breaking away from her, Dylan spoke with more vehemence than he'd intended. "Maggie, I'm serious, we need to leave." He was feeling utterly disillusioned. This was not what he wanted and sadly, it seemed that neither was Maggie after all. Maybe he wasn't the kind of guy who could fall in love. He never had before and prior to that brief glimpse back at the inn, he'd never given it much thought. He'd always been happy with his commitment-free life, but Maggie had opened his eyes to the possibility of a partner for life and then, before he'd had an opportunity to experience what it truly meant to be in love, it had disappeared.

Dylan grabbed Maggie's hand roughly and pulled her towards the horses, where a dazed looking Alec still stood waiting. "Are you alright, Alec? You look like you might pass out," Dylan observed.

"I be fine. Just verra tired all of a sudden. I dinnae ken why," he said, as he yawned again.

"We'll be heading back to the castle now. You can rest when we get there." Dylan gave Maggie a leg up onto her horse, carefully avoiding eye contact.

"Thank ye, love," Maggie cooed. Dylan fought the urge to cringe. As he turned to his own horse, out of the corner of his eye he noticed Alec swaying on his feet. Reacting swiftly, he reached Alec before he hit the ground and the young lad collapsed into Dylan's arms.

"Oh, my," Maggie exclaimed, although she hardly seemed alarmed. "I guess we'll need to stay here for now." She started to dismount, but Dylan put up a hand to stop her.

"Let me try to wake him. The poor little guy must be exhausted. Alec? Alec, wake up!" Dylan gently shook him, but had no luck. Alec continued sleeping deeply. "Something's wrong," Dylan muttered to himself. He threw Alec over his shoulder, amazed at how soundly he was sleeping and by how light he was. He briefly recalled what Maggie had suggested about Alec being a woman, but right now, it was more important to get back to the castle.

Maggie appeared to be in quite a huff as she watched Dylan get himself onto his horse, shifting Alec around until he had him settled comfortably in front of himself. Dylan called softly to Alec's horse and when Blue was close enough, he leaned over to grab the reins in order to pony her alongside.

"Maggie, I have something I need to ask you," Dylan carefully guided the horses through the brush.

"Of course. Anything," Maggie responded, with a thin smile on her lips.

"Did you put some sort of spell on Alec?" Dylan suddenly asked. "You know, to make him sleep?" Dylan cast an uneasy glance back at Maggie, who seemed startled by his question.

"Why would I do that?" she asked. She had quickly regained her composure and appeared quite peeved by his question.

"I don't know. I just wondered. Don't you think it's rather odd that Alec would fall into such a deep sleep?"

"I did nothing to Alec. If anyone is up to something, I believe 'tis Alec himself. Ever since he's arrived, all sorts of strange things have been happening. I cannae believe you would accuse me of, of—" Maggie sniffled and brushed a nonexistent tear away from her cheek.

Dylan suddenly felt terrible for insinuating that Maggie was at fault. "I'm sorry, Maggie. I didn't mean to accuse you. I guess all the strange happenings have me second-guessing everything. I know you wouldn't do anything to hurt anyone. Please, don't cry." He slowed his horse and waited for Maggie to come up alongside him, and then took her hand in his. Maybe she was right about Alec and he did have something to do with what was going on. Things *had* started to happen after he arrived with Angus. But why would he put himself to sleep? That part didn't make any sense at all… unless Alec *wanted* Dylan to believe that Maggie was up to no good. This was all very unsettling. He was going to have to dig deeper if he was going to get to the bottom of this. "Maggie, tell me something," Dylan carefully worded his question as she pulled her hand away from his. "What exactly are you doing here in Breaghacraig? Is something going on that you aren't sharing with me?"

She seemed to think about this question for a moment before she responded. "Well, if ye must know, while I came here to spend time with ye, I've found myself thrown into the middle of someone else's witchcraft. Someone who wishes harm to the MacKenzie Clan." Brielle nodded towards Alec, where he lay peacefully sleeping in Dylan's arms.

Dylan didn't want to argue the point with her, so he let it drop. Again, he thought before speaking. "Maggie, if something is going on here that involves witchcraft and the MacKenzies, don't you think you should tell them?"

She acted as if he'd just suggested that she share some top-secret information with them. "I dinnae see what good it would do for me to tell them. They'd nae believe me and it might complicate matters."

"I don't know how much more complicated things can get after yesterday." Dylan adjusted Alec in his arms as Breaghacraig came into view.

"I ken things will get worse before they get better," Brielle said with a snicker.

"It's not a laughing matter, Maggie." Dylan couldn't believe she was taking this so lightly, when moments before she had been in tears.

"Nae. Yer right. Although a wee bit of levity never hurts, wouldn't you say?"

Dylan didn't answer her. He was lost in his own thoughts. So many things were pressing on him. Should he believe Maggie? Was Alec a witch? What things were going to get worse? He'd ponder those questions when he was alone. For now, he had to make sure Alec was okay.

Chapter 9

Upon reaching Breaghacraig, they were met by a visibly shaken Angus. "What's happened?" he questioned. Reaching up, he gently took Alec from Dylan's arms. Again, Maggie's suggestion that Alec was not a lad came to Dylan's mind as he watched Angus gently cradle Alec against his shoulder.

"I'm not sure. He said he was tired and before I knew what was happening, he passed out. I tried to wake him, but I couldn't," Dylan explained.

"Let's get him inside, maybe we can rouse him there," Angus said.

"Maggie, are you coming?" Dylan asked.

"I'll be along shortly, I've some things to see to," Maggie said, as she turned her horse away from them.

Angus appeared relieved when Maggie and her horse walked away and Dylan had to admit to himself, that after what happened on the ride back, he was as well. He needed some space to reassess things. He dismounted and handed his horse to one of the stable boys.

Angus was running for the castle doors and Dylan had to hurry to catch up with him.

"Irene!" Angus called.

"Aye. I'm here," Irene replied as she hurried towards them. What's happened?"

"I believe 'tis a spell that's making wee Alec sleep. I dinnae ken what to do." Angus hurried past Irene and into the Great Hall.

Dylan thought carefully about that. Maggie swore she hadn't put a spell on Alec, but what if she really had been responsible? Was it so they could spend more time alone together, or was there some other, more sinister reason?

"Bring him here," Irene led the way to a nearby table where she indicated Angus should lay Alec. She reached for a pitcher of water and a cloth, which she wet and gently used to wipe Alec's face. As she swabbed his skin, the cloth removed much of the dirt he seemed to be perpetually covered in. Irene examined him carefully. "'Tis a sweet face he has, once the dirt has been removed."

"Do you think he'll be alright?" Dylan asked. He stared down at Alec's face and experienced a flash of recognition. *Who is he... or she?*

"Aye. He's in a verra deep sleep, but otherwise he seems fine. He's not warm to the touch and his breathing seems normal," Irene announced.

Dylan sighed in relief.

"Why dinnae ye take him to yer room, Angus, and let him sleep. If he doesnae wake by the morning, we'll worry then."

Angus nodded. "Aye. 'Tis sound advice. Mayhap I can contact Edna in the meantime, to see if she knows what to do."

"Do you need any help, Angus?" Dylan asked.

"Nae, lad, I'll see to him. Thank ye." Angus picked Alec up and held his limp body in his arms.

Dylan watched as Angus carried Alec from the room. He had a strange sensation in his gut. The questions were piling up and he was determined to find the answers, but first he had to find Maggie.

* * *

Maggie said she hadn't done anything, but it was obvious she could easily have done so. *She's a witch; it would probably be easy for her.*

Dylan walked across the open field, which led to the bluff overlooking the ocean. There in the distance, he could see Maggie, her back to him, staring out to sea. Dark clouds were gathering and a chill wind whipped through the air. She stood perfectly still and it wasn't until he was right behind her that she turned and faced him. Her facial expression gave nothing away.

"Hi. I've been trying to find you. I thought you had some things to take care of and would be coming right back," Dylan said, as he looked deeply into her eyes - in search of what, he didn't know.

"I wanted to be alone so I came out here. 'Twas verra upsetting to me that you would think I, of all people, could harm Alec, or anyone else here at Breaghacraig."

He wouldn't apologize again. Where there had been tears before, now all Dylan saw was defiance. He heard it as well. Her voice sounded bitter to his ears, and his mind went back to when they first met and he'd thought she had the sweetest voice he'd ever heard. He didn't like being lied to, but he had no evidence he could use to accuse her... yet.

"Well, if you're done being alone, I think it's going to rain soon. We should get back before it starts." He held out his hand to her and after a moment's hesitation, she took it. Her hand felt cold in his, so he rubbed it between his own to try and warm her. Nothing seemed to help - her fingers remained icy. "A good hot meal will go a long way to making you feel better. You'll see." Dylan wondered if he should talk to Angus about this. Angus had kept his distance from Maggie since their arrival, which seemed odd, since he was a very protective and kind man, but he certainly didn't seem to want much to do with his own niece. *I wonder why*, Dylan thought to himself.

Maggie didn't utter a word during the walk and when they arrived back at the great hall, everyone had gathered for dinner. Jenna waved at Dylan from across the room and Chester, who had been on his way to greet him, suddenly decided to head in the opposite direction. Dylan glanced Maggie's way and for just a moment he thought he saw a haggard old woman standing in her place, but then she was gone and the alluring red-haired, green-eyed beauty was back. *What was that?* He needed to get his head back in the game, all the crazy thoughts he'd been having were starting to make him imagine things.

They were greeted warmly by the others and Dylan noticed that Angus was missing from the table. *He must still be with Alec.* Throughout dinner, he kept a wary eye on Maggie and wondered if he'd be able to figure this out before something really bad happened.

* * *

"Maggie, 'tis yer Aunt Edna. Can ye hear me?" Edna's melodic voice was singing in Maggie's ears as she struggled to open her eyes. "Keep yer eyes closed, there's no need to open them, ye cannae see me anyway. I've removed the spell, but you need to rest so that your body can recover from Brielle's evil spell. Why did ye nae protect yerself, Maggie? Didnae I tell ye how important that was?"

"I'm sorry, Aunt Edna. Brielle showed up out of nowhere and I was so upset that she was joining Dylan and me on our ride, that it totally slipped my mind. I realized when it was too late that I was in trouble," Maggie explained.

"Dinnae let it happen again. Ye must be on yer guard at all times."

"Auntie, I'm not sure what I'm doing here and I'm not sure what to do about Brielle."

"Rest now, Maggie, dear. Ye'll have yer answers soon enough, love."

Edna's voice drifted away and Maggie slept soundly and peacefully through the rest of the night.

* * *

"I've asked the boys to bring a tub for ye. Stay where ye be until they're done filling it." Angus was sitting at her bedside, holding her hand, concern causing his brow to wrinkle. "Are ye well, Maggie? I've been so worried fer ye."

"I'm fine, Uncle. Auntie has lifted the spell. She spoke with me during the night," Maggie responded.

"I don't understand this at all, lass. Brielle is as bad as they come. I cannae, for the life of me understand how the others dinnae see it. She looks like an evil old bat to me eyes."

"I know, Uncle, but ye and I ken who she really is. Yes, they're nice to her, but as ye've told me, that's just the kind of people they are. I think they really arenae terribly fond of her. The thing that upsets me the most is that Dylan, of all people, cannae see it. I thought fer sure he'd know it wasn't me, but even though I know he's under her spell, I can't help but worry that he's smitten with her." Maggie lowered her eyes so Angus wouldn't see the tears threatening to spill. She wanted to cry, but she had to be strong. There was still much to do.

"I dinnae believe that. He is a smart lad. He kens the truth of it, believe me." Angus lifted Maggie's chin to gauge her reaction.

There was a knock at the door and when Angus opened it, the lads entered, first with the tub and then with buckets of steaming water, one after the other. Maggie was excited to take a bath, but she'd let the water cool down just a bit before getting in. She waited until the lads left before speaking again.

"Uncle, I saw him kiss her. How could he do that?" Maggie questioned.

"A man can kiss a woman for many reasons, but not all of them are for love," Angus appeared uncomfortable discussing Dylan with her. "I'm sure things will become clearer soon. Be patient. And now I am going to go get some food. I'm surprised ye cannae hear my tummy grumbling. Take yer nice warm bath and I'll bring something back for ye."

Maggie had to laugh. Angus was nae one to ever miss a meal. "Thank ye, Uncle Angus. I love ye verra much."

Angus ducked his head and darted to the door. "I love ye verra much, as well," he hurriedly said as he bolted from the room.

* * *

Hiding in the shadows, Dylan felt a bit guilty as he waited for Angus to head into the great hall and out of sight. He was going to check in on Alec and make sure he was alright and if he was awake, maybe he could shed some light on Maggie's accusations. He mounted the stairs and headed down the passageway to the door of Alec's room. Not hearing anything coming from inside, Dylan wondered if Alec might still be asleep. If so, he didn't want to disturb him. He checked the door and finding it unlocked, opened it and went in.

"Dylan!" a surprised voice said.

Dylan let his eyes adjust to the dimness of the room and searched for the source of the voice. What he saw shocked him so much that he couldn't speak. There, standing in front of him, with a plaid clutched to his chest was Alec, but it wasn't really Alec. The clothing he had been wearing was pooled at his feet and with the cap and cape gone, Dylan could see for the first time that this was Maggie. *His Maggie.* He went to her and putting his hands on her upper arms, looked deep into her eyes. "It's you," was all he could manage to say.

"Aye. 'Tis me," was Maggie's soft response.

He didn't know whether to kiss her or kill her. "You've been disguising yourself as Alec this whole time?" His voice registered the incredulity he felt. "Why? Why were you hiding from me? And who is that other woman who's obviously pretending to be you?"

"I wasnae hiding from ye, Dylan. I have a job to do and up until this moment, it has been best that I remain disguised. And in answer to your question, that woman is an evil witch who wants to harm the MacKenzies and you." Maggie shifted uncomfortably in his grip.

Dylan was suddenly aware of the fact that a very naked Maggie stood before him, trying to cover herself with a thin piece of fabric clutched to her chest and that he was perhaps holding onto her arms a little too tightly. He was also aware of the fact that for the first time in weeks, he felt that spark he'd been missing. He tenderly dipped his head and placed a soft kiss on Maggie's lips. "It *is* you," he whispered. "All this time I thought she was you and I couldn't understand why I didn't feel anything for her. Now, in these few short minutes that I've known it's really you, my body is responding in a way it never did with her." He pulled her into his embrace and hugged her tightly to his chest. Letting go was not an option.

* * *

"Dylan, I cannae breathe, but please dinnae stop holding me," Maggie said into his chest.

"I'm sorry." He loosened his grip just a bit.

Maggie held onto him, not wanting this moment to end, the plaid slowly slipping from her grasp. She could feel something firm, poking her in the belly. Maggie had an idea of what it might be, but she had so little experience with men, she truly couldn't be sure. She only knew what she'd been told by the other girls in the village. She tipped her head back, looked up into his soft brown eyes and forgot for a moment that she was angry with him. Angry for the way he'd kissed Brielle yesterday. She stiffened in his embrace, remembering her disappointment at seeing them together, how it had been like a punch to the gut. Pushing him away, she quickly scooped up the plaid and covered herself.

"I was just about to take a bath. Perhaps we can talk about this later, when I'm done. My water's cooling." Maggie was torn, she wanted him to stay, but she knew it was wrong for him to do so, especially when his true feelings were not clear. She walked to the door and waited for him to walk through. "We have a lot to discuss. I willnae keep ye waiting long." She closed the door in his face.

* * *

Dylan slumped to the floor outside Maggie's room. He sat with his back against the door, confusing thoughts swirling through his brain. *So there are two Maggies. One who is Maggie and Alec and one who is Maggie and an evil witch.* How could he be sure that this Maggie was the real one? Wasn't it possible that he was being fooled once again? No. He had felt something very different with this Maggie. The real Maggie. That spark was definitely still there. No denying it. He hadn't felt anything at all when he kissed the other Maggie. In fact, it had been as if he was kissing someone very unappealing. Then he remembered the image that had flashed before his eyes last night. The image of a haggard old woman. He nearly gagged at the memory of kissing her. He'd be forced to wait for Maggie to explain everything to him, and he decided he wasn't going anywhere until she did.

A short while later, Dylan heard footsteps coming up the stairs and as he waited, Angus stopped dead in his tracks at the sight of him.

"What are ye waiting here for, lad?" Angus asked. He was carrying a plate of food that Dylan assumed must be for Maggie.

"I know," was all that Dylan said.

"I'm sorry, what do ye ken?"

"I know that Maggie is Alec. I walked in on her as she was getting ready for her bath and saw her with my own two eyes." Dylan realized a moment too late that he probably shouldn't have told Angus that he'd just walked in on his naked niece.

The look on Angus' face was a mixture of anger and amusement. "I see," was all he said in response.

"I'm sorry. I didn't know it was her. I came to speak with Alec and I didn't want to disturb him if he was sleeping—"

Angus held up a hand to stop him from speaking. "So why are ye sitting out here?"

"She showed me out of the room and said we'd talk later. I'm waiting right here, until that happens."

"Alright, then." Angus knocked on the door and Maggie opened it, clothed once again as Alec. Dylan was disappointed, but now that he knew, he could see the girl who had sparked his interest and been on his mind since he left her back in Glendaloch. "Join us, Dylan. We've much to share."

Dylan rose and entered the room, not taking his eyes off Maggie for a second. She sat on the edge of the bed and took a bite of the food Angus had brought for her. "Thank ye, Uncle," she said politely. Her eyes swept from Angus to Dylan and back again.

"I understand that Dylan walked in on ye earlier," Angus said. "I'm here to protect ye from all threats." He made a point of catching Dylan's eye. Dylan lowered his gaze appropriately.

"Nothing happened," Maggie explained hastily. "I sent him out as quickly as I could. Ye ken we were both shocked to see each other."

Dylan nodded his head in agreement, feeling as if he was twelve years old again, being reprimanded for kissing one of the girls behind the school auditorium. "I'm sorry, sir. If I'd known it was Maggie in here, I wouldn't have just walked in." *Of course he would, who was he trying to kid?*

"See that ye behave as a gentleman with my niece," Angus ordered in a very stern voice.

"I will. Always," Dylan stammered.

"We have much to discuss," Maggie said and then told Dylan everything, from the vision Edna had experienced, right up to this very moment.

"Is there a plan?" Dylan asked. He had listened intently to everything both Angus and Maggie had to say and not once did he hear what the ultimate goal was, or how they were going to achieve it.

"No," Maggie appeared ashamed. "We havenae been told what the plan is or even why this is happening."

"Then how are you supposed to stop her? We need a plan," Dylan stated firmly.

"We?" Maggie asked. "Aunt Edna never said that ye were supposed to be involved."

"Aye. She's right," Angus added.

"I'm already involved. I've been spending a lot of time with Brielle and I don't like the fact that she was trying to use me for whatever her purpose is. I'm helping and you can't stop me." Dylan put his foot down and was quietly pleased when he got no argument from anyone.

"Okay," Maggie agreed. "Ye can help."

"I think the first thing you should do, is let the others know who you really are," Dylan announced.

"I dinnae believe that would be wise," Maggie said. Angus however, seemed to be giving the suggestion some serious thought.

"He could be right," Angus said. "If ye tell everyone who ye really are, that could force Brielle's hand. She cannae continue to do damage here, if everyone is on to her."

"But Auntie Edna hasnae told us it's alright to do so," Maggie said, worry furrowing her brow.

"Maggie, I think it's time for ye to be in charge of yer own destiny. Edna isnae here, but I believe she'd agree with whatever decision you come to," Angus offered.

"Okay. Let's say we do that. What's the outcome? Does she just leave? Or, does she stay here and become angry and try to destroy everyone and everything?" Maggie was frightened by that prospect.

"We won't know unless we try. And you've done a good job of thwarting her at every turn so far. I have faith that you can do this, Maggie." Dylan stood and walked over to her. He held out his hand for Maggie to take and when she did, he knelt in front of her. "I will protect you, I promise."

Angus cleared his throat and came to Maggie's side. He laid a hand on her shoulder. "I'll do the same, lass. Ye've no need to fear."

"And I'll protect ye both. Whenever we need to be anywhere near Brielle, I will cover us all with a spell of protection. Her witchcraft willnae be able to penetrate it. Aunt Edna taught me well." Dylan could see the confidence rising in Maggie. It showed in the way she stood a little taller, head held high and a sparkle in her eyes. They would do this together. The three of them.

Chapter 10

As they headed down the stairs, Maggie, having discarded her cap and hood, caught the curious gazes of the soldiers in the barracks. She walked past proudly, holding hands with Dylan and Angus. Further curious looks came their way as they headed for the great hall, where they intended to meet up with the others, who should be finishing their breakfast.

As they approached, it was apparent that something was not right. Loud noises and yelling spilled from the hall as Cailin burst through the doors. He stormed past them with a brusque, "Get out of me way."

"I've never seen him so angry," Dylan observed.

"'Tis not like him at all, from what I ken," Angus answered.

"We need to get in there. Something's wrong." Maggie tore her gaze from Cailin's fleeing figure and back toward the castle entry. She didn't like what she was hearing from inside. She pulled Angus and Dylan along with her and passed swiftly through the doors, to discover a chaotic scene. Ashley was in tears. Cormac and Robert were on the verge of fisticuffs and Jenna and Irene were at their men's sides, glaring at each other. Others in the hall were also indulging in spats of their own. "Oh, no! This is Brielle's doing," Maggie said. She let go of the two men's hands and focused on the room. "Calmness reign at the castle this day. Make their anger go away. Peace and quiet once again. Settle upon these women and men. So mote it be."

Abruptly everything came to a standstill. Robert seemed surprised to discover himself holding onto the front of Cormac's shirt. He let go and glanced around at the others. Irene and Jenna looked embarrassed and Ashley stopped crying, wiping at her eyes. As if on cue, all eyes turned to Maggie and the men behind her. Expressions morphed from curiosity to astonishment.

"Maggie, why are ye dressed in Alec's clothing?" Irene asked.

"I have some news to share with ye all," Maggie said. "Dylan, can ye bring Cailin back here, please?"

"Sure." Dylan turned to leave, just as Cailin re-entered the hall.

"I dinnae ken what came over me, but I found myself out on the practice field, beating the life out of a bale of straw." Cailin appeared frazzled, and ran a hand through his hair.

"I believe ye were all under a spell," Maggie explained. "And 'tis nae the first time."

"A spell that you cast!" Brielle, still disguised as Maggie, had followed Cailin inside.

If they were astonished before, the castle residents now seemed unable to comprehend what they were seeing. Their heads turned from Maggie to Brielle and back again.

"What goes on here?" Robert demanded.

"She's pretending to be me, to confuse you all," Brielle stated, calmly eyeing the others.

"Yer the one who's in disguise, Brielle." Maggie's eyes were alight with anger. "Ye came here to hurt these good people. I was sent by my Aunt Edna to send ye on yer way, isnae that right Uncle Angus?"

"Aye, Maggie, 'tis true." Angus cast his gaze slowly over the others in the group, making eye contact with each in turn.

"'Tis a lie," Brielle announced. "Ye've obviously bewitched my good uncle. She's been at the heart of all of these problems! The bread in the kitchen, the horses escaping, the apple orchard and this morning's events. If ye think on it, ye'll surely see I'm telling the truth!"

The room came alive with multiple voices, questioning what they were hearing.

Maggie spoke up. "Dinnae believe her! It was I who broke the spells that she cast in the first place!"

"I know my own niece," Angus affirmed, "and she came with me to Breaghacraig, disguised as Alec. Ye can be assured I am telling the truth."

"He's right," Dylan added. "Even I was fooled by Brielle. From the moment she arrived, I've always thought something was off and if you think about it Jenna, you remember she didn't even recognize you when you saw her. When I went to check on Alec this morning and I found Maggie - *my Maggie* - I knew what a fool I'd been. One look at her and there was no doubt in my mind." He took Maggie's hand in his. "This Maggie is the true Maggie. She would never do anything to hurt any of you."

Robert pointed to Brielle. "Cailin, Cormac, seize her. She'll need to be locked away before she does any more harm," Robert stated. Cailin and Cormac strode to Brielle's side. Before Brielle could react, Maggie cast a spell, freezing her in place. Unable to move, Brielle was no longer a threat, but to be on the safe side, Maggie cast a spell of protection over Cailin and Cormac.

"Ye cannae do this to me! Ye'll regret it," Brielle shrieked. Cailin and Cormac each grabbed one of her arms. Brielle struggled to no avail. Her frustration at being unable to break Maggie's spell was evident in her expression.

"Lock her up, lads," Robert ordered, as Brielle was dragged from the room. "We dinnae want her to escape."

Chester wriggled out of his hiding spot beneath the table and ran to Dylan, practically turning himself inside out in his excitement. He hadn't gone near Dylan since Brielle was around.

"Hello, Chester," Maggie said, reaching her hand out to pet him. "'Tis good to see you again."

"There, we have further proof! Chester hasnae left Cormac's side since ye've been spending all yer time with Brielle. I understand why, now." Robert smiled as he watched the dog wriggling every which way, as Maggie and Dylan showered him with attention.

"Well, I for one, am very relieved," Irene said. "I havenae had many good thoughts for that woman. Something about her set me on edge, from the very moment I met her."

"I knew there was something odd about her. She had no idea who I was when she first arrived and I was pretty sure after spending a few days with her in Glendaloch that she would remember me," Jenna agreed.

Maggie left Dylan's side and walked across to Jenna. "I'm sorry she deceived ye in my name. I couldnae forget ye - or ye, Ashley." She hugged both women, one after the other before turning to Irene. "Irene, I'm so glad to meet ye. I've always wanted to visit Breaghacraig; I just never thought it would be under these circumstances."

"Now we must decide what we're to do with Brielle," Angus announced. "Edna didnae make her intentions clear to us and I believe things have moved far more quickly than she anticipated."

"Maggie, why did ye nae tell us who ye were right from the start?" Robert asked.

"Aye. I was wondering the same," Cailin added.

"When Edna told me she wanted me to come to Breaghacraig to rid ye of Brielle, she said it was important that I be in disguise. I wasnae certain why. The only ones who knew my true identity were Edna, Angus and Brielle," Maggie explained. "I'm sorry to have fooled ye fer so long, but I believe that Edna was trying to avoid the confusion that was sure to set in when ye had two Maggie's in yer presence. Brielle may have reacted badly and done more damage if she had been found out sooner." Maggie anxiously twirled her fingers through her hair. "We managed to surprise her today, and that worked to our advantage."

"Are we safe from her now? Or can she harm us from her cell below stairs?" Robert asked.

"I hope so, but I'm not sure what she is truly capable of. So far I've been able to stop her from doing any real harm, but she is a powerful witch and I don't believe we've seen the worst of what she can do. I have cast a spell on her that will temporarily keep her from mischief. I will need to find a more permanent solution, though. I would like to speak with her first, if someone can show me the way."

Maggie observed the others in the room. They all still appeared to be stunned by the events of the past few minutes and it took another minute before anyone responded.

Robert spoke. "Of course, as soon as Cormac and Cailin come back, I'll have one of them escort ye down to see her. Why do ye nae sit and eat a bite first? Ye must be verra hungry after that long sleep ye had."

"Aye. Uncle Angus brought me some food, but in our hurry to come and explain things to ye, I'm afraid I didn't eat much," Maggie smiled. "And I didn't eat more than a bannock and a pear yesterday." Her eyes surveyed all the warm and welcoming faces of the MacKenzie's and she suddenly felt very much at home.

"How do ye feel this morn?" Irene asked. "We were all quite worried about ye when ye wouldnae wake yesterday."

"I'm fine. Aunt Edna helped me escape from the spell Brielle cast, and then I slept peacefully throughout the rest of the night."

It seemed to Maggie as if she were on display for the next few minutes. She and Dylan helped themselves to some food and Maggie looked up to discover everyone else watching her intently as she ate.

Angus cleared his throat and their attention turned to him. "Mayhap we should let these two have their breakfast in peace."

"Aye. I'll see where Cailin and Cormac have gone off to and I'll send one of them back for ye, Maggie," Robert said as he turned to leave the room.

"Thank ye," she agreed, around a mouthful of bannocks.

The group turned in unison and filed out of the hall, leaving Maggie and Dylan alone. As soon as they were gone, Dylan sat back in his chair and put an arm around Maggie's shoulders. "I'm so happy you're really here now."

Her heart sang when she heard his words. Maggie was beyond elated to be seated next to him, the warmth of his touch making its way through her clothing and flowing deep inside. How could she have doubted him? "I've been here all along, Dylan." She thought for a moment before she continued. "I was wondering why ye continued to kiss Brielle, if ye didnae enjoy it?" Maggie asked the question as casually as possible shovelling food around on her trencher in hopes that her jealousy wouldn't be revealed.

Dylan cleared his throat and when Maggie looked up, he smiled, melting her heart. "Maggie, I kissed her because I was trying to recapture what I'd felt between us. When I first met you back at the inn, I felt an immediate connection. It was something I'd never experienced before and I knew it was something special. So, when Brielle showed up here, disguised as you, I had no idea she was someone else trying to trick us. Those feelings I had for you were suddenly gone and I didn't understand why. I guess I kept hoping that things would settle down between us, that maybe because we'd been separated for a while, we had to get to know one another again, maybe that would help to find it. I thought if I kissed Brielle, because I thought she *was* you, it would eventually come back, but it didn't."

"So you didn't enjoy kissing her at all?" Maggie questioned.

Dylan shook his head. "Not in the slightest."

"Not even one tiny bit?" Maggie asked.

"Not even one tiny bit." Dylan lifted her chin with his fingertips and gazed into her eyes. "Come, sit here with me."

Maggie found herself being drawn up out of her chair and onto his lap. She was the witch, but he was the one who'd cast a spell over her. They were sitting so close; she could feel his breath on her face and feel the truth of his words as something hard poked against her thigh. Gathering all her courage, for she had never been a verra forward girl, Maggie turned her head and kissed him. The sensation that ran through her body was amazing. She kissed him some more and he kissed her back, drawing her closer. She could feel the hard muscles of his chest and the strength of his arms, caged as she was inside them. Maggie wanted to run her hands all over him, but she didn't dare. Should she continue to kiss him, or should she stop? Her inexperience in these matters had her head spinning. She didnae wish him to think her easy, even though for him, she most definitely wanted to be. Gasping for breath, Maggie pushed herself back and quickly turned her face away as a blush formed on her cheeks.

"Maggie, look at me," Dylan said.

Red-faced, she did as he asked. "I'm sorry. I don't know what came over me."

"Don't apologize. I enjoyed it and I'd like to enjoy it again. I know that this isn't the right time, and definitely not the right place, but promise me we'll do this again... soon."

"Aye," she blurted out. Kicking herself, she couldn't believe how eager she had sounded. Wasn't it better to play hard to get? "Aye, soon. First we must take care of the Brielle problem."

Footsteps warned them that someone was approaching and Maggie stood up abruptly, so as not to be caught behaving like a besotted schoolgirl.

"Maggie," Cailin's voice rang through the empty hall. "Robert says I'm to take ye to see Brielle."

"Aye, please. Dylan, will ye join me?" Maggie hoped he would agree. She really didnae wish to face Brielle on her own, but there were questions that needed answering.

"Of course. I was planning on it," Dylan responded.

"I'll be joining ye as well," Cailin said. "There's strength in numbers, ye ken." He led the way down a passageway, which took them from the hall and into a dimly lit stairway and then down into the underground levels of the castle. "She's down at the verra end there and hopefully far enough away so she cannae use her witchcraft to seek aid in escaping."

"'Tis a bit creepy," Maggie said, as a shiver ran across her skin. Dylan clasped her hand and pulled her closer to him. "Is anyone else down here?"

"Nae," Cailin said. "None but Latharn, I've left him here to guard her. He'll nae let her out, no matter what she might say."

"I'm nae so worried about what she might say, but what she might do. She is a witch, ye ken and while I was able to stop her from casting spells, it was only temporary. I'm sure she'll be able to overcome my spell at some point soon, and then I don't know what we can expect." Maggie strained her eyes to see in the darkness. The torch that Cailin carried did little to light their path, and his large frame kept her from seeing what was in front of them. Finally, she could distinguish another glowing torch up ahead and as they approached, Maggie could see Latharn seated in a chair outside of a locked door. He stood as soon as he saw them.

"How has she been behaving?" Cailin asked.

"Quiet," Latharn responded.

Maggie stood on tiptoes and peeked through the barred opening into Brielle's cell. "I must speak with her, Cailin."

Cailin pulled the chair Latharn had been seated on closer to the door. He held out his hand to Maggie. "Step up onto the chair. I'd prefer that ye speak with her through the opening."

"Dinnae think that a wooden door, no matter how thick can protect ye," Brielle shouted from inside her cell. "I'll get my power back soon enough and ye'll be sorry for ever thinking that ye could get the better of me."

"We'd nae be foolish enough to believe that," Maggie answered. "Brielle, what is it ye were trying to accomplish here?"

"Did yer auntie nae tell ye? Why did she send ye here on a fool's errand to try to stop me, when mayhap it should have been Herself to do so?"

"Edna cannae leave because she is the keeper of the bridge in Glendaloch. She sent me, because she couldnae come," Maggie replied.

"So, she didnae tell ye why she sent ye." Brielle laughed scornfully. "That sounds just like Edna. Sending a wee babe to do her bidding in her stead."

"I am nae a wee babe," Maggie retorted. It occurred to her that she was beginning to sound defensive. "If ye know so much, why am I here?"

"Yer here, because Edna was afraid to go up against me in a battle for the bridge. She didnae wish to die." Brielle laughed maniacally. "As soon as I've defeated ye, I will be the keeper of the bridge. That was our agreement - Edna's and mine. I can do so much with control of the bridge! So many on this side, would pay me handsomely to allow them to travel forward in time to gather riches, or go back in time to change the outcomes of their fate." Brielle paused, as if waiting for a reply. "So, ye've nothing to say?" she asked.

Maggie said nothing, preferring instead to let Brielle continue.

"I knew ye were coming and I disguised myself as ye because I knew the MacKenzies and Dylan would welcome me with open arms. Once I was here and accepted as ye, it would make my work much easier. I had only started to play with them, when ye arrived, spoiling my fun. Edna was quick to send ye here. Her love of the MacKenzie Clan is great and I used that to my advantage."

Maggie was shocked by this information. So this was all really about the bridge, and Edna had been willing to sacrifice her niece in hopes of defeating Brielle. "How did ye ken I was coming?" Maggie asked.

"Were ye nae listening to me, lass? Yer auntie told me. In order to save the MacKenzie Clan from destruction, yer auntie agreed that we would fight for the bridge, of course, as I'm sure ye ken, I enjoy nothing more than causing a wee bit of trouble, and if I'm bored and left to me own devices, well… The sight of the clan running for their lives in the apple orchard was invigorating to say the least. And the water, the horses and the bread dough all helped relieve my ennui. As for ye, yer auntie wouldnae come, so she sent another witch, but she didnae send the right witch. Ye'll be easy to destroy." As she spoke, Brielle's voice took on a whole different tone, sounding as if she'd aged one hundred years in the last few minutes. "Yer auntie sacrificed you. As I've said, once I've defeated ye, the bridge is mine. Yer auntie swore to it."

Maggie couldnae speak. She was shocked by this revelation and as she peered through the opening at Brielle, she saw her body gradually changing, just as her voice had. She was growing old and haggard before Maggie's eyes. Her eyes blazed with an angry fire and Maggie quickly placed a wall of protection spell around herself and the others in the passageway. Dylan, who stood behind her to keep her from toppling off the chair, tightened his grip on her legs. Maggie glanced down and saw concern written all over his face. Cailin and Latharn appeared to be just as worried.

"What's wrong, my dear, cat got yer tongue?" Cackling laughter echoed throughout the passageway and Maggie suddenly realized that this was going to be the most difficult thing she'd ever done in her life. She was going to have to rid the world of Brielle. It was so out of her nature to destroy anything, let alone another human being. Granted, Brielle was an evil witch, but still, could Maggie bring herself to do it? If it came right down to it, could she kill Brielle? The question echoed in her head until she almost screamed in frustration. Catching herself, she tapped Dylan's shoulder to let him know she wanted to get down. He lifted her from the chair and set her on wobbly feet, steadying her as he folded his arms across her chest and pulled her back into his embrace. Everyone, it seemed had been stunned into silence.

"Let's get out of here," Maggie said.

"I'll go find Robert. He needs to know what has happened here," Cailin stated. "Latharn, I'll send Fergus to relieve ye later. I dinnae need to remind ye not to leave yer post under any circumstance."

"Aye," Latharn said as he moved his chair back against the wall.

"Latharn, I've put a spell of protection on ye. She cannae harm ye," Maggie said.

"Aye, thank ye, miss." Latharn peered through the opening at Brielle and he visibly shuddered at the sight.

"Cailin, I'll do the same for Fergus as soon as we're out of here." As Maggie turned to leave, she took one last look at Latharn, who had seated himself on the chair once again. He was a brave man from what she'd seen of him and strong, but would he be strong enough to withstand an assault from Brielle - she could only hope.

Chapter 11

"Maggie, wait!" Dylan had to run to catch up with her as she fled the castle. "Maggie, it's okay. Everything's going to be okay." Dylan grabbed her arm and pulled her around to face him.

"I can't believe it! I can't believe Auntie Edna would do this to me!" Maggie's reddened face displayed her anger and frustration. Tears spilled from her eyes and Dylan wanted more than anything to find a way to comfort her.

"Do you think perhaps Brielle isn't being totally honest with you?" Dylan tried to keep his voice calm and soothing, hoping to ease Maggie's anxiety over her aunt's betrayal.

"I dinnae ken. It doesnae make any sense. I know Edna didnae give me all the details and I've felt like a fish out of water from the minute I arrived, as I've tried to make my way through this. She should have told me the whole story. I would have helped her, regardless of the reasons."

"There has to be something more to this. I know she's a bit of a meddler, or at least that's the impression I've gotten from Jenna and Ashley, but she always seems to have the best of intentions. Jenna and Ashley were angry with her interfering to begin with, but they came around when they found Cormac and Cailin and realized that Edna had done what she had to do to get them together."

"Aye. I ken that, but this is different. She's nae matchmaking here. This is dangerous! What am I supposed to do? How do I defeat Brielle without killing her? How do I do it without getting myself or someone else killed?"

"I don't know, Maggie, but we'll do it together. I'll help you and protect you as much as I possibly can." Maggie clenched her teeth tightly together and Dylan ran his finger along her jawline, in an effort to ease the tension he saw there. The energy she was emitting was strong and filled with static electricity. Were those real sparks flashing in her eyes, or was he seeing things? As Maggie leaned into him, the hair on his arms stood on end. Dylan took a deep breath to ground himself and in doing so, brought Maggie back from the brink of imploding with fury. "Come with me. Let's go for a ride and put some of that energy to good use." He offered her what he hoped was his most charming smile and Maggie nodded in agreement.

"I'd like that. I need time to think, to figure out what to do next," Maggie said.

"Maggie!" Angus was heading their way and he didn't look happy.

"Uncle," Maggie responded.

"Is it true? Cailin told me what happened down in the dungeons. I cannae believe Edna would do this. Yer her niece and to think she knowingly sent ye into the lion's den, all for the sake of that damn bridge! I cannae tolerate this kind of deceit! She has gone too far this time. She didnae even confide in me, her own husband, with this crazy scheme of hers." Angus, in his usual fatherly fashion, wrapped an arm around Maggie and held her close. "I can tell ye this, my sweet Maggie, I will protect ye, no matter what happens. I willnae let that witch Brielle harm ye in any way."

"I ken that, Uncle, but I dinnae want anyone to get hurt," Maggie responded. "Dinnae be angry with Auntie Edna, Uncle. She's trying to protect the MacKenzies, not just the bridge. We must believe in Auntie and not fall prey to Brielle's lies." Maggie laid a gentle hand on Angus' arm. "I'm going to go riding with Dylan, to try and clear my head and figure out how to handle this situation."

"Do ye need me to go along with ye?" Angus asked. He sent a warning glare in Dylan's direction.

"Nae, Uncle, I'll be fine. Dinnae worry about me," Maggie said. She gave Angus a big hug and kissed his cheek. "I'll be fine," she repeated, when he appeared as if he might protest.

"I'll keep an eye on her, Angus. I promise." Dylan wanted to reassure Angus. He knew that he was a very protective man and felt it was his duty to watch over his niece.

"Make sure 'tis just yer eyes, lad," Angus warned.

"Yes, sir," Dylan said. He had a great deal of respect for Angus and all the men at Breaghacraig. They were men of honor and he hoped that they felt the same about him, although just now, Angus certainly seemed to be questioning it. Dylan would prove himself to him. He wanted Maggie in his life and he wouldn't do anything to jeopardize his chances.

"Fine then, see that yer back here before sunset, or I'll come looking fer ye." Angus turned away and headed back towards the great hall.

"Well, I guess we know what Angus is worried about," Dylan chuckled.

"Aye. He's a good man, Dylan." Maggie searched his face and Dylan smiled again to put her at ease.

"I know he is, but I don't think he trusts me with you."

"Does he have reason not to?" Maggie teased.

As they prepared to leave, Cailin came around the corner with Fergus. "Maggie, I've brought Fergus."

"Of course, Fergus, come stand here for a moment," Maggie said.

Fergus stood perfectly still while Maggie placed her spell on him and when she was done said, "Thank ye, Miss."

"You're welcome, Fergus. We'll be gone for a few hours, Cailin, but I feel confident that Brielle won't cause any problems while I'm gone, I've charmed her cell, so she canna escape." Maggie turned her horse towards the gate and said to Dylan, "Let's go. I need to get as far away from Brielle as possible. I dinnae know if she can read my thoughts or if she can sense my presence, but if I'm going to plan her demise, I need to be sure she doesnae know what I'm up to."

* * *

Brielle sat in her cell, waiting for an opportunity to escape and it seemed as if the time had come. She heard the sound of footsteps coming down the passageway and could feel the presence of the kitchen maid, Sophia. *She's here to visit her man, but she doesnae have the benefit of Maggie's spell of protection.* Brielle snickered softly to herself.

"Latharn," Sophia called nervously as she approached. "It's dark down here. I wanted to make sure you were okay. I've brought you something to eat."

Brielle heard Latharn get to his feet as Sophia neared his position. "Sophia!" The warmth in Latharn voice made Brielle want to gag. *Love is for fools,* she thought. *Are they kissing out there?* The prospect disgusted her, even as she listened intently to the sounds she heard coming through the door. A moment or two later, she head Latharn speak again. "Sophia ye shouldnae be here. 'Tis verra dangerous."

"I'm only staying for a minute. Mary would be so angry with me if she knew I were here, but I know you haven't eaten since breakfast."

"Thank ye fer bringing me food. I be verra hungry."

"I be verra hungry, too," Brielle shouted.

Silence was the only response she received. After a moment or two, she could hear whispering between Latharn and Sophia. They obviously didn't know that with a simple little spell, she could hear them, as clearly as if they were speaking aloud.

"She scares me," Sophia said. "How long do you have to stay down here?"

"Not much longer. Cailin will send someone else to relieve me from guard duty soon." The sound of Latharn settling back in his chair echoed down the passageway.

"Girl," Brielle called. "'Tis hard to breathe down here. Dinnae ye think?" She wove a spell and cast it upon Sophia.

"Latharn, I... I..." The alarm in Sophia's voice was evident, her fear obvious.

Brielle cackled as she listened to Sophia gasping desperately for breath.

"Sophia, are ye nae well?" Latharn's voice was full of concern.

This will be child's play, Brielle thought happily to herself.

The sounds of Sophia struggling for air and of Latharn, scrambling to her aid filled Brielle's cell and surrounded her like a warm, comforting blanket.

"Witch, what have ye done to Sophia?" Latharn sounded alarmed.

"Nae a thing that cannae be undone, if ye open this door and let me out," Brielle said. "She willnae last much longer. Do ye really want her death on yer conscience?"

She didn't have to wait long for her answer, as she heard the jingling of keys and the sound of the lock releasing. He pushed the door open and Brielle sailed past him and down the passageway.

"Wait! What about Sophia? Ye said ye'd undo yer spell," Latharn shouted.

Brielle cast a glance back to where he was crouched over Sophia, who lay still in his arms. "I did say that, didnae I. So be it." With a flick of Brielle's wrist and a burst of light from her fingers, Sophia gasped and gulped air into her lungs. Before Latharn could move, Brielle turned three times on the spot and disappeared from his sight.

* * *

Sunshine filtered through the trees, casting intricate, shadowy designs on the pine needle covered path and a crisp breeze was a strong reminder that autumn would soon turn to winter. Maggie took a deep breath and enjoyed the scent of the pine trees, so fresh and comforting. She pulled the hood of her cloak close around her head in an attempt to keep warm. Dylan rode alongside her and reached out to hold her hand.

"This was a good idea ye had, Dylan," Maggie said. Despite the chill in the air, she was happy to be here with him. They reached a narrow spot in the road and Dylan let go of her hand. He moved his horse ahead of her and led the way.

"I'm glad we could spend some time alone together." He turned in his saddle to look back at Maggie. "I've missed you since I've been here."

"But ye had Brielle. Ye thought she was me," Maggie reminded him.

"I missed the Maggie from Glendaloch. I missed *you*. And I was sad that the feelings I'd been experiencing had changed. I should have realized from the very beginning that it wasn't you. It never felt right and now that I know the truth, it sickens me to think I actually kissed that evil woman." He made a face that communicated his disgust and had Maggie giggling. "Hey, don't laugh at me. I didn't know!"

"I'm sorry. Yer right, but I wasnae laughing at what ye said though. 'Twas the face ye made." Maggie could hear the sound of rushing water and wondered where they were headed, when the path suddenly opened out to reveal a large pool of water surrounded by enormous boulders. Maggie craned her neck back and shielded her eyes from the bright sunlight, in order to get a look at the beautiful waterfall cascading into the pool and the rainbow it created in its mist. "Dylan, this is beautiful. How did ye find this place?"

"I go out riding nearly every day. Exploring really. I stumbled upon it a few weeks back and I wanted to share it with you."

Maggie could see him watching her, out of the corner of her eye. She slowly turned her gaze on him and without thinking wriggled down from her horse and walked to his side. Placing a hand on his knee, she looked up at him, fully appreciating the handsome man he was. Dylan dismounted and before she had a chance to speak, she was in his arms and he was kissing her. His lips were sweet and warm and she let herself fall deeper under his spell. This was what she'd dreamed of and she was not disappointed. It was everything she had wanted, everything she needed in this moment. She could forget about all the other craziness happening in her world and focus on this kiss. Her hands crept up from his chest to wrap around his neck as she pressed herself as close to him as she could possibly get, wanting full body contact with his amazingly strong and chiseled frame. The kiss turned into another and then another. Their movements grew almost frantic with desire. She wanted him so much it was almost painful, but it was a good kind of pain. The kind that let her know how right this was. She had been wrong to think that love was not for her. Here it was, right in front of her and she wanted all of it. She didn't know if Dylan loved her, but she knew without a doubt how she felt about him.

* * *

He wanted to tell her he loved her, but he caught himself, uncertain of how she felt about him. He'd hold on to that pronouncement for a while longer. He really hadn't known Maggie for very long. Just a short time in Glendaloch, and then, when he left for Breaghacraig, he'd been left with the unsettling feeling that without her, something was missing from his life. It had only been a short time since he'd found out she was the real Maggie and there was so much turmoil happening around them, it didn't seem like the best time to announce his feelings. It would be better to concentrate on getting rid of Brielle first, and then he'd be free to tell her how he felt. The kisses they'd shared had been the best he'd ever experienced, and he hoped Maggie thought so too. It was important to him to please her. He wanted her to be happy and without worry. Brielle was the main source of Maggie's current concerns, and he was going to do everything in his power to change that situation. Dylan settled back against a warm boulder, Maggie wrapped in his arms, enjoying the sounds of the water dropping down over the falls and the peacefulness that he felt with her close to his heart.

"Maggie, are you comfortable?" Dylan asked.

"Aye." Maggie replied. "I could sit here with ye forever." She turned in his arms to see his face better. She caressed his cheek and couldn't help herself as she ran her fingers through the riot of blonde curls that framed his handsome face. The sensory experience she was having cleared her mind of any and all other thoughts. Dylan was the only thing on her mind now. She turned her lips up towards his and he covered them with his own. He roamed his hands over her body and made his way inside her shirt, fondling her breasts with strong, callused fingers. Maggie found she wanted more. She moaned, pushing herself against his hands. Undoing the laces of her liene, Dylan freed her breasts for exploration with both his tongue and lips. The pounding urge between her thighs grew so strong; Maggie turned herself completely in Dylan's arms so she could straddle him and wrap her legs around his waist. She rubbed the source of the throbbing ache she felt against Dylan's hard manhood, searching for relief. It only served to create a more titillating sensation. One that felt so good, she forgot completely about anything and everything that was not Dylan.

Dylan repositioned her, so that she lay under him on the large boulder they had settled on. The roughness of the rock beneath her back only served to heighten her excitement. Dylan began to search the waistband of her trewes with his fingers, while she slid her hands up beneath his kilt and felt the tightness of his buttocks. She was keenly aware of the fact that this was the first time she'd ever done something quite so bold. She felt like a real woman here in Dylan's arms, wanting him more than she had ever thought possible and if things went the way she wanted, having him, and soon.

* * *

This all felt so amazingly good. Dylan didn't want to stop, but he knew he needed to. He'd made a promise to Angus and he intended to keep it. "Maggie, we have to stop," he croaked.

"Why?" she asked. She spoke like a woman in a sensual haze, which he could fully appreciate, because he was right there with her.

"I respect you too much, to take you for the first time right here on this rock," he managed to say.

"But what if I want ye to take me right here on this rock?" she asked, licking her lips in a way that was driving him to distraction.

"I promised your Uncle Angus that nothing was going to happen and I intend to keep my promise." The most amazing, sparkling green eyes stared up at him with a yearning that told him exactly what she wanted. He wanted to give it to her, but he had to keep his word. If there was one thing he'd learned since being here with the MacKenzies, it was that a man was only as good as his word. Although, Maggie's pouty lips were calling to be kissed. Before he forgot himself and his word to Angus, Dylan unceremoniously pushed himself up and away from Maggie and removing his kilt, he jumped into the icy cold water, which definitely put a damper on his aroused state.

* * *

"Dylan, what are you doing?" Maggie exclaimed.

"Cooling things down," he gasped as he swam back to the rocks and climbed out of the water.

Maggie giggled at the soaking wet man standing in front of her and the gooseflesh that covered his body. She grabbed his kilt and hurriedly brought it across to him. "Dry yerself off! Ye'll likely freeze to death if ye don't." She felt badly that she had caused him such discomfort. Maggie ran to her horse in search of something else to help him dry off.

"It's alright, Maggie. I'll be fine. Don't worry." He shook his watery locks out of his eyes and continued drying himself with the kilt. "I think I've got a dry one in my saddlebag." Maggie went in search of it and was pleased to discover he was right.

"Here," she said. She turned her back while he donned it, not wanting to tempt fate. She desperately needed a swim in those icy waters herself. "Are you decent?" she asked.

"Yeah, I am." Dylan came up behind her and wrapped his arms around her waist. "You still feel cold," she said, noticing the iciness of his body up against her back.

"I'm fine, and I hate to mention it, but Angus will be angry if we don't get back soon."

* * *

Dylan kissed the top of her head and breathed in her heady floral scent. Everything about Maggie was perfect, from her coppery locks, to the smattering of freckles that ran across her nose and over her cheeks, to the emerald green of her eyes. She was his and he felt an instinctive need to protect and care for her.

Maggie turned in his arms and gazed up into his eyes, with what he could recognize as the same intense longing he had been experiencing. He had to force himself to ignore it, although he had a head full of sensual images, they would have to remain that way for the time being.

"Must we really go back?" Maggie asked.

"As much as I'd like to stay here with you forever, I'm afraid Angus would track us down and skin me alive." Dylan grew serious for a moment. "I can't say I'd blame him. The thoughts going through my head at this very moment are anything but pure."

"I believe I ken yer meaning," Maggie stood on tiptoe and offered him one more kiss. This one was sweet and tender, but her red, swollen lips were testament to the passionate kisses they'd just shared. He only hoped Angus wouldn't notice, or he'd be in a whole lot of trouble.

"I've never been one to turn down temptation, but in this case I'm going to make an exception."

"But why?" Maggie asked.

"Because I care about you." And he really did care about her. More than he'd cared about anyone else in his life. Of course, he loved Jenna and Chester, but Maggie was different. His relationship with her was going to be life changing. He could feel it.

Walking back to the horses, Dylan kept Maggie close by his side, not wanting to give up that connection he'd been experiencing and enjoying. He helped her mount her horse, knowing she was perfectly capable of doing it herself, but that gentlemanly instinct took over and left him no choice. For her part, Maggie looked ready to tell him she could do it herself, but at the last minute, she seemed to think better of it and allowed his help.

As they nudged their horses in the direction of the castle, Dylan noticed that Maggie grew obviously concerned over something. "Is everything okay, Maggie?"

"No. I dinnae think so. Something's wrong back at Breaghacraig. We'd better hurry." Without waiting for Dylan, Maggie spurred her horse into a gallop and headed off through the trees.

* * *

"Maggie," Angus said, sounding confused. "I thought you were out with Dylan."

"I was Uncle, but I'm back now. I was looking for ye, as I have need of yer help." Brielle had disguised herself as Maggie yet again. She had scanned the immediate area with her mind and was aware that Maggie was not nearby. She used that fact to her advantage. It hadn't taken much to get that besotted Latharn to open the door to her cell and thus facilitate her escape. Men were so weak when it came to the women they loved. It was guaranteed to work in her favor, every time. Now in order to continue with her plans, she was going to need Angus and she made sure to mimic Maggie better than she ever had before. She'd need to, in order to convince Angus to go with her. Brielle needed to get him out of the courtyard and away from the others.

"Just what exactly do ye need my help with?" Angus asked.

"Come with me, Uncle. I have something I must show ye."

"Is it something to do with Brielle?" Angus sounded as if his curiosity had been piqued.

"Yes. I believe ye will find it most interesting." Brielle took Angus by the arm and led him out through the postern gate, nodding at the guard as they passed. "It's just this way." She led him along the outer wall of the castle, far away from prying eyes. Stopping without warning, Angus was just about to speak when Brielle cast a sleeping spell on him and he collapsed in a heap at her feet. She laughed quietly at the sight of the huge highlander, lying helplessly in front of her. Brielle whirled continually on the spot, picking up speed and then disappearing, taking Angus along with her.

Chapter 12

The smell of baking bread and the happy expression on Mary's face had Jenna feeling triumphant with her accomplishments in the kitchen. This was probably the first day since she'd been at Breaghacraig, when Mary had not scolded her for one thing or another. Jenna had come to love Mary and her *set-in-her-ways* handling of anything to do with food or the kitchen. It had taken some time, but Jenna had eventually won her over and that made her happy. She wanted so much to fit in here at Breaghacraig. She had everything she could possibly want - the man of her dreams, her best friend and now sister-in-law, and a new family who let her know in so many ways, how loved she was. Life at Breaghacraig had been perfect. Sure, she missed all the modern conveniences of the twenty first century, but she had gladly given it all up for her man. Cormac was more than she'd ever hoped for. He was kind, loving and he knew how to make her laugh. She realized now, after being here and being his wife for a while, that she had really been quite awful to him when they first met and she was happy he hadn't let that get in the way of winning her over. Lost in her own thoughts, Jenna almost missed the arrival of Latharn and Sophia as they practically fell into the kitchen. It appeared as if Sophia couldn't go another step further, so Latharn picked her up and carried her to a nearby chair.

Latharn was alarmed about something; Jenna had never seen him so frazzled before. He was normally a very levelheaded man, but Sophia was special to him and he was obviously very upset about something that had happened.

"What's wrong?" Jenna asked, glancing across to Mary, hoping for some hint of what had happened.

"The witch, Brielle, has escaped! She tried to kill Sophia!" Latharn appeared terribly embarrassed about something.

"Oh, my, Sophia, are you okay?" Jenna asked.

"Here, lass, drink this." Mary handed Sophia a cup of whiskey and held her hand as she brought it to her lips and took a big gulp, coughing and sputtering as it went down.

Latharn seemed unable to move and he couldn't take his eyes off Sophia. Jenna could see how concerned he was about her and wanted to put him at ease.

"Latharn, you go and get help. Mary and I will make sure no further harm comes to Sophia." Latharn hesitated for only a moment, before he turned and ran down the passageway, calling for Cailin and Cormac.

Sophia was gasping for breath and Mary tried to get her to drink some more whiskey. "Just a small sip, lass. Ye took a wee bit much the last time."

Sophia did as Mary suggested, and with Mary's soft motherly voice soothing her, Sophia was finally able to speak. "I couldn't breathe. She made it so I couldn't breathe! I must have passed out and the next thing I knew, Latharn was helping me into the kitchen. I was so scared! I thought I was going to die, but now she's escaped and who knows what she'll do!" Sophia seemed as if she might be about to start crying. "Latharn had no choice. He unlocked the door for her. She would have killed me, if he hadn't."

"It's okay, Sophia. They'll find Brielle and deal with her before she can cause any more trouble." Jenna hoped she sounded convincing, because she was anything but confident they could stop that witch. Worry for Cormac and the others began to seep into her brain, filling her with dread. *Please, don't let any harm come to Cormac,* she prayed. He had become her world and it would kill her if anything happened to him. "I'm going to find Ashley and Irene. I'll be right back. Stay here."

"Dinnae ye fash, Jenna. I'll take care of Sophia and if the witch is unlucky enough to find herself here in my kitchen, she'll be verra sorry." Mary waved a large piece of firewood in the air. Jenna couldn't help but smile despite her concerns, as she left the kitchen in search of her friends.

* * *

"Cailin! Cormac!" Latharn stumbled out of the castle and into the bright afternoon sun.

"Aye, Latharn," Cormac answered. "What's wrong? Ye look terrible." And then as if realizing the problem, Cormac continued. "Who's watching Brielle?"

"That's what I've come to tell ye. She's escaped!" Latharn was doubled over, hands on knees as he tried to catch his breath.

"Explain," Cormac demanded.

Cailin and Robert came running towards them from the practice field. "What's all the commotion?" Robert asked.

"Latharn is just about to tell us. It seems Brielle has escaped," Cormac responded swiftly.

All three men stood together, silently waiting for Latharn to speak. Latharn was ashamed of himself for letting Brielle out, but he had to save Sophia. He loved her and he wouldnae allow anyone to harm her. He just wished he had been able to do more to stop the witch before she got away. Taking a deep breath, Latharn told the men exactly what had happened. He mentally prepared himself for the berating he was certain would follow, but much to his surprise, there was total silence.

"I'm verra sorry," Latharn said. "It was wrong of me, but I couldnae let her harm Sophia."

Again, he waited for someone to pummel him, or at the very least, have him taken away and locked up.

"'Tis nae yer fault, lad. Any one of us would have done the exact same thing if it had been our woman she'd bespelled, and that is what Brielle was counting on. She knew ye wouldnae stand by and watch as she sucked the verra life out of Sophia." Robert paced back and forth. "We must locate her immediately!"

"Aye, but how?" Cailin asked. "We have nae idea where she is or what she might do next. We should send the women off to Ewan's castle, until we have everything under control. I dinnae trust that Brielle wouldnae try to harm Ashley or our baby. I think it's best for them to seek refuge with yer brother for the time being."

"Yer right," Robert agreed. "Latharn, start spreading the word that the women and children are to leave the castle as soon as possible."

"Aye, sir," Latharn said. He walked away swiftly to do as he had been told, relieved that Sophia would soon be out of harm's way.

* * *

Jenna found Irene and Ashley sitting by the fire, sewing baby clothes. They both looked up as she hurriedly entered room.

Ashley held up the little outfit she was working on, "Jenna, what do you think? Isn't it the cutest little thing you've ever seen?"

Jenna was sure she looked anything but interested in baby clothes, at that particular moment.

"What's wrong, Jenna," Irene asked, taking note of Jenna's worried expression. She stood up and hurried across to Jenna, taking her hand. "Tell us."

"Brielle has escaped. We don't know where she is," Jenna said, managing to calm herself enough to fill them in on the details. "We need to find the men."

Ashley put down her sewing and joined them. "We'll all go."

They were just about to leave when Latharn came rushing through the doors. "My ladies, yer husbands have requested that ye prepare to leave. Ye will be escorted to Sir Ewan's castle as soon as yer ready."

"What? I'm not going anywhere without Cormac," Jenna protested.

"Sir Robert has ordered that all the women and children are to leave the castle. 'Tis fer yer own safety," Latharn responded, looking as if he fervently hoped Jenna wouldn't continue to argue with him.

"Where are they?" Ashley asked.

"They were in the courtyard, making arrangements to see you all to safety," Latharn explained.

"Thank you, Latharn. We'll get ready to leave," Irene announced firmly. "Jenna, Ashley, I ken ye dinnae wish to leave yer husbands, but Robert is right. We dinnae ken what this witch is capable of. So far, her mischief hasnae done more than cause chaos and a few wee injuries, but now that she understands we ken who she is, there's nae telling what she may be capable of."

Jenna gave that some thought and realized that leaving would be for the best. She was worried about Ashley and the baby, and Irene and her children, not to mention all the other innocents who might find themselves in the path of Brielle's ire. "Let's get ready then."

* * *

Hours later, the courtyard was lined with wagons, being loaded with passengers and their belongings. Maggie and Dylan charged through the gates atop their horses and came to an abrupt halt near the stables, where they quickly dismounted and ran to discover what was happening.

Seeing Jenna, the two of them headed her way. "What's going on?" Maggie demanded.

"Brielle has escaped and we don't know where she is. Robert thought it best for all of the women and children to leave the castle and head to Ewan and Lena's for our safety," Jenna answered. It was obvious from her composure that she was nervous. She kept searching the area and relief spread across her face when Cormac made his way through the others to reach her. He pulled her into his arms and held her tightly. "I'm scared, Cormac," she told him.

"All will be well, Jenna. Dinnae be afraid," Cormac responded.

"I can't help it. What if something happens to you? I can't bear to think about it," she replied.

"Then dinnae," Cormac smiled down at her and plunked a kiss on her forehead. "I love ye, Jenna, and I'm nae about to leave ye."

Maggie watched and realized she wasn't jealous of these exchanges anymore. She finally had Dylan for her own and the possibility of love was alive in her. Cormac escorted Jenna to her horse, Rose, and helped her mount. Maggie searched for Cailin and Ashley and giggled as they argued over whether Ashley was riding her horse or travelling in a wagon. It was obvious which Ashley preferred and it was the exact opposite of what Cailin wanted.

"Ashley, ye cannae sit astride yer horse for that length of time! 'Tis much safer for ye and the babe to ride in the wagon." The pained expression on Cailin's face must have gotten to Ashley, because she finally gave in. Cailin picked her up and settled her next to the driver, but before he did, he gave her a very passionate kiss goodbye. Ashley held on to him tightly as if she didnae ever wish to let go.

"Ahem," Robert cleared his throat. "Enough already, you two. It's time for ye to be on yer way. Cailin, let go of yer wife. Ye'll see her again, soon enough."

"Is that a promise, Robert?" Ashley asked.

"Aye. I promise. I dinnae wish to be away from me own wife and family any more than ye wish to be away from yer husband." Robert perused the courtyard and approached Maggie. "Maggie are ye sure ye willnae join the women? I'd feel better if ye did."

"Aye, Robert. I'm the only one who can deal with Brielle and it will be better for all if I remain and fight her with my witchcraft." Robert nodded his agreement and Maggie watched as he ensured all the wagons were secure and everyone was ready to leave. He kissed

Irene and each of their children goodbye and then waved the wagons on through the gates.

It took some time for everyone to leave and those staying behind stood and watched until the very last wagon was out of sight.

"Robert, have you seen my Uncle Angus?" Maggie suddenly grew concerned. She realized that in all the upheaval, she hadn't seen Angus since coming back with Dylan.

"Nae, lass, I havenae. Mayhap he has gone to his quarters to rest," Robert suggested.

"It wouldnae be like him to miss all the commotion that's been happening out here. I hope he's not sick." Maggie immediately discounted the thought. It seemed more likely that his disappearance had something to do with Brielle and the idea terrified her. "Dylan, let's go and see if we can find him."

They headed off towards the barracks and straight up the stairs to the room Maggie had been sharing with Angus. Maggie knocked and stood for a moment with her ear to the door, and when she didn't hear anything, she opened it. He wasn't there.

"Where could he be?" Maggie asked.

"I don't know, but I don't like this," Dylan answered.

Their room looked very much the same as it had earlier today. Nothing appeared out of place and although Maggie searched carefully, she couldn't find any clues that would lead her to her uncle.

Dylan and Maggie hurried back downstairs and into the stable, in search of Angus' horse. Much to their dismay, Archie still stood in his stall. The stable boys hadn't seen Angus in quite some time, although they admitted they had been very busy preparing horses for the trip to Ewan's and might not have noticed if he had visited the stable.

Robert had followed them and when he realized they still hadn't found Angus, he tried to reassure Maggie. "I'll have the castle searched, from top to bottom. We'll find him." He turned and strode away swiftly, calling to some of the men as he did so.

Distraught, Maggie slumped against a stall door. "We should never have left the castle this afternoon. If I had been here, this nae would have happened."

"We don't know anything yet, Maggie. There are still plenty of places he could be."

"Do ye truly believe that, Dylan?" Maggie shook her head in disbelief.

"No, I don't," Dylan admitted. "I guess I'm feeling the same way you are. I suspect Brielle has him." Dylan grabbed Maggie by the hand. "Let's go. We can't give up until we've searched everywhere."

They joined the other searchers as they went through every room in the castle and every outbuilding. They even investigated the nearby crofter's cottages and the path along the bluff. Nothing. Angus was nowhere to be found.

"What could she possibly want with Angus?" Dylan questioned, after they had exhausted their search efforts.

"I believe she kens it will hurt Edna... and me," Maggie replied. She was having a hard time sitting still, anxiety pouring from her in waves. "I must find him!" *I feel so helpless,* were the words she didn't dare speak aloud. *Is there anything I can do to stop her? I dinnae even know where she is!*

Dylan gathered her into his arms and held her close. Maggie could hear the steady rhythm of his heart beating in his chest and it gave her some comfort. In this moment, at least one thing in her life was steady and stable. She knew Dylan was there for her, no matter what. His presence helped her to deal with what was turning out to be the worst moment of her life.

When they had run out of places to search, everyone gathered in the courtyard. Robert, Cailin and Cormac tried valiantly to hide their distress from Maggie, but the distress of not knowing what to do next had overcome everyone. You could hear a pin drop in the courtyard, and that alone spoke volumes.

* * *

Angus awoke in a dark, dank cave, with no idea of how he had gotten there. "Where am I?" he croaked.

"Ye've finally awoken, and it's about time" Brielle's voice was harsh, the words spoken close to his ear. "Welcome to my home away from home," she announced. She laughed low in her throat and Angus shivered at the sound. "Dinnae fear. I dinnae wish to harm ye - unless I be forced to."

Angus didn't respond to the threat, he knew there was no point in it. Instead, he concentrated on surreptitiously surveying the cave for an escape route. Light cast from a fire burning in the center of the cavern allowed him to see that they were apparently hidden deep inside a rocky hideaway. He couldn't distinguish any daylight and had no idea whether it was night or day outside.

"Escape willnae be possible, my handsome one," Brielle seemed to be reading his mind. She ran a sharp pointed fingernail through his hair, making him cringe. "Yer wife takes ye fer granted, doesnae she? She sent ye here to protect yer niece, with no care for what the out-come might be. All she cares about is the bridge, isnae that right?"

Was that right? The thoughts in his head were all jumbled as if he'd been drinking heavily, and listening to Brielle, Angus started to think that maybe she was right. Her suggestions played havoc with his rational mind and his emotions, and he wondered if what she was say-ing might actually be the truth. If he was honest with himself, he had wondered much the same thing of late. The bridge had become an ob-session for Edna in recent years. She couldnae leave it for more than a day or two and even then, she worried endlessly about it. He loved Edna more than life itself, but lately, he had to admit he'd found him-self wondering if she felt the same way about him, or if he'd taken a backseat to the importance of the bridge. "Nae. Edna cares for much more than the bridge," Angus said with conviction. *The spell Brielle's put on me is what's leading me to believe her lies.*

"She is a witch, ye ken, and as a witch, she will never behave the way ye expect her to. Her magick will always be first, a fact I suspect ye already are aware of," Brielle continued, as if Angus hadn't said anything at all.

How was it that Brielle knew exactly what he was thinking? It couldnae be a fair fight if she knew what he was going to do or say, before he did it. Frustration was mounting in his chest. His only hope was that the people of Breaghacraig had noticed he was missing and Robert would send out a search party for him.

Again, Brielle stunned him with her knowledge of his thoughts. Had she created some sort of spell to read his mind while he was unconscious? "The others have spent the whole day searching for ye, but they've found nary a clue as to where ye may be. So, ye'd best get comfortable here. I have food and water for ye and unlike yer wife - I'll take good care of ye. Such a handsome man, 'tis a shame ye've been treated so badly." Brielle seemed poised to touch Angus' cheek with her icy cold fingers, but Angus ducked out of the way. Brielle shook her head. "Tsk, tsk, ye dinnae wish to anger me, Angus. I shall be yer savior and ye'll be grateful to me, once I've rid ye of that pesky wife. I may have to rid ye of yer niece as well, but that cannae be helped."

Brielle puttered around the cavern, collecting herbs, candles, something that appeared to be a bone, and a clay pot. Placing the herbs into the pot, she muttered a barely audible incantation while lighting the candles and placing them in crevices gouged into the walls of the cavern. She crushed the herbs with the bone, using it as a rudimentary pestle. Apparently satisfied with her efforts, Brielle reached for a vial on a rock shelf behind her; picking it up, she placed the vial close to the fire. As Angus watched, the liquid inside the glass tube bubbled, which seemed to elate Brielle. She removed the cork stopper and poured the red liquid into the bowl holding the crushed herbs, mixing the liquid and herbs together with the bone. He had no idea what she was up to, but he had no doubt that no good would come from it. His biggest concern was for the safety of his wife, niece and the people at Breaghacraig.

Brielle continued her incantation, but Angus stopped listening. He assumed while she was focused on her spell, she couldnae read his thoughts, so he used the time to try and formulate a plan. He stood up and wandered around the cavern, surprised to learn that no matter where he looked, he was surrounded by solid rock walls. There was no entrance or exit visible to him. He suffered a moment of claustrophobia, but was careful to hide it, not wanting Brielle to know. He was going to have to bide his time while he formulated a plan. If he killed Brielle now, without knowing how to get out, he might never escape. This cavern could become his tomb. If he had no other choice, then that would be his fate, but he decided he should wait to see what Brielle's plans might be.

* * *

"Yer back," a woman's voice came from behind them and they all turned in unison to see who it was.

"Mary what are ye doin' here? Ye were to leave with the others," Robert shouted.

"Of course I wouldnae leave. Someone needs to feed the lot of ye," Mary stood calmly, in apparent defiance of Robert's orders. "Come, I've prepared a simple meal fer ye. 'Tis the best I could do, as I've nae had much help. I tried me best to put the stable boys to work, but they dinnae ken the difference between a pot and a ladle." She chuckled at her own joke.

Mary led them into the great hall where she'd set up a huge pot of soup, several loaves of bread, butter, honey and pitchers of ale. "Ye'll have to serve yerselves, as all the servants are gone." The group of men stood staring in wonder at the table holding the food. "Come now, ye must eat. Ye need yer strength, if yer to fight that troublemaking witch." Mary placed a bowl in Robert's hands and pointed towards the table. Robert took the not-so-subtle hint and filled his bowl. The others followed suit and before long, everyone was seated and eating. Mary's nurturing presence warmed the room and brought a sense of normalcy to an otherwise strange situation.

"Mary, please join us," Robert requested.

"I've already eaten, sir, but thank ye for the offer," Mary answered.

The room began to hum with low voices, speaking between mouthfuls of food. Maggie and Dylan sat close together, each resting a hand on the other's knee. Maggie was trying hard not to break down in tears. She was so worried about Angus. She had promised Aunt Edna that they would protect one another. She should never have gone riding with Dylan. It was a terrible mistake. If she had stayed behind, she might have been able to stop Brielle, and if they'd let Angus join them, he'd still be here. Maggie found she had no appetite, she was so sick with fear for him.

"Maggie, you really need to eat. Mary's right, you'll need your strength to fight Brielle," Dylan said, offering her gentle encouragement.

"Yer right," Maggie agreed. She ate, though it was without enjoyment. The scenarios running through her head were anything but comforting. Self-doubt swept through her brain like water furrowing a path that would eventually flood everything surrounding it. When she was a child, she had dreamed of being a witch like her auntie, but she had never dreamed it would be like this. She never expected her abilities would lead her to this place and time and to the task that lay ahead of her. *What if I fail? What will happen then? How will I face Auntie Edna?* She didn't dare think of what might happen to Angus. Maggie continued eating, until all the soup in her bowl was gone and surveying the men gathered in the room, she suddenly regained her confidence. She wasn't alone. She had Dylan and all the others, who had stayed behind to find Angus and fight Brielle. They would succeed - she was suddenly certain of it.

Dylan must have noticed the change in her demeanor and attributed it to the food. "See, I told you eating would help."

Maggie didn't want him to know that the food had nothing to do with it. She appreciated that he was trying to take care of her and it was so sweet and loving that she wished she could allow him to handle all of the things she didn't care to face. But she couldn't. Maggie stood, and gaining control of her voice announced to the room something she now knew to be true. "I have something to say and I'd like you all to listen carefully." Heads turned in her direction, giving her their full attention. "I believe Brielle will come back here to challenge me. I have nae doubt she will bring Angus with her, and use him as a shield in her efforts to defeat me. I ken this is nae yer battle. 'Tis mine. I would appreciate it if ye would all stand with me when the time comes, but ye dinnae have any obligation to become involved. I understand if ye would prefer to leave and join the others.

A loud uproar washed over the room as everyone tried to speak at once.

"Silence!" Robert shouted and the room stilled instantly. Robert turned his attention to her and smiled warmly. "Maggie, this is our fight. Brielle has come into the MacKenzie castle and endangered the lives of everyone. I ken ye feel the heavy burden of responsibility yer auntie has entrusted to ye, but we willnae desert ye. We stand with ye, every last one of us. Ye will prevail. We will see to it." Cailin and Cormac stood and raised their cups. Latharn, Dougal, Donal, Fergus, and every other man who'd stayed behind also stood with their cups raised in the air. "To victory and to ye, Maggie," Robert announced. "With yer help, we will win this battle."

Maggie's cheeks heated at this show of solidarity. She was touched by their desire to stand by her. She and Dylan raised their cups as well. "To victory," Maggie said. They all drank and the atmosphere, which had been dour throughout the meal, grew lighter and more liberated. The men's voices returned to their normal loud tones and some even laughed with one another. "This is much better," Maggie said to Dylan. "I'm feeling hopeful for a change."

"You'll have all the support you need, Maggie. You can do this," Dylan reassured her.

"I *will* do this." Maggie smiled confidently at Dylan. *I won't fail.*

Chapter 13

Edna paced angrily back and forth in front of the fireplace. She knew exactly what was happening at Breaghacraig and she knew there was nothing she could do about it.

"Brielle!" She called out to her nemesis through the fireplace, which was, for Edna, the equivalent of a cell phone. "Brielle, answer me! I know ye can hear me." Patience was not something Edna Campbell had an abundance of, and Brielle was trying every last shred of it right now. She waited momentarily for a response, and when one wasn't forthcoming she opened her mouth, ready to call to Brielle again, but just as she was about to yell, she heard Brielle's grating voice.

"Alright, alright. I can hear you," Brielle grumbled. "What could ye possibly want with me? Oh, that's right, I have yer verra handsome husband here with me. I've just been telling him how deceitful ye've been with him. He wasnae happy to hear it."

"I have not been deceitful! Yer twisting the truth. Let me speak with him. I ken yer blocking me from him and from Maggie." Edna was furious. Thank goodness, no one other than Teddy, her long-time friend and confidant, was around to witness what was happening. The inn was closed for the evening and Teddy sat in his usual corner spot, while Edna stood alone by the fire in the dining room, contemplating Brielle's demise. She wished she could do it herself, but Brielle had threatened the MacKenzie clan with destruction, unless Edna sent Maggie in her place to Breaghacraig. Edna hadn't anticipated that by having Angus accompany Maggie, Brielle would have the perfect weapon to use against her. "Did ye hear me, Brielle? Let me speak with my husband!"

"I'm afraid that willnae be possible. He doesnae wish to speak with ye, now or ever." Brielle laughed maniacally. "Ye'd best be prepared to hand that bridge over to me, as I'm sure to easily defeat the little lass ye sent in yer stead." Edna could hear more snickering laughter from Brielle. "Everyone here believes that the only thing ye care about is the bridge, Edna. They believe everything I've told them. They believe you'd sacrifice their lives for the bridge. Now isn't that something? They believe ye lied to them. I wonder why? Could it be because you've done it before?"

Edna knew Brielle was trying to rile her. How could anyone believe that Edna cared more for the bridge than she cared about Maggie, Angus and the MacKenzies? "If ye believe ye'll win this, Brielle, ye have another thing coming. Maggie will surprise ye. She's an even more powerful witch than I am." Even as she spoke, Edna felt a shiver of apprehension travel up her spine, wondering how much truth Brielle was speaking amongst her lies. Yes, Edna had lied in the past, but it had never been malicious. Instead, it had been her way of helping the people of Breaghacraig to meet their true loves. What was so wrong with that? She wondered now, in this situation, if perhaps it had been the wrong thing to do.

"She may well be powerful, but she doesnae ken it and after I'm done with her, our bet will be complete and I shall have the bridge and yer life. That was our agreement, wasnae it?"

"'Twas nae an agreement!" Edna protested. "Ye left me with nae choice! I did what I had to do and believe me when I tell ye, ye'll pay for it, especially if any harm comes to Angus or Maggie."

"Any harm that comes to them is yer doing, Edna!" With Brielle's furious response, the crackling of the fire in the dining room grew louder and flames shot from the hearth.. Teddy ducked beneath his table, covering his face and head with his hands.

"Damn ye, Brielle!" Edna cursed. She quickly jumped out of the way of the errant flames, and with a wave of her hands and a steely gaze, put the fire out before it did any real damage. Fire had always been Brielle's strongest power. Edna wished she had remembered to tell Maggie about that. *Maggie is a smart girl* she thought to herself. *She'll know what needs to be done.* Edna extinguished the fire in the hearth, abruptly ending the communication with Brielle.

"Are ye okay, Teddy?" she asked.

Teddy crawled out from under the table and dusted himself off before he settled back in his chair. "Aye. Fine."

Edna's thoughts turned back to Maggie and Angus. She only wished that she could be there, to help Maggie and to get Angus away from Brielle's evil clutches. A shiver of fear trickled through her body at the thought of the danger they were both in.

* * *

What is she up to? Angus thought, as he sat with his back against the cave wall. Brielle had a strange expression on her face. "Are ye well, Brielle?" he asked, not out of any concern for the woman, but rather out of curiosity and frustration at not knowing what was going on.

"Aye. All is verra well." Brielle turned slowly to face him. "I was just speaking with yer wife. She doesnae miss ye! She told me so herself."

"Dinnae bother lying to me. I know me wife. She may nae always be forthcoming, but I do ken that she loves me and I love her, no matter what rubbish ye be spouting at me." Angus watched Brielle carefully to see her reaction, but none came. She merely shrugged and took a seat opposite him.

"'Twill be morning soon and ye and I have work to do. Ye'd best get yer rest." She closed her eyes and made herself comfortable. "And dinnae get any ideas. Even in my sleep, I ken where ye are and what ye be doing."

Angus was not surprised by this announcement. He had figured as much already and so didn't bother to answer her. Instead, he closed his own eyes. Brielle was right about one thing. He was going to need his sleep, to cope with whatever took place on the morn.

* * *

Dylan led Maggie to his chambers inside the castle, with Chester happily following along behind them. Since Brielle was no longer in residence, Dylan's room was his once again and he had decided to let Maggie have it for the night. She, more than any of them, needed a good night's sleep and he intended that she would get it in his bed.

"Dylan, I dinnae need to sleep here. I'm quite comfortable in the barracks," Maggie argued.

"That was fine when your uncle was there with you, but a woman alone shouldn't be sleeping out there with all those men."

"But this is yer room, Dylan. I cannae take it away from ye."

"You're not taking it from me. I'm giving it to you. I'll sleep in the barracks."

They arrived at the door to his bedchamber and Dylan opened it for her. He didn't step through, instead letting Maggie go in and then he stood in the doorway.

"Would ye like to come in?" Maggie asked shyly.

"No, it's okay. I'm pretty tired. I think I'll just head off to bed. I'll see you in the morning." He leaned in to give her a brief kiss good-night, and suddenly found himself glued to the spot. Sweet, sweet Maggie. How could he even think of leaving her here by herself? The kiss lit a fire in him, warming him from head to toe. His hands moved of their own accord, rubbing over her shoulders and down her arms, while hers were planted squarely on his chest. He wanted her so badly it hurt. Pulling her even closer, he savored every taste, every touch, and every tantalizing sensation that rushed over him. When he finally managed to come up for air, he spoke breathlessly. "Maggie, I have to go, before we do something you might regret."

"I'd never regret it, Dylan. Yer the man I want to be my first," Maggie gazed up at him dreamily.

"You're first!" Dylan was blindsided by this announcement. "That's a huge responsibility, Maggie. I think we should definitely wait." What was he thinking? He'd never said that to a woman before - not once in his life, but here he was, trying to protect Maggie from himself. Why hadn't she mentioned this to him when they were at the waterfall? If he'd known, he would never have let things go so far. No, he was determined to wait. *And why am I waiting?* He groaned aloud, when Maggie reached down and brushed her fingers along his hardness, which protruded from the front of his kilt. "Maggie, please. You don't know what you're asking." He was practically panting with desire now. She had him worked into a frenzy and if he didn't bolt now, he never would. Dylan backed up to create some distance between them.

"Don't ye want me, Dylan?" Maggie appeared hurt by his rejection.

"Oh, Maggie, no! I want you more than I can say, but this is not right. I want to be your first, I really do, but I... I..." He had to leave - now. "Chester, stay here with Maggie." Dylan spun on his heels and strode away, leaving Maggie standing in the doorway, confused and forlorn.

* * *

"What just happened?" Maggie said to Chester. She slumped heavily onto the bed, wondering if she'd been too forward with Dylan. Chester curled up on the floor next to the bed and gazed up at Maggie with sad, dark eyes. She was a bit embarrassed by her actions. She had thought for sure that Dylan would like what she was doing, and he had, at least for a little while and then - boom - he had taken off down the passageway as if his kilt was on fire. She had a lot to learn about men. Maybe Dylan was right. This might not be the best night to learn.

She couldn't help but wonder though, had she misread the signs and the things he'd said to her? Her inexperience in these matters was showing and it was doing a number on her self-confidence. She needed another woman to talk to, but unfortunately, they were all miles away. Uncle Angus was a good listener and he gave good advice, but he wasn't here either and this wasn't a conversation she wanted to have with him, anyway. Thoughts of Angus abruptly made her feel guilty and selfish. She reached out to him with her mind and she could sense that he had not been harmed, but she could also feel Brielle's malevolent intentions swimming around his psyche.

Maggie got undressed and snuggled into the bed, pulling the furs up and over her head. As a child, this had always been her way of hiding from the world and tonight she wanted to be that carefree child once again, hiding from all the bad things out there.

It wasn't working. Her head was full of both possible and impossible scenarios, and none of them ended well. Was she having premonitions of things to come, or was she just feeling unworthy of the responsibility that had been placed on her shoulders? Her thoughts swirled around and around, resembling leaves caught in an eddy. "Good night, Chester." Closing her eyes, Maggie focused firmly on good thoughts and outcomes, until she was finally able to fall asleep.

* * *

Loud pounding on the door startled Maggie out of a sound sleep. "Maggie!" called Robert.

"Aye," Maggie answered. She rubbed the sleep from her eyes and squinted at the sun shining through the windows, landing directly on her. She noticed that Chester was gone and the door stood slightly ajar.

"May I come in, lass?" Robert asked. From the sound of his voice, Maggie knew it must be urgent.

"Aye."

The door flew open and Robert entered, closing it behind him. "Maggie, Brielle is in the courtyard and she has Angus. She's threatening to kill him, if ye dinnae join her immediately."

"I'll be right there. I must dress first," Maggie replied. She glanced around for her clothes, remembering she'd strewn them about the floor with no regard before getting into bed. Robert observed her search and understood what she needed. He bent down and picked up her belongings, throwing them onto the bed. Maggie blushed. "I need a moment of privacy, if ye dinnae mind."

It was Robert's turn to appear embarrassed, two spots of color appearing on his shaven cheeks. "I'm sorry. Of course. I'll be waiting right outside yer door. The men are gathering in the courtyard, to be of service to ye if need be."

"Thank ye," Maggie put one leg out from under the covers tentatively and watched as Robert backed out of the room. *This is it. No escaping it.* She threw her clothes on quickly and upon opening the door, discovered that Robert had been leaning on the wood as he almost fell into the room. He caught himself just in time, and took her by the arm to lead her outside. Maggie really didn't need his help, but he had such a tight grip on her arm, she decided not to try to free herself, instead running along at his side. It was apparent from his haste that he was deeply worried about the situation they faced.

As the castle doors opened, Robert turned to her. "We're here to help ye, remember that."

"I will," Maggie said. She drew herself up to her full height and emerged into the sunlight, taking a deep breath.

A dozen large highlanders stood at the base of the castle steps, waiting for her. Others lined the battlements. They were all there - Dylan, Cailin, Cormac, Latharn and many others whom she'd met in the past few days. It gave her confidence a boost as she stood looking out over all of them. They were armed to the teeth with swords, bows and dirks. She had no doubt they would fight to the death, to rid their world of Brielle. Maggie didn't have any more time for self-doubt, so she addressed them with the most confidence she could possibly muster. "Thank ye all for yer support. 'Twill nae be easy, but I believe we'll be the victors."

The men all cheered and raised their weapons high in the air.

"Does anyone have my weapons?" Maggie asked quietly.

Dylan stepped forward, carrying the weapons she had brought with her from Glendaloch. The same weapons Uncle Angus had trained her to use and that had been magically charmed by her Aunt Edna. Maggie briefly closed her eyes and took a deep breath. She came down the steps and walked to the center of the courtyard to face Brielle, who stood about fifty feet away. The men followed, forming a solid wall behind her. Spotting a large lump next to Brielle, Maggie realized that it was Angus curled up in a ball. Why wasn't he standing?

"What have ye done to my uncle?" Maggie asked, deliberately making her voice loud enough so that Brielle would hear from her position near the gate.

"He's merely resting," Brielle answered. It seemed obvious to everyone that she was lying. Why would he choose this moment to rest? It was more likely he was under some spell Brielle had cast.

"If ye wish to fight me, I'm here. Let Angus go. He has no part in this." Maggie did her best to keep her voice from quivering and her legs from shaking.

"He has much to do with this. He will stay where he is." Brielle no longer appeared to be Maggie's doppelganger. She stood before them in what Maggie suspected was her true appearance, but as they watched, she turned herself into an innocent-looking young girl of roughly twelve years of age. Maggie knitted her eyebrows together as she watched. *She's trying to make us see her as a sympathetic creature, so we won't harm her.* Maggie wasn't about to fall for that and as she glanced back at the men, their expressions confirmed they were of the same mind.

"Maggie, I am going to give ye a choice. I can give ye yer uncle and we'll agree that I am the victor, or ye can continue on with this ridiculous battle yer auntie has arranged." Brielle announced this in the sweet voice of a child and with the laugh of an evil witch. Her eyes glowed and embers shot from them, landing on Angus's body. Brielle raised her hand, and as if she were a puppeteer pulling the strings of a marionette, Angus began to rise at her side. He was unconscious, limp and obviously unable to stand on his own. Maggie and the others couldn't tell if he was alive or already dead.

Maggie fought the urge to run to him and instead waited where she was, for Brielle to make her next move. Patience was needed and she dug deep to find it.

"Well, what's yer answer?" Brielle tapped her foot impatiently and spun Angus on the spot like a top. "Do ye wish me to harm him, or nae?"

"Nae. I dinnae wish ye to harm him, but how do I know ye havenae already done so, and how do I know ye willnae harm us all once ye have yer way?"

"Hmmm… Mayhap yer right. Ye dinnae ken. Ye'll have to trust me, willnae ye?" Brielle began lifting Angus into the air.

As Maggie watched, his feet left the ground, and Brielle, seemingly fascinated as she sent Angus higher and higher into the air, watched avidly as well. It was obvious that this was not going to end well, so, while Brielle was preoccupied with her handiwork, Maggie grabbed her bow and one of the charmed arrows Edna had provided and took aim. She needed to shoot straight and true if she were to pierce Brielle's heart. Her own heart pounded in her chest and her hands shook with the effort, but Maggie still pulled back on the bow with all her might. Just as she was about to let the arrow fly, Brielle turned and glared at her. Eyes the color of molten lava, she transformed back from the young girl to the evil old witch in the blink of an eye. Maggie quickly adjusted her shot and sent the arrow sailing in Brielle's direction, just as the witch flung a helpless Angus towards them, followed by dozens of flaming arrows that appeared out of nowhere. Maggie's own arrow dodged to the right and left as it travelled through the air, avoiding the flaming missiles and seeking Brielle's heart. Brielle spun away and moved in a different direction, but the arrow continued on its path, straight towards her. The men behind Maggie began to duck and dodge the flaming missiles as they approached their positions. Angus hit the ground with a sickening thud, the sound sending shivers of apprehension through Maggie's skin. Dylan and Cormac risked themselves to drag Angus out of harm's way and shielded him from the burning arrows that rained down around them. Maggie stood her ground, firm in her resolve to rid the world of Brielle's evil. She watched Brielle intently and the flames of each arrow fizzled out as soon as they reached her vicinity. She was beginning to understand her own level of power and could sense that she was a far stronger witch than she had ever imagined. The expression on Brielle's face confirmed she knew it too. She had obviously thought that she could beat Maggie easily and now, Brielle was beginning to realize that was not going to be the case.

In that moment of realization, Maggie's magical arrow reached Brielle and Maggie couldn't tell if it met its mark, or if Brielle had simply disappeared. A cloud of black mist where Brielle had stood spun like a miniature tornado and then it was gone. Maggie's arrow lay on the ground where Brielle had been standing, still in one piece. Maggie ran across to the spot where Brielle had been. She searched the ground for any clues to confirm she had been successful, but there was nothing to be seen. Dylan ran to her, astonishment clear in his expression. He scanned the ground as Maggie had, but he came up with something she had missed. There, hidden by the fletching of the arrow, was an onyx amulet attached to a thin black ribbon. Dylan picked it up and nearly dropped it when it seared his skin. Maggie quickly took it away from him and passed her hand over the burn, healing his hand instantly.

"Was that hers?" Dylan asked, staring at his healed hand in wonder.

"Aye. I believe 'twas. I'm nae sure what to do with it." The amulet lay in Maggie's hand, the heat not affecting her at all. It was an unusual piece. Not much to look at, but there was something about it that left her wondering. *Where was Brielle? Why did she leave this here?* "Do ye think my arrow hit its mark?"

"I don't know. It was hard to see anything. As soon as the arrow reached her, that black tornado appeared. Do you think she might have gotten away?"

"Not if I truly hit my mark, but I'm afraid I didn't and she probably escaped unharmed. As for this amulet, I'm going to save it to give to Aunt Edna. She'll know what to do with it." Maggie looked back and seeing Angus motionless on the ground, asked the question she was afraid to hear the answer to. "Is he alive?"

"Yes. He's barely breathing though," Dylan took her hand and they rushed across to where Angus lay, surrounded by the Breaghacraig men.

No one said a word as Maggie knelt beside Angus and took his hand. "Uncle, speak to me," Maggie pleaded, but he didn't utter a word. She passed her hands over him, in an attempt to heal any broken bones or other invisible wounds, but it was to no avail. Maggie was very frightened. What had Brielle done to him? She knew Brielle was capable of putting someone into a deep sleep, but this was something far different. Angus' breathing was shallow and his skin was cold to the touch. Maggie didn't know what she could do to save him, so she did the only thing she could think of and talked to him.

"Uncle Angus, I hope ye can hear me. I need ye to stay here with me. Remember we were going to take care of each other. I ken I have nae held up my end of the bargain, but I cannae imagine my life without ye, Uncle. Auntie Edna needs ye as well. Yer the one man who can calm her frazzled nerves. She listens to ye and nae one else. I dinnae ken what would happen if ye left us." Tears fell from Maggie's eyes and she attempted to wipe them away, but they fell faster than she could catch them. Dylan put a comforting arm around her shoulders and she lay her head on his chest and cried even harder. Robert quietly told the men to disperse and leave them be. They shuffled away with many a backward glance.

"Maggie, my dear, let Cormac and Cailin carry Angus inside to a soft, warm bed," Robert suggested. Maggie nodded her agreement, but kept a tearful eye on the men as they carefully lifted Angus and brought him inside.

Maggie knew she looked a mess - red, puffy eyes and a tear-stained face most likely. Using the hem of her cape, she did her best to scrub away the tears and by doing so, regained her composure. Her uncle needed her to be strong now; falling apart wouldn't help him or anyone else. She sniffled one last time and said, "I dinnae believe Brielle's dead, nor do I think she's gone. I can sense her presence." Maggie cast her gaze around the courtyard and on past the gates. "She's gone just far enough away that I can't get to her, but close enough that I can still feel the evil emanating from her."

"How will we find her?" Dylan's brow wrinkled as if he was worrying about what might come next.

"We won't need to… Brielle will find *me*. She'll want her amulet back." Maggie nodded as if she were agreeing with herself. "I must leave Breaghacraig. Brielle's already done enough damage here. If I can draw her away - somewhere so she can't harm anyone else, then it will be a fair fight."

Dylan shook his head stubbornly. "I'm going with you, Maggie. We're a team."

"Dylan, I must do this alone. I cannae risk any harm coming to ye because of me."

"And I can't risk any harm coming to *you*, because I'm not there to protect you."

Maggie bristled at the suggestion. "I am perfectly capable of taking care of myself," she snapped.

"I know you are and I didn't mean to imply you couldn't, but I'd feel better, knowing I was there if you needed me." Dylan knew he had to keep his male ego in check. He wanted to protect Maggie and take care of her. He'd never felt that way about any other woman before Maggie came into his life and he didn't quite know what to do with those feelings. Hanging around with a bunch of medieval highlanders hadn't helped. They were all about protecting their women, but both Cormac and Cailin had somehow learned how to deal with strong-willed women from the future and still protect them, without Ashley and Jenna protesting. He made a mental note to ask them how they did it.

"I'm sorry." Maggie twirled her hair around her finger. "It's just that I'm afraid she'll hurt ye, like she did Uncle Angus."

Dylan smiled. The way she played with her hair when she was nervous was very endearing. "I can't guarantee that I won't get hurt, but I'll do my best not to. I want to do this with you. I want to be there with you when you take her down." Dylan tried to gauge Maggie's reaction to what he was saying. She didn't say anything in response, but he suspected she might be softening to the idea. He decided to plough on and bring up a worry he had over the amulet. Who knew what it was and what it could do? "One question, though. What would happen if you destroyed the amulet?" Dylan wondered if by destroying the amulet, it would somehow destroy Brielle. But if that were the case, why would Brielle have left it when she disappeared?

"I don't really know. I think she left it behind on purpose. I think I'll need it to locate her. If I destroyed the amulet, it possibly would destroy Brielle, but I cannae be certain of it. It could be that she left the amulet here accidentally and that mistake will lead to her downfall, but I'm going to have to take a wait and see approach."

"Better safe than sorry… right?" Dylan took her hand in his, loving the way it fit so perfectly. "What do you say, Maggie? Can I go with you?"

He could see she was pretending to give it some thought. "Well, okay, as long as ye dinnae interfere or get in the way. Magick is a powerful thing, Dylan, I ken ye know that." He watched as she changed from serious to smiling in a single beat. "Let's go check on Angus, shall we? And I'm going to try to contact Aunt Edna for some help." Maggie had a sneaking suspicion she would need all the help she could get.

Chapter 14

Edna knew something was wrong, she could feel it in every cell of her being. "Angus," she cried. "Angus, my love, nae ye! This was never what was supposed to happen. Ye must fight this, love. Fight it with all ye have in ye." Edna drew on every ounce of power she had, trying to get through to him.

Brielle had used every trick in the book to get to Edna, and now she was attempting to take Angus away. *I won't let you take him! As I live and breathe, Brielle, ye will pay for this. Ye will pay!* Even as she heard the faint cackling laughter of her nemesis, Edna positioned herself in her usual spot by the fire and stared into the flames. She searched the fiery embers until she saw Angus, lying motionless on a bed and barely clinging to life. She fought hard to keep her emotions under control. It would do him no good if she were to fall apart now. Sending waves of healing energy his way, she had to fight her way through the shield Brielle had placed around him, designed specifically to keep Edna out. It took all Edna had in her and she could feel her energy swiftly flagging, but she finally managed to shatter the veil of evil that surrounded him. She watched and waited and then she saw it. A slight movement of his eyelid. A twitch. And then another. His eyes remained closed, but the subtle movement was all Edna needed to reach out to her husband and send words of encouragement she knew he would hear. "Angus, my love, hold on. I'm here to help ye, but ye'll need to help yerself, as well."

Another small movement caught Edna's eye, this time his lips moved slightly, as if he wished to speak. Ideally, it would have been better to be right there with him, touching him to assist in breaking the spell, but instead, Edna found herself both miles and centuries away from her love. Edna continued her healing work, and as if in answer to her prayers, she saw Maggie and Dylan enter the room where Angus lay. Maggie walked over to Angus and placed a hand on his chest. It was the therapeutic touch needed to complete their task and as Maggie touched Angus, the link between Maggie and Edna grew stronger.

"Maggie, work with me," Edna pleaded.

"Auntie, I can hear ye. What would ye have me do?" Maggie's connection with Edna allowed her to hear her aunt's voice clearly, while Dylan, on the other hand, heard nothing.

"Do exactly what ye are doing, Maggie. Send yer healing into him while I do the same. With double the magick, we should be able to save him."

Edna watched as Maggie concentrated on Angus. She could feel the energy Maggie was sending through him and Edna was pleased by the strength of the magick she felt there. Maggie was coming into her own at the perfect time. Between the two of them, Angus would be saved. Edna experienced a great sense of relief. The healing flowed back and forth between Maggie and Edna as it passed through Angus. Dylan stood back near the door, watching intently. Edna surmised he had decided it best to stay out of the way and she appreciated his perceptive nature. He would be a good match for Maggie and the perfect addition to the family, if things worked out the way she had planned they would.

Angus groaned loudly, startling them all.

"Uncle Angus, it's me, Maggie. Auntie Edna is helping too. Please wake up, Uncle." Maggie moved to hold his hand and his fingers closed around hers. "I think we've done it, Auntie," she cried. "He's squeezing my hand."

Relief flooded through Edna, exactly as she knew it was through Maggie. "Good work, Maggie. Ye did it! I couldn't have done it on my own. Brielle used verra powerful magick on Angus and neither of us would have been able to break the spell alone."

Maggie leaned down and lovingly stroked Angus' cheek. He slowly opened his eyes and scanned the room. "What's this all about? Dinnae look at me as though I were a dead man." Angus struggled to sit up and Maggie did her best to hold him down. Dylan came to her aid and lowered Angus back down onto the bed.

"You have to rest, Angus. You've been under Brielle's spell for quite a while." Dylan sat on the edge of the bed.

"Was it that bad, lad?" Angus appeared to be seriously considering what Dylan had just said.

"It was. We were all very worried about you. How do you feel?" Dylan asked.

"I feel like a huge weight has been lifted off of me. Brielle forced me to drink some dreadful tasting concoction. I couldnae move, I couldnae fight it, no matter how hard I tried." His focus switched from Dylan to Maggie. "Thank ye, lass. I ken ye saved me life."

"I couldnae have done it without Auntie Edna," Maggie said.

"Where are ye, love? I cannae see ye, but I ken yer here." An exhausted Angus searched the room with his eyes for his wife, but couldn't locate her.

Unlike the way she had spoken with Maggie, Edna's voice now came from the fireplace and both Angus and Dylan could hear her. "I'm here, Angus, back at the inn. I was so worried for ye. Thank heavens yer safe now. I dinnae know what I would've done without ye."

"We have much to talk about, Edna, but it will have to wait, as I'm verra tired." With that announcement, Angus fell into a deep, but thankfully natural sleep.

"Auntie, he's right. There is much we must speak of," Maggie said. "I have so many questions. I found Brielle's talisman. I don't know if she left it on purpose or if it was an accident. Do you ken what it is?"

"Aye, it is the key to her power. She didnae leave it and she will want it back. Be careful, she will do anything she must to have it returned to her possession," Edna explained.

"Auntie, Brielle told us that the whole reason you sent me was to fight for the bridge. Is that the truth? I don't understand why you couldn't have done it. I'm confused about so many things."

"Yer right, Maggie, there is much to talk about and we will, but now is not the time. Ye must find Brielle before she hurts someone else." Edna was suffering a guilty conscience and it was weighing heavily on her mind. She hadn't been totally truthful with Maggie or Angus when she sent them off to Breaghacraig. "I cannae hold my focus for much longer and my fire is dying on this end. I have faith that ye can do this, Maggie. I love ye, child." Edna closed the connection to the sixteenth century and wept. She had almost lost her husband and her niece was still in grave danger. *How did I let this happen?*

* * *

Maggie moved away from the bed where Angus now slept comfortably. She was shaking from the effort she had put forth to heal him. Glancing in Dylan's direction, she saw him smiling at her. It was a soft, warm smile that made her heart sing. He came to her and she relaxed into his arms.

"It's okay, Maggie. It's over for now." Dylan rubbed her arms and back soothingly.

"Oh, Dylan, I was so afraid. I thought we were going to lose him." Dylan's strength flowed into her, giving her the comfort she needed. "I don't know if I can go on fighting her. Maybe I'm the wrong witch to deal with this. She's so strong."

"She's strong, but you're stronger, Maggie. You can do this. One step at a time. Don't think too far ahead, if you do you'll overwhelm yourself." Dylan continued stroking her and holding her close. "I'm here for you. I won't interfere, but I'm here if you need me."

"I do need you, Dylan," Maggie's eyes lifted to his and then lowered to his lips. She wanted so badly to kiss him, but felt this might be a very inappropriate time. Before she could make a decision, Dylan's mouth found hers, his lips gently pressing and his tongue tempting and teasing. Maggie responded like a woman in great need of nourishment. She put everything she had into answering his kisses with her own. A moment ago, this had seemed the wrong time and place, but now it seemed it was exactly the right time. Dylan cradled her head in his hands, holding her in place as Maggie's hands went to his chest, exploring the hard muscle beneath his liene. She heard a whimpering sound. Had it come from her? No. She was reasonably sure it hadn't. She continued to enjoy the warm, wet kisses she had wanted for so long. She heard the whimpering sound again and this time Dylan's head shot up. They both scanned the room, searching for the source of the noise and when they finally found it, Dylan and Maggie released one another simultaneously.

Chester stood in the doorway looking quite a mess, blood was dripping from a wound that wasn't clearly visible, and onto the floor. They both ran across the room to him and dropping to their knees, did their best to find the wound. Dylan ran his hands over Chester, covering every inch of his fur. As he approached Chester's hind leg, the dog yelped in pain.

"It's okay, Chester. It's okay." Dylan calmly reassured the dog. "What happened to you?"

Maggie scrambled around Chester to the site of the injury and gasped when she finally saw the wound. It was deep and had a foul odor emanating from it. It had been hard to notice at first because of Chester's black fur, which had camouflaged the injury, making it almost invisible. "It looks as if someone stabbed him," she observed anxiously. "Don't worry, I can fix this. It will be a piece of cake compared to healing Angus." Maggie placed her hand over the wound and muttered a healing incantation as she did so. Chester visibly relaxed and leaned into her. "There, there, Chester. Yer going to be fine. Dinnae fret, my sweet." Once again, Maggie focused her healing powers on the wound and as she watched, it closed up right before her eyes. Had she not seen it firsthand, she wouldnae have believed it were possible. She released a big breath she hadn't realized she'd been holding. "Wow! Did ye see that?" she asked Dylan.

* * *

Dylan sat beside her on the floor, his eyes filled with admiration for what she had just achieved. He had seen a lot of amazing things today - things that tested even *his* usual acceptance of all things weird and unusual. "Maggie, you're absolutely amazing! Thank you." Dylan cradled Chester's huge head between his hands. "Chester, who did this to you?" Chester cocked his head to one side, as if he understood exactly what Dylan was asking him. "If only he could talk."

"He was missing from your room this morning when I woke. When was the last time you saw him?" Maggie asked.

Dylan gave this question some thought. "Last night when I left him with you, but since we've been here, it's been hard to keep track of him. He wanders off on his own all the time, something he couldn't do back in San Francisco. He loves everyone here and follows anyone he thinks is headed off on a fun adventure."

"I'd bet anything that Brielle had something to do with this," Maggie announced firmly. Dylan watched her as she silently contemplated a much-happier Chester. "The wound itself had the touch of dark magick surrounding it. Chester, can ye try to tell me who did this to ye." She sat perfectly still, closing her eyes and listening intently.

"Are you trying to talk to Chester?" Dylan asked with a touch of disbelief.

"Shhh… I cannae hear him if yer talking to me." Maggie tipped her head to one side and Chester wriggled closer to her. He lifted his head and sniffed her hair, nuzzling against her ear. Maggie began to giggle. "Chester, yer tickling me. Uh-huh... Uh-huh... I see." Maggie raised her head and turned to Dylan who was watching the exchange with bemusement. "It *was* Brielle, just as I suspected. Chester saw her earlier today when she first arrived in the courtyard and he ran down and tried to rescue Angus. She slashed at him with a dirk, which I'm sure was probably charmed, but he was able to get away with only the one wound. He hid until after she disappeared and then came to find you. And it's a verra good thing that he did. The dirk had some kind of poison on it, which entered his body when he was stabbed. It created that horrible odor we could smell. Since I knew it was there, I was able to drain it from his bloodstream. It would have killed him if he hadn't found us soon. Oh, and he says he's verra sorry he's been avoiding you lately."

"Are you telling me that Chester can *talk* to you?" Dylan knew he no doubt looked as bewildered as he felt.

"I wouldn't say *talk,* but I seem to be able to read his thoughts. That's the best way I can describe it. I see pictures relating to what he's thinking." Maggie eyed Dylan anxiously, wondering if he would believe her.

Dylan leaned in and drew her close. Chester licked Maggie's hand and then laid his head in Dylan's lap contentedly.

"Chester, don't get too comfortable," Dylan warned the dog. "Maggie and I have things to do. You stay here with Angus, boy." With a quiet yap, Chester repositioned himself so that he was curled up on the floor by the bed.

"We should go," Maggie announced. "I'll go to the kitchen to ask Mary for some food and supplies. You go to the stable and get the horses. I'll meet you in the courtyard." She gave Dylan a quick peck on the cheek and quickly left the room.

"Chester, take good care of Angus. We'll be back soon." The dog lifted his head and uttered a low bark in response.

Leaving the room, Dylan hurried towards the stables. He trusted Maggie implicitly, but he was a little apprehensive about this undertaking. He shook his head at himself. Who was he kidding? He was a lot apprehensive.

* * *

They met in the courtyard - Dylan with the horses and Maggie, accompanied by Mary and what seemed to be enough food to feed an army. Mary was quite proud of her efforts and Maggie had decided it was better not to argue with her about what they needed to take. Mary was used to equipping the men - all of the men - with whatever they might need for a journey away from the castle. She had packed far more than Maggie felt was necessary, but as Mary was the one with the experience, Maggie had quietly accepted her decisions. Along with co- pious amounts of food, Mary had rounded up clean plaids and a bottle of Sir Robert's finest whiskey. Maggie quietly smiled to herself as she watched Mary handing things to Dylan, who packed them expertly into their saddlebags. They rolled the plaids and tied them to the saddles and while Mary nervously fidgeted, Dylan found a safe spot for the bottle of whiskey.

Just before they were ready to leave, Maggie thanked Mary for her help. "'Tis nothing. I wish ye a safe journey. Take care and come back safely to us." Mary seemed ready to cry as Dylan threw an arm around her shoulders and gave her a gentle squeeze. She covered her face with her hands and hurriedly left them, rushing back towards the kitchens.

"All set?" Dylan asked.

"All set." Maggie adjusted her saddle and with a leg up from Dyl- an, climbed atop her horse.

"Where to?" Dylan mounted and then nudged his own horse to- wards the gates.

"Something is telling me we should take the road back towards the bridge. I believe that's where we'll find her."

"Let's go, then."

As they approached the gate, Robert, Cailin and Cormac came rushing from the castle.

"Wait!" Robert ordered.

Maggie and Dylan stopped dead in their tracks and turned in their saddles to look back at the others. The three men came rushing to their side. "If yer going in search of the witch, we'll be joining ye," Cormac announced firmly.

Maggie and Dylan exchanged questioning glances before Maggie looked back down at Cormac.

"That wouldnae be a good idea," Maggie said. "Ye must stay here. Brielle may come back and ye'll need to be here, to defend Breaghacraig."

"Jenna will be most upset if some harm comes to ye, Dylan." Cormac took hold of Dylan's reins.

"Don't worry, Cormac. We're going to be fine." Maggie did her best to sound as if she believed in what she was saying. "We'll be back, before ye know it."

"I left Chester here with Angus. Take care of him for me, will you?" Dylan reached out to clasp Cormac's shoulder and for a long moment, Maggie wasn't certain Cormac would agree.

"What if ye cannae defeat Brielle?" Cailin asked. "What will happen then?"

"That's why ye need to be here. All of ye. I have faith that I can stop her, but just in case something goes wrong, ye must stay here to finish the job and to protect your home from her."

Cormac reluctantly let go of Dylan's reins and Maggie breathed a sigh of relief. It seemed they were going to let them go off on their own and Maggie would prefer it that way. In her time at Breaghacraig, she had seen how they all loved one another unconditionally, and would be deeply scarred by the loss of any one of their clan. The thought of Ashley, Jenna or Irene being left without the men they loved, wasnae something she wished to have resting on her shoulders. She was going to take care of this. It's what she had been training for and what she now understood was her destiny. No matter what happened, she had confidence that she would prevail. She was surprised by the level of her confidence. When she had first started this journey, Maggie had been apprehensive and unsure of herself, but now she had a newfound sense of who she really was and what she was capable of achieving. She also knew what was at stake if she were to lose to Brielle. With Dylan by her side, Maggie was sure this was one battle she would win. With that thought firmly in mind, they left Breaghacraig behind and began the search for Brielle.

Chapter 15

"Well, mother, I am off to undo the damage I have done." Sir Richard sat atop his large black destrier, tall, handsome and dressed all in black. "I will be back as soon as I can, but in the meantime, I know you will run the castle as smoothly as if I were still here. If you need any help, Edward will be of assistance." He nodded to his brother, who stood protectively by his mother's side. Edward was young, but he was capable. He was already as tall as Richard was and still growing. He was going to be a fine man, and Richard hoped he would be a man unscarred by life's emotional upheavals.

"I am so proud of you, Richard. You are a good man, no matter what you've done in the past. You will make it right and then you'll come back home and we'll find you a wife to love." Lady Catherine watched her son with a mother's love in her eyes. Richard could see it and for the first time in a long time, he thought himself worthy of that love. He bowed very formally to his mother, a sign of the respect he had for her and the regard he held her in, and then trotted off through the gates.

As he rode, Richard felt as if a burden had been lifted from his shoulders. Of course, he had absolutely no idea how he was going to stop Brielle, or if the MacKenzies would be able to forgive him, but it didn't matter. What really mattered was that he had experienced an awakening of sorts and he was very happy about it. It was as if he had suddenly, and very unexpectedly, grown a conscience. He attributed it to the nightmares that had plagued him, but where once he had cursed them, now he was grateful, for they had allowed him to see the error of his ways. He had chosen to make this journey alone and he was glad he had. It gave him the peace and quiet he needed to think. He was also more aware of the beauty of his surroundings, enjoying the scenery he was passing and humming to himself as he travelled. It was a perfect day and nothing could spoil it for him.

* * *

Brielle sat perched among the branches of a large pine tree, hidden from view. From her hiding place, she watched as Sir Richard approached. Was he smiling? She did not recall him ever looking happy in their past acquaintance. If she remembered correctly, a scowl was more likely to appear on his face, than any other expression. And what was that noise she heard? Was he *humming*? Her face pinched as she silently observed him. This was an extremely unusual state of affairs. What could have put him in such a good mood? Her curiosity was growing by leaps and bounds, but caution dictated she should wait and observe, before she made her presence known. Until then, she would simply follow his progress.

She was playing a waiting game on all fronts today. Brielle was also awaiting the arrival of her enemy, Maggie. *I know she seeks me out, but she will only find me when I want to be found. I'll teach her a lesson she will never forget. How dare she think she can destroy me and live to tell the tale?* Anger bubbled up inside Brielle's chest. This was supposed to have been much easier. She had no idea when she had proposed this arrangement that Maggie would be such a worthy opponent. Brielle wanted that bridge and she was determined to get it. She would destroy Edna in the process, along with anyone else who got in her way. Then she'd be respected and feared by everyone. She snickered to herself for a moment, and then transforming herself into a hawk, she soared off to find another spot from which she could spy on Richard.

* * *

Richard watched the hawk sailing off into the distance. He needed to find a spot to camp for the night and he thought he had spied an area up ahead that would work for him. He needed to take some time to think carefully about Brielle and how best to convince her to leave the MacKenzie clan alone. She'd probably think him crazy for cancelling their plans, but he knew he had to try. Off to his right and through the trees, he saw the clearing he had sought, situated beside a small creek. It was a perfect place to stop for the night. He dismounted and unsaddled his horse, leaving the destrier to graze peacefully nearby while he set about making camp. Richard gathered kindling, collected some water from the creek and started a fire. Once it was blazing brightly and there was no risk it would extinguish, he went through his saddlebags in search of food. He'd probably need to do some hunting tomorrow, but for now, he had plenty to eat from his own kitchen at home. Richard found he was rather enjoying this solitary expedition. It was rare for Richard to find himself alone, his men were usually with him whenever he travelled away from the castle. Of course, there was that time when he'd travelled to the future, courtesy of Edna Campbell. He had been alone then, but that was different. There were people everywhere in the future, and the peace and quiet he now relished so deeply was nowhere to be found. There was always some sort of noise assailing his ears in the twenty first century. He sighed heavily, just thinking about it. It had been an adventure and one that not many had the opportunity to have, but he'd wanted more than anything to return to his own time, to the people he knew and the things he was familiar with. He wondered if the time travelers he had met a short time ago were still in his time; or if they had been able to return home. What would it be like to be forced to stay in a time that was not your own? It didn't matter either way, he was back where he belonged and if they were not, there was nothing Richard could do to change their situation. In deep contemplation, Richard finished his meal and settled by the banks of the creek. He'd enjoy this time alone and as for Brielle, he still wasn't sure how he would convince her to abandon her plans. He was determined to speak with her, but what he said would be important if he didn't wish to end up a pile of ashes at her feet.

* * *

Nestled below a rocky outcropping, Dylan spotted a small stone cottage with a moss-covered roof. No smoke rose from its chimney, so he was hopeful that it was unoccupied and that they could make the cottage their shelter for the night.

"We'll need a place to rest for the night," Dylan announced, pointing to the cottage, "and this looks like it might be the perfect place." Glancing Maggie's way, he noticed that she was beginning to slump in her saddle. "You must be exhausted," he said.

"Me? No, I'm fine." Maggie sat up taller, as though determined to convince him she was fine.

Dylan knew she wouldn't admit to being tired, so he decided to force the issue a little. "You might not be, but I am. I'd like to stop."

"Okay, we can do that," she agreed.

"This way," he said, guiding his horse towards the cottage.

"Do you think anyone's living there?" Maggie asked.

"It doesn't look like it, but I'll go and check it out, to be sure it's okay for us to stay there." Dylan dismounted and cautiously approached the doorway. He wanted to be sure this wasn't a trap set for them by Brielle. "Hello!" he called. No one answered, so he peeked inside. He discovered a neat room, just large enough for the small table and chairs it held, along with a bed and a good-sized fireplace. He headed back to the door to tell Maggie it appeared safe. "No one's here, but I think it will be okay for us to stay here tonight."

There was a cloth wrapped parcel lying on the bed and Dylan walked over to examine its contents. Inside he found a note, written in a fine hand. *Ye have found a safe haven for the night. We are away for a while, but please feel free to use our cottage, we only ask that ye treat it as ye would yer own home. This parcel contains clean bedding and there is firewood to help keep ye warm. There is a river not too far from here for water. If ye would, kindly replace any firewood that ye may use. We'll not be back until the spring, so welcome and enjoy.*

"It's like we were meant to find this place," Maggie said. "Do you think Brielle had anything to do with this?" Maggie appeared spooked by the note. "It seems a bit odd to find such a finely written note, as if whoever it was expected us."

"If it was Brielle, it just makes our job a little easier, don't you think?" Dylan asked.

"I suppose so," Maggie answered. "Maybe we can stop looking and wait right here for her."

"I'm going to unsaddle the horses, I'll be right back." Dylan hurried out the door and completed his task in record time. He couldn't rid himself of thinking about the prospect of spending the night under the same roof, and possibly in the same bed, with Maggie. His kilt was doing a poor job of hiding his rampant desires. He stood outside the door for a long moment before entering, trying to get himself under control. He had to think of something that would tamp down the rising urgency of his need to be with Maggie. He certainly didn't want to frighten her. She had told him he would be her first and he wanted more than anything to do things the right way. He mentally shook himself. What was he thinking? She might not even want him tonight! Maggie might want to wait; these weren't exactly ideal conditions for romance, not with the threat of Brielle hanging over their heads. With that thought in mind, Dylan walked through the doorway. It would be difficult, but he would do his best to behave and keep his lustful thoughts to himself.

Maggie was making up the bed with the items that had been left for that purpose, including soft, warm fur throws. She also set the food Mary had given them on the table. Dylan headed over to the fireplace and Maggie stopped him. "Don't worry about the fire; I can get it going in no time."

"Are you sure? I'm pretty good at starting a fire. It's really no trouble."

Maggie laughed. "Get some wood and I'll show you how a witch starts a fire."

Dylan obliged her and gathering kindling and firewood, placed it all in the hearth. "Okay. We're good to go."

Maggie walked across to the fireplace and gave Dylan a wink. She passed her hand over the wood, and instantly, a crackling fire appeared in the hearth, the warmth quickly spreading into the small room.

"Impressive," Dylan admitted. He was glad he hadn't made a fool of himself, trying to do what Maggie had just managed to do in a split-second.

"Just a little something I learned from Edna," Maggie replied. "Shall we eat?"

"I'm hungry. What did Mary give us?" Dylan poked his nose into the saddlebags he'd brought inside and finding them empty went to the table to see what Maggie had set out. Mary's specialty was bridies. These meat pasties were Dylan's favorite and he was excited to discover she'd included enough for dinner tonight with some leftover for breakfast in the morning. She had also packed cheese, bread, bannocks and fruit. They were definitely not going to go hungry. He held up the bottle of whiskey. "For later," he said.

Maggie took a seat and he joined her. With a snap of her fingers, Maggie lit the candle in the middle of the table and between that and the fire a nice cozy glow filled the cottage. Dylan thought it was very romantic and he wondered if Maggie would agree.

"I certainly would agree," Maggie said. She laughed and he assumed it was because of the astonished expression, which had no doubt spread across his face.

"Did you just read my thoughts?" he asked in disbelief.

"Aye," she answered, "I believe I did."

"I'm going to have to be careful about what I'm thinking, I guess." Dylan cocked an eyebrow, secretly worrying that she had read all of his recent thoughts, including his errant desire which he struggled hard to control.

"Don't worry. I cannae seem to do it all the time," Maggie reassured him. "I just catch bits and pieces."

"So, you haven't been inside my head all day then?"

"No, of course not. It wouldnae be polite to read people's thoughts without their permission." Maggie eyed him shyly when he raised a questioning eyebrow. "I'm sorry. I guess by my own standards, I was impolite because I read yer thoughts. I won't do it again."

"Good. Because I wouldn't want you to know what I've been thinking all this time." He offered her a dazzling smile.

"I don't have to be inside yer head to ken what ye've been thinking, Mr. Sinclair. It's written all over yer face." Maggie giggled and it soon morphed into uncontrollable laughter.

Dylan surmised it must be his expression that had her in stitches. He hadn't known his emotions were so transparent. He'd been doing his best to hide his desire and apparently had failed miserably.

"Okay, okay, you can stop laughing at me now. I can't help how I feel about you, you know." Dylan rose from his chair and pulled Maggie up to join him. Suddenly he was feeling very warm. The close proximity of Maggie's body was certainly heating things up. Lifting her chin with his finger, he held it there while he placed several small kisses on her very soft and inviting lips. Before he could stop himself he had her securely anchored in his arms and was kissing her senseless.

* * *

His kisses were exactly what Maggie had been craving all day. How lucky that they had found this wonderful little hideaway in the woods! It was the perfect place, as far as she was concerned. She wasn't sure exactly what to expect, but she knew what she wanted and what she wanted was Dylan. She hoped she wasn't being too forward, but she desperately needed to get that shirt off of him. She undid the laces at the neck and pulled it from his kilt. She ran quivering hands up beneath the silky material, relishing the feel of soft warm skin over rock hard muscle. She let herself drift into a place where nothing mattered but what she was feeling. No thoughts interfered with her actions. This was where she wanted to be and Dylan was the man she wanted to be with.

Dylan pulled his shirt up and over his head, revealing a sight that took Maggie's breath away. Her hands had a mind of their own as they traced every inch of him - chest, shoulders, and perfect washboard abs. A sensation resembling butterflies furiously beating their wings filled her belly and a pulsing ache spread between her thighs. She reached for the belt that held his kilt in place, but Dylan gripped her hands in his, stopping her movements.

"Maggie, are you sure?" He looked deeply into her eyes, searching for her answer.

"Verra sure," she whispered into his chest as she peppered it with little kisses and flicks of her tongue. She went back to work on the belt and this time Dylan helped her, dropping the kilt to his feet. He kicked it out of the way and his boots came off next. He was totally and completely naked and Maggie just stared at him in wonder. She'd never seen a completely naked man before. Well, that wasn't completely true. She'd seen Dylan at the waterfall that day not so long ago, but it had been a brief view and he'd been soaking wet and cold. This was different. Her eyes travelled over him from head to toe. She had to admit she was a little embarrassed, but Dylan didn't seem to mind one bit.

"Your turn," he said as he began removing her clothes, all the while kissing her. One hand twisted into her hair while the other hand drew her shirt off. Next came her boots and pants. The cool air sent gooseflesh spreading across her skin and she pressed herself up against Dylan seeking his warmth. He picked her up and reverently placed her on the bed, his eyes burning a sensual path from her eyes, down to her lips, on to her breasts and further. She could hardly breathe for excitement and nerves, and she nearly groaned when he lowered himself to lay atop her. The sensation of having every inch of him covering her own body was sheer ecstasy. It seemed every single part of him was touching some part of her.

"Maggie," Dylan's voice sent shivers of delight rippling through her limbs. "This is your first time, right?"

She nodded shyly.

"It might hurt for a moment or two, but I promise I'll make it up to you. Are you okay with that?"

She nodded again.

"Don't worry. We'll work up to it." He ran his hand down the side of her face, lovingly caressing her cheek. Shifting his weight to the side, he sought out her breasts with his mouth and tongue, slowly driving her crazy. A moan escaped her lips and she could feel Dylan's mouth turn up into a slow smile as a low chuckle erupted from his throat. She closed her eyes and enjoyed the moment, the touch of his mouth on her and then he moved again, focusing his attention on her belly. He circled her navel with his tongue, and she bucked beneath him. It tickled a little, but in a wonderful way and she stifled a giggle. As Dylan continued kissing and licking her belly, he lowered his hands to a different part of her body. The spot between her legs, which had been aching so badly for him, now enjoyed the gentle caress of his fingers. His thumb found a particularly sensitive spot and she jumped. "Does that feel good?" he asked, continuing to circle that very sensitive nub.

Couldn't he tell? It felt better than anything ever had before. "Mmm…" she moaned helplessly. "Mmm…"

Dylan pulled himself further down her body until his mouth was where his hands had been and his hands grabbed her buttocks, holding her still. "Dylan," she cried.

"Don't worry, I've got you," Dylan said, sounding very certain as his tongue did things to her that she had never anticipated. An unusual sensation started building inside her body. Part aching, part tingling - her breathing quickened, and while she didn't have a clue where this was all leading - she wanted to get there with every fiber of her being. Dylan was an expert it seemed. All sense of time and space left her as she floated in ecstasy with his touch. The sensation continued to build and she could scarcely bear it, and suddenly, when she thought she could take no more her body shook and bucked, and she experienced a release she had never experienced before. She thought it was over, but still Dylan continued licking and suckling against her, and she tangled her fingers in his silky soft hair holding him against her. She thought she might expire right there on the spot, and then it happened a second time. Maggie was certain she was having an out of body experience, and she moaned in delight at the sheer pleasure coursing through her body. Dylan's fingers continued to massage her gently, but he lifted himself back up over her body, his mouth on hers, his tongue probing. She responded by throwing her arms around his neck and holding him close. Her body arched up to meet his as his kisses left her mouth and headed to her throat and then his mouth was next to her ears. "Are you ready?" he asked. "I'll go slow, but you let me know if you want me to stop, okay?"

"Yes." She wouldn't ask him to stop. She wanted to feel him inside of her and nothing was going to get in the way of that.

Dylan moved to cover her with his body again. The hard shaft of his penis poked her as he positioned himself between her legs. He moved again, this time inside of her and then in one swift movement, he slid all the way in and she experienced a sharp, burning pain. "Are you okay?" he asked. He stopped moving, watching her face worriedly for her reaction.

"I'm good," she assured him. "Please, don't stop."

Dylan slowly began moving inside her and Maggie experienced that same growing excitement she had enjoyed before. She held tightly to his shoulders for a moment or two, as she adjusted to his movements and then she let her hands wander down his back to grip his buttocks. The muscles tensed and released between her fingers as he plunged into her. His breathing quickened and he dove deeper with each pump of his hips. She cried out, spasms of pleasure rocking her body for the third time and a moment later, Dylan joined her, growling as he poured his release into her. Rolling to his side, he pulled her with him and she rested her head on his chest. They lay that way, catching their breath, the crackling of the fire the only sound in the small cottage.

"That was beautiful," Maggie said, when she finally found her voice. "Amazingly beautiful."

"No pain next time. From now on, it will only be pleasure," Dylan said in response.

Maggie smiled and snuggled closer to Dylan. He secured her tightly to his side with his arm, and with the flickering flames casting shadows around them, they both fell asleep, happy and sated.

Chapter 16

The sound of someone singing woke him. Dylan stretched and opened his eyes to discover Maggie happily setting out food and drink. "Good morning, beautiful," he said, drinking in the sight of a tumble of red hair and smiling green eyes.

"Good afternoon," she corrected, running across to the bed and throwing herself on top of him.

He caught her in his arms, thinking to himself that he was the luckiest man alive. Dylan couldn't believe the happiness he enjoyed as he nuzzled her neck, her scent drifting to his nose and sending an alert throughout his body. In the past, he was always out the door before there was any time for talking, sharing or getting close. He couldn't imagine doing that now, not with Maggie. He wanted to spend every waking - and every sleeping - moment with her.

Maggie pulled herself up so she could straddle him with her legs. She giggled and wriggled against his groin. "What's this I feel?" A seductive smile caressed her lips.

"I think you know what it is." Dylan grabbed her waist, deftly lifting her and switching places, putting her beneath him. He flipped his hair out of his face, so he could get a better look at her. Again, he considered how lucky he was to have found her.

"Are we going to do it again?" Maggie asked with a knowing smile.

"I think we are," Dylan responded with a smug smile. "And I think I've created a monster." He tickled her sides and she squirmed with laughter, trying to get away. "Where do you think you're going, miss? I'm not done with you yet."

Squeals of laughter echoed throughout the room as they wrestled with each other on the bed, until Dylan stopped teasing and began to kiss her. Maggie's soft moan let him know she wanted more, but the sound of hoof beats from close by had both of them freezing on the spot and listening to the clip clopping as the sound approached the cottage. Dylan leaped out of bed and swiftly wrapped his kilt around him, while Maggie scurried about the room searching for her own clothes.

"Stay here," Dylan ordered.

Maggie threw her clothes on as quickly as she could manage and much to Dylan's dismay, she followed him to the closed door. He shook his head, knowing there was no time to argue with her, they needed to find out who was approaching. Pulling open the door, he saw a lone rider heading their way. The man was dressed in black from head to toe and rode a massive black destrier. Dylan was immediately on guard. "Maggie, get my sword. I left it inside."

Maggie did as he asked, retrieving the sword from beside the fireplace and handing it to Dylan. The rider stopped just short of the cottage and casually dismounted.

"Good morning," he said. "I was passing by and noticed smoke coming from the chimney. I thought I'd stop by, to see who was here."

Dylan silently sized the man up, wondering if he'd be able to take him in a fight. He had gotten quite good with a sword, thanks to the MacKenzies' practice sessions. Even so, he hoped he wouldn't have to use the skill now.

The black-clad man continued. "My name is Sir Richard Jefford. I'm travelling north to visit some," he hesitated for only a split-second and then continued, placing emphasis on the last word, "friends."

Maggie poked Dylan in the back and Dylan turned to glance at her. She raised her eyebrows and widened her eyes in an exaggerated gesture, which he assumed she thought he'd recognize.

"Sir Richard, it's a pleasure to meet you. I'm Dylan Sinclair and this is Maggie MacKinnon."

Sir Richard bowed in Maggie's direction, giving her curious clothing the once-over as he did so. "Is this your cottage?" Richard asked.

"No. We're also travelling. We arrived here yesterday afternoon and found a note from the owners, giving travelers permission to use it as shelter." Maggie continued to elbow him, but he ignored her for the moment. "We were just about to break our fast," Dylan lied. "Would you care to join us?"

"I would love to join you. Are you certain you wouldn't mind? Miss MacKinnon seems a little distressed by my presence." Richard nodded his head in Maggie's direction.

"I wasn't expecting company. One can never be too careful," Maggie responded. Dylan couldn't imagine what was wrong, but as soon as he and Maggie were alone for a moment, he was going to find out.

"I'll just take care of my horse then." Richard unsaddled his horse and left the massive destrier to graze, before heading back to join them. He had a relaxed manner about him and Dylan decided there was nothing to worry about from the newly arrived stranger. He was generally good at reading people and this guy didn't seem as if he was interested in causing trouble. Just in case, though, he'd keep his sword close by. Dylan directed Richard inside and Maggie went first, stomping on Dylan's foot as she swept past him.

"Is she upset about something?" Richard questioned as he passed.

Dylan merely shrugged his shoulders and followed them inside.

* * *

Maggie sat on the edge of the bed, sullenly staring daggers at them, while Dylan and Richard sat at the table and helped themselves to the food. She couldn't believe that Dylan hadn't understood that she was trying to give him a warning. From what she had heard about Sir Richard, the man was no doubt up to something. She assumed he was heading to Breaghacraig, to cause more trouble for the MacKenzies. Auntie Edna had warned Maggie that he was in league with Brielle. This was not good. She had to find a way to get Dylan alone to tell him, but all she could do for now was watch as he sat having a friendly conversation with a man, who was in her mind, their enemy. The only good thing about the situation was that Richard had no idea who they were.

"I'm on my way to visit the MacKenzies," Richard announced.

"The MacKenzies? What a coincidence—"

Maggie jumped to her feet before Dylan could utter another word. "Dylan, might I have a word with ye please?"

"Sure, Maggie. What is it?" Dylan asked.

"Alone, please." Maggie knew this was all piquing Sir Richard's curiosity, but she had to tell Dylan about the man, before he said something that could only lead to trouble.

"Okay, no problem." Dylan stood and turned towards Sir Richard. "I'm sorry. Please excuse me for a minute. Go ahead and enjoy the food."

Richard merely smiled warmly, and tucked into the food on the table in front of him.

Once outside, Maggie began to gesture animatedly at Dylan, her voice a loud whisper. "Are ye crazy? Don't ye know who that is?"

"I'm afraid not, but I'm assuming you're about to tell me," Dylan retorted, sounding bemused.

"I tried to warn ye before ye invited him in to eat with us!" Maggie said. She was so frustrated, she was sure there must be visible steam coming out of her ears.

"I thought you were just upset because he'd interrupted us before I made love to you again," he teased.

"Dylan, this is serious. Sir Richard is an enemy to the MacKenzies! He has done nothing but cause trouble for them for many years and Auntie Edna told me he's working with Brielle to destroy them, once and for all."

Dylan lapsed into silence. His brow furrowed as he considered what she had just said.

"What are we going to do?" Maggie asked impatiently, when a response wasn't forthcoming.

"Well, you know that old saying about keeping your friends close and your enemies closer? We're sticking to him like glue." Dylan disarmed her with a sweet smile. "You're going to have to try and be nicer to him, Maggie. He already thinks something's up."

"Okay, I see yer point," Maggie admitted. "I'll be nice, but he'll nae doubt be wondering what we're out here talking about."

Dylan winked at her. "Don't worry. I'll take care of it."

Heading back inside, they found Sir Richard sitting in exactly the same spot they had left him in, happily eating. "Ah, you're back. These meat pasties are wonderful. Did you make these, Maggie?"

"Yes, I did," she lied. She had almost said no, but then she would have had to tell him where she got them, and she wasnae very good at thinking up stories on the spot.

"I'm sorry about Maggie's attitude before, Richard," Dylan said. "Maggie's a bit upset because we were just about to, well, you know…" Dylan winked conspiratorially at Richard.

Richard didn't miss a beat, shaking his head and giving a hearty chuckle. "I'm very sorry for the interruption, Dylan. Bad timing on my part. If I had known, I certainly would have waited outside."

Maggie cringed with embarrassment. She couldn't believe Dylan would admit something like that! And now, Richard was looking at her as if she were a wanton woman. The nerve of them both! Her temper got the better of her, and before she could stop herself, she grabbed a ewer of water and spilled it all over Dylan's head.

The look of disbelief on Dylan's face was comical. Maggie watched as Sir Richard tried to hide his own face, obviously struggling to cover his amusement. The best he could do was to try and conceal it by coughing loudly. Maggie stormed out of the cottage, leaving the two men together and baffled as to what had just happened.

* * *

"I believe she's angry with you," Sir Richard chuckled. "Women don't like their deepest, darkest secrets revealed, you know. Especially to a stranger."

Dylan sat in a puddle of water; his hair was soaked, as was his kilt. "I know that *now*. I'll be more careful in the future."

"Where are you from Dylan? I detect an unusual accent," Richard said.

Dylan had to think on his feet here. He couldn't say America, as that might rouse Sir Richard's suspicions. He bought himself some time by rising and finding a cloth to dry himself off. "It is unusual, isn't it? I've travelled quite extensively since I was a lad. I've lived in more places than I can count, and I guess I picked up a bit of an accent from each of those places. It's made me the man I am today."

Sir Richard nodded. "Before you went out to speak with your lady, we were talking about the MacKenzies."

"Were we?" Dylan said vaguely, hoping he could keep Richard from asking too many questions.

"Yes. I said that I was on my way to see them and you said it was a coincidence. I got the impression you might know them."

"Not really. I mean, Maggie and I spent a night at Breaghacraig. They were very kind and gracious hosts." Dylan waited for a reaction, but when there wasn't one, he continued. "You say they're old friends of yours?"

"Not friends, really. We've had some problems in the past, but I'm on my way to give them my sincerest apologies for past transgressions, and to see if we can start over again. I've done some things I'm quite ashamed of and I'm proud to say I'm a changed man. I'd like them to know that."

Dylan felt he was a good judge of character and he listened carefully for any sign that Sir Richard was not being truthful, but he got the sense that the man really did want to make amends. "It takes a big man to admit when he's been wrong. I admire that."

"I only hope I'm not too late. You see, there's someone else who is intent on harming them, and I'd like to warn them if possible."

"It sounds like they have lots of enemies," Dylan said, testing Richard.

"No. Not so many," Richard said. "Just myself and this other party I spoke of. I no longer consider them enemies though, and if I can help them dispense of this new threat, my conscience will be clear."

"Then what will you do?" Dylan was curious as to what was motivating Sir Richard.

"I'll go back to my own home and live my life. I've spent far too many years, blaming others for my own mistakes. I'd like to become the man I was meant to be, but who lost his way when he lost his first love and spent far too many years seeking revenge."

Dylan could see that Sir Richard was genuinely sad as he discussed his past. He didn't know all the particulars, but he could tell there was sincerity in the words being spoken. "Sounds like you're doing the right thing."

"That is my hope. I am not a wise man, and I have a lot to learn, but I will give you this one piece of advice with regard to your young lady, Maggie. If you truly love her, and she loves you, don't make light of her feelings. She seems a good woman, who deserves your respect. I believe you may owe her an apology for sharing your secret with me."

"I believe you're correct. I'm going to go find her. Thanks for the words of wisdom."

Dylan left Richard behind in the cottage as he set off to find Maggie.

* * *

Maggie sat on the ground just outside the cottage door. She had been listening intently through the door, to everything that passed between Dylan and Sir Richard and she wasn't sure what to think. She had been led to believe Sir Richard was a very bad man. Now she wasn't so sure that impression was accurate.

"I guess I didn't have to search too far for you. Were you sitting right here all along?" Dylan asked when he pulled open the door.

Maggie couldn't help but giggle at his disheveled appearance, with his damp hair and sopping wet kilt, he resembled a drowned rat. "Sorry about the water. I guess I let my temper get the better of me."

"Let's go for a walk," Dylan suggested. "We need to talk."

Maggie took Dylan's hand and followed him, as he walked towards the river. She glanced around and found a large, flat boulder for them to sit on. "Over there," she said, pointing it out to Dylan.

Once they were settled together on the boulder, Dylan took Maggie's hands in his. "Maggie, first I want to apologize for telling Sir Richard what I did. I didn't realize it would embarrass you like that."

"I know. I understand now, it was the perfect thing for you to tell him under the circumstances. It made complete sense and it worked. So, you're forgiven."

"You heard everything, right? What do you think of his story?" Dylan asked.

"I don't know. He doesn't sound anything like the evil monster Aunt Edna told me he was. Do you think he's putting on an act for our benefit?" Maggie questioned doubtfully.

"I suppose it's possible, but I'm reasonably good at reading people, and I don't think he's lying." Dylan picked up a stone and skipped it across the creek.

"That was pretty good," Maggie commented. She picked up a rock of her own, and tried to mimic what Dylan had done. It skipped, but not nearly as many times as Dylan's.

"I think we should just play it by ear. Maybe we should stick with Sir Richard and see what he's up to, if anything. If we can convince him to stay here with us for another day or two, maybe we can come up with some reason to head back to Breaghacraig. What do you think?"

"How will we get him to stay here with us? I'm sure he just wants to be on his way. And what about Brielle? We can't just give up our search for her." Maggie noted.

"Brielle! He says he's trying to stop her. Maybe if you could find a way to get her to come to us, we could solve all our problems at once." Dylan waited for her to answer, but Maggie suddenly found herself mesmerized by how handsome he was. She wanted this mess to be over and done with, so she could have him all to herself and stop worrying. "Hey, what are you thinking about?" Dylan asked.

Maggie was embarrassed to be caught daydreaming about Dylan in the midst of a crisis. "Oh... it's nothing. If I can get her here, I think it might work. It would certainly be a way of confirming if Sir Richard is telling the truth before he goes on to Breaghacraig. You know, maybe we've been going about this the wrong way. I have her talisman. She surely wants it back, so instead of us searching for her, we let her find us." Maggie smiled triumphantly. "That's the new plan."

"Okay, I'll see what I can do to get Sir Richard to stay. Try not to get mad at me though, if I say something you don't like," he teased.

Maggie punched him in the arm and laughed when he feigned injury. Dylan scooped her into his arms and planted a kiss on her lips and once again, Maggie was sad that they had so much to do before they could enjoy each other again. He put her down and they began walking back to the cottage. A chill ran down Maggie's spine and she shivered.

"You cold?" Dylan asked, gathering her closer.

She wasn't cold, but she didn't want to alarm him. She could sense Brielle and she was nearby.

* * *

Surrounded by birds, sitting high up in one of the trees, Brielle had been observing the activity going on at the small stone cottage. "What goes on there?" she asked the birds. She received no response; the birds seemed content to ignore her, instead preening at their shiny black feathers with their strong, curved beaks. "I ken ye dinnae care," she complained to her silent friends. "But they're up to something. Sir Richard is with them. Why? Mayhap that will be to my advantage. He can deal with the man, while I deal with the witch." A thought occurred to her, "But what if he betrays me? Hmm… No matter. If he does, he'll pay for his betrayal right along with the rest of them." Brielle kept watch as Dylan and Maggie went back inside. "That one senses I'm here," she observed, pointing one gnarled finger in Maggie's direction. Brielle cackled and the sound rang through the tree, scaring some of the birds into flight. "Don't leave me, my friends." She held out her hand and one lone bird hopped along the branch and then onto her outstretched arm. He tipped his head from side-to-side, intelligent eyes sizing her up.

"Caw, caw," the bird cried.

"Yes, I must be careful. She is much stronger than I anticipated, but I will outsmart her, never fear. You'll see," Brielle spoke to the bird as if he could understand her. She stroked his soft feathers with her hand. "Yes, you will see and so will they. They'll all learn they can't win against me." Reaching into her pocket, Brielle removed a piece of fruit, which she held out to the bird. He grabbed it from her fingers and fluttered off her hand, stopping further down the branch to eat. Some of the others came back, realizing that Brielle had food and not wanting to miss out. She gladly shared what little she had with her feathered friends. She loved perching in the uppermost branches of the tallest trees. She could see for miles in every direction and rarely did anyone other than the birds know she was there.

"Time grows short; I must make my move soon. She has my amulet and I must have it back. Maggie has no idea the power it holds, nor what she could do with it and she mustn't find out. You won't tell her, will you?" The birds had settled around her once again, sated by their small treat, their feathers plumped up around their small bodies and eyes closing to nap. Brielle stayed where she was and watched the cottage, until long after the sky had grown dark and the wind began howling through the branches of the tree.

Chapter 17

In between greeting guests who were arriving in her dining room, Edna Campbell paced back and forth restlessly. She felt disconnected from Maggie and Angus, and had no idea what was happening between them and Brielle. She had done her best, as promised, to change Richard's conniving ways with the nightmares she had sent to haunt his sleep. Hopefully it had worked. Edna had always believed that everyone had good qualities and sometimes they just needed a little assistance to reveal them. Sir Richard needed a woman in his life, but until he found one to replace Irene, he would never be content. The nightmares had been meant to wake him up to the possibilities that lay in front of him. To make him see how his behavior had adversely affected him and caused him to make bad choices. It had initially been difficult for Edna to see Sir Richard as a good man, who had simply lost his way, but she'd done it, and now she desperately needed to know what was going on in medieval Scotland. She had tried contacting Maggie, but Brielle was blocking her again. She'd try again later, in the hope that Brielle might grow preoccupied with something else and lose concentration. It was the only way she'd be able to talk to Maggie, unless she could find a way to force her way through Brielle's block again. She'd done it once before, when Angus needed her so desperately, so it was always possible she could manage to do it again if the circumstances were right. She just didn't know what the right circumstances might be.

Pacing in front of the fireplace had become a ritual for Edna. Day after day, she paced back and forth, staring into the flames, waiting for a glimpse into what was happening with those she loved. The weight of the world seemed to be sitting on her shoulders and she couldn't shake it. Responsibility for all that was happening weighed heavily on her mind. Edna had been less than forthcoming with the truth about Brielle, but at the time, she'd felt she had no choice. In truth, the bridge was only a small part of the reason she had sent Maggie back in time. If she lost the bridge, then so be it. Of far more concern was Brielle's threat to the MacKenzies. She couldn't ignore Brielle's challenge. If she did, the MacKenzies would surely pay and Edna couldn't allow that. They were innocent victims in all of this and she would nae see any harm come to them. Hadn't she sent Ashley to Cailin and then Cormac to Jenna? Now that they were all happy and in love, she would be damned if she let Brielle take that away from them. She clenched her fists and gritted her teeth, just thinking about it.

"Edna?"

"Yes," Edna responded, turning to her friend and helper, Teddy. "What's wrong, Teddy?"

"I was going to ask you the same thing," Teddy answered.

"I'm so worried about Maggie and Angus, and I'm frustrated that I'm in the dark as to what's happening." Edna walked to the bar and poured herself a glass of wine. "Maybe this will help," she said, offering Teddy a reassuring smile.

Teddy didn't say anything. Instead, he held out his hand to Edna. Tipping her head to the side, she gave him a questioning look, but gave him her hand. Teddy led her back to his favorite corner of the dining room. It was where he kept watch over everything and everyone as they came and went. He even had a view of the street outside the inn. Edna sat with him and saw the world from his perspective. The dimly lit space created a cocoon for Teddy. It was his safe spot and he wanted to share it with Edna. She'd known Teddy since he was a small child and they'd developed a special bond over the years. Most people thought of Teddy as odd and avoided him, but not Edna. Edna loved all the things that made Teddy different. People didn't know him, didn't see him through her eyes, but if they could, they'd see he was loyal, kind, smart and trustworthy. In fact, since Edna had taken him under her wing, the people of the village had become more accepting of him and many had befriended him. He was awkward at carrying on a conversation, but that didn't matter a whit to Edna. She was happy to do all the talking and Teddy was a good listener. She appreciated the fact that here and now, Teddy was trying to make her feel safe and comforted, so she settled back and enjoyed his quiet company and her glass of wine.

* * *

The more she got to know Sir Richard, the harder it was for Maggie to believe he was guilty of the crimes Edna accused him of. He was very chivalrous, helping her gather wood for their fire, while Dylan tended to the horses. He had offered to collect water from the river and seemingly worried that they would not have enough food for the evening meal, Sir Richard had found a wicker trap around the back of the cottage and offered to catch a fish for their dinner. Maggie followed him down to the river, curious to see just how successful his fishing would be.

"The water is very clear," Richard said. "Look you can see the fish there among the larger rocks." He pointed to a spot near a huge boulder. "We'll set our trap here." He placed the trap, which he had baited with some of the meat from the bridies, into the water and then sat back on a boulder. "Now, we wait."

Maggie stood awkwardly to one side, but after a few minutes decided it wouldn't hurt to sit with Richard. "Have you fished with one of those before," she asked.

"Yes, many times. They work best in a stream or river like this one." He checked the trap and then sat back down again.

Maggie surreptitiously studied Sir Richard from beneath her lowered lashes, and decided he was really quite handsome. She was puzzled as to why he wasn't married. "Sir Richard, may I ask ye a question?"

"Please, call me Richard," he offered pleasantly. "What would you like to know?"

"Why is it that ye arenae married? A handsome man like yerself should have many women to choose from."

For a long moment, Richard remained silent, staring at the slowly moving river and Maggie began to worry that she'd offended him. He drew his gaze from the river and turned to face her before he spoke. "Because, my dear, I am a fool. I fell in love once, a long time ago and she didnae feel the same for me. In fact, she loved another man. I let my heart turn cold to everyone but her. It set me on a path that I am sorry to say, has left me alone and deeply regretful of the decisions I've made."

"I'm sorry," Maggie said, and she really meant the sentiment. She knew the woman he was speaking of was Irene. She had heard the story from Edna, but had always imagined the Sir Richard who loved Irene as being an unattractive and unappealing man. This Richard, sitting beside her by the river's edge, was neither of those. "Will that change now, do ye think?"

Richard appeared touched by her concern. "I can only hope it will. There are steps I must take to ensure it, but if I can accomplish them, who knows? Anything may be possible." He smiled; a warm, friendly and open smile, and Maggie decided that she rather liked him and thought she would do whatever was within her power to help him.

The sound of splashing water caught their attention.

"Look there, we've caught a very nice fish. He seems large enough to feed the three of us, I'd say." Richard laughed with delight as he pulled the trap from the water. He'd caught a huge trout and seemed gleeful about his success. "Shall we go show your man what we've caught? Come." He offered Maggie a hand to help her up and Maggie accepted his assistance without concern.

"This will make us a fine meal," Maggie agreed. She liked that he'd called Dylan *her man*. She certainly thought of him as such and she liked the sound of it. He *was* her man, she thought happily.

* * *

Later in the afternoon, Maggie and Dylan went in search of edible wild plants to go along with their fish dinner. Maggie, who was very familiar with what was safe to eat and what was poisonous, due to years of wandering the countryside near her home, led the way and pointed out things Dylan should pick. Her mother and Edna had given her a topnotch education, with many warnings about taking care when choosing plants to eat. They gathered a good quantity and headed back to the cottage, where Richard had cleaned the fish and prepared it for cooking. Maggie wrapped the greens around the fish and placed it, along with some water, in a heavy pan. The three of them settled back and waited for their meal to be ready, Dylan and Richard casually discussing fishing and hunting.

When the fish was almost cooked, Maggie rummaged through their saddlebags, hoping to find something she could use to make a sauce. She used some apple cider, combining it with herbs they had found while foraging, along with some of the now-stale bread, a handful of dried fruit and a touch of the whiskey. "This may not be verra good, but it's all I've got to work with." Removing the fish from the pan, she added her sauce ingredients and stirred continuously until the bread had broken down and it had thickened nicely. "Shall we give it a try?" Maggie asked, returning the fish to the pan.

They sat on the floor near the fire and ate communally from the pan Maggie had used for cooking. "This is delicious, Maggie," Richard complimented. "Very, very good."

Dylan nodded in agreement, shoveling another spoonful into his mouth.

"Are ye sure it's not just that yer terribly hungry?" Maggie questioned with a grin, but from the smiling faces staring back at her, she could tell they were truly enjoying it. Maggie reached for the rest of the stale bread and tore off a chunk, passing the remainder to Dylan and then Richard. It was perfect for sopping up the juices from the pan and left them all completely sated.

* * *

The sky had darkened outside of the little cottage, but the hearth cast a cheery, warm glow about the one room cottage. Richard proved to be quite the gifted storyteller, keeping them entertained with tales of romance and adventure long into the night.

Richard was surprised to find himself happier than he could ever remember being before. Once he had cast off the anger and jealousy that had held him captive for much of his life, he found that he could genuinely enjoy the company of others. Dylan and Maggie had accepted and welcomed him into their temporary home. He felt comfortable and at ease with them, in a way he hadn't experienced even with those who had sworn to be his loyal friends. "This has been most enjoyable," Richard proclaimed.

"It has," Dylan replied.

"You have both been so welcoming and generous with what you have shared. If there is ever anything I can do for you, simply ask. I will be happy to be of service." Richard poked at the fire and added more wood. The air outside had grown colder and the little cottage, while small and cozy, was not without drafts.

"I'm so happy ye decided to stay the night with us," Maggie said. "I wish we were travelling together. Ye are verra good company."

"As are you," Richard agreed. "Unfortunately, we are headed in opposite directions. You head south, I believe you said."

"Aye. We have something we must accomplish and then we'll be heading back to the north."

Maggie's statement piqued Richard's curiosity. "What must you do? Perhaps I can be of assistance and then we could travel north together?"

* * *

After Richard's announcement, Maggie turned to gaze at Dylan with an unspoken question in her eyes. "I think it's okay to tell him," he said.

"Tell me what?" Richard asked.

"Well, ye see - Dylan and I - we know who ye are. We've heard stories about ye." Maggie hesitated a moment, seeing the shocked expression on Richard's face. "We've just travelled from the MacKenzie's castle in search of a witch named Brielle. I must stop her before she destroys the MacKenzie clan."

"I see," Richard said. His face, which had been so happy moments before, had turned ashen on hearing this news. "Why didn't you tell me immediately... that you knew who I was?"

"Well, based on what we'd been told, I wasnae sure at first whether we could trust ye. After getting to know ye a little better, I have to admit to feeling completely different. I understand that ye've done some things yer ashamed of. Haven't we all? The point is, ye have changed for the better. Dylan and I both believe that now and Aunt Edna will be so pleased to hear it."

"You're Edna's niece?" asked an astonished Richard.

"Yes, I am." Maggie scooted closer to Dylan, who put an arm around her shoulders and hugged her close. You should also know that neither one of us is from this time. We're both from the future."

"That explains the accent," Richard said to Dylan.

"Richard, we didn't want to deceive you," Dylan said. "You can surely understand our hesitation in telling you the truth at first."

"I can. I completely understand and I'm not upset with you. I would have done the exact same thing in your position. I've no doubt you've heard some very horrible things about me." Maggie tried to interrupt, but he held up his hand to stop her. "They were, for the most part true and I did it all without a care of the consequences for those affected by my actions. I was a despicable human being. I did whatever I had to do, to get what I felt was rightfully mine. Now that I look back on it, I can see clearly that Irene was never mine. She always held Robert's heart close to her own. Through it all, I have to admit to feeling extremely lucky that no one was killed by my blind vengeance." He lowered his head in shame. "The one person I need to apologize to, more than any other is Ashley. There is no excuse for what I did to her and I'm sure she will never forgive me. I had some very bad men in my employ. They treated her horribly and I allowed it, and then I added to that bad treatment, by being equally cruel. She was an innocent victim of my need to make Irene mine. When I think about what I did, it truly sickens me."

"We'll help you in any way that we can, Richard. It won't be easy, but I'm sure they will at least listen to what you have to say." Maggie strongly believed that Richard was telling the truth, relying on her gut instincts.

"Thank you, Maggie. Your kindness is most generous and that gives me hope that with time, others may see me differently. Perhaps I'm not as hopeless as I thought." He smiled sadly at them. "You must let me help you with Brielle. After all, I am to blame for her presence among the MacKenzie clan."

"I don't think you can take one hundred percent of the blame, Richard," Maggie suggested.

"You may change your mind about that when you hear my tale," Richard said. "You do know that I've been to your future time, don't you?" he asked.

Maggie nodded, "I do, but I don't think Dylan was aware of that."

"No. I didn't know that," Dylan added, appearing surprised to hear it.

"Well, I crossed the bridge through time and found myself in Glendaloch, where you're from, Maggie. It was quite a shock to me, but I made the best of it, even after your aunt had me arrested." Richard laughed remembering the experience. "I was eventually released for lack of evidence and when I was finally able to get back across the bridge to my own time, I was quite angry with your Aunt Edna and the entire MacKenzie Clan. I couldn't wait to get my revenge on them for what I perceived as their unjustified mistreatment of me." Richard paused momentarily, gathering his thoughts. "Of course, now, I can see that everything they did was completely justified and I was deserving of everything that came my way." Richard stood and stretched his legs. "But at that point, my only thoughts were of revenge. Upon my return, I met some time travelers in the woods - a man and woman. After a brief conversation, I understood that while *they* were not sure of their final destination, I knew they were looking for Breaghacraig, and I travelled with them for a while as the man explained to me what he was after. We decided that he needed a potion, something that would put the men of the castle to sleep so he could rescue his wife from Cormac MacBayne,"

"That was Jonathan and Sophia," Dylan said somewhat astounded by this news. "They were looking for my cousin, Jenna, who wasn't his wife anymore, by the way. He lied to you."

"I see that my behavior has affected you and your family as well, Dylan. I apologize," Richard said, sounding deeply regretful.

"Go on with yer story," Maggie prodded.

"I agreed to help this Jonathan by introducing him to a witch I knew who lived nearby. That would be Brielle. She provided him with the sleeping draught they needed and they went off on their way. I was planning to head back home to gather my men and to plot my next assault on the MacKenzies, when I thought I might be able to use this witch to finally get my revenge on them. I told her about my journey to the future and that a man, or woman could travel there and come back with information that might make them very rich, or that they might travel back in time to change their future. She knew of the bridge, but had never thought that it could be used to her benefit. It was at that moment she decided she had to have control of the bridge. Brielle and I spoke about it at length. We discussed your Aunt Edna and then the MacKenzies. I knew that Edna would never want any harm to come to the MacKenzies and I expressed this to Brielle. She was convinced that she had a plan in mind that would work to get her the bridge and me the revenge I sought."

"With or without you, Brielle wants control of that bridge," Maggie stated.

"I understand that, but I can't help but wonder if I didn't put the thought in her head, would she have done this?"

"I don't know the answer to that question, but I do know that she hates my Aunt Edna, because she refused to let Brielle cross the bridge many years ago, and it was probably just a matter of time before she would have figured out that the best way to hurt her was by hurting the MacKenzies, taking the bridge, or both," Maggie offered.

"I'm afraid I didn't really care what her motivation might be at the time. I just saw her as a way to do more damage to the MacKenzies and to get back at Edna." He turned his gaze towards the fire, seeming embarrassed by his own callousness.

Maggie spent a few minutes explaining everything Brielle had done at Breaghacraig, how she had disguised herself as Maggie, tried to kill Angus and that she and Dylan had left Breaghacraig in an attempt to keep her from doing further damage there. Their hope was that she would want her talisman back so badly that she'd come to them. Richard sat silently, listening carefully to what she said and when she finished she could tell from his expression he was thinking seriously. His brow was wrinkled and he sat tapping his lips steadily with one finger.

"Do you think she'll come here?" he asked.

"I believe she's here already. I can feel her presence nearby. I don't think it will be long now before she shows herself and then I'm not sure what's going to happen," Maggie shivered at the thought. She still hadn't come to grips with the fact that she might have to kill Brielle to end the threat she posed.

For a few minutes, the crackling and popping of the fire was the only sound in the room. "I'd like to stay with you. I believe I can help, if you'll allow it." Richard finally said.

Dylan gave Maggie another gentle squeeze. "I'm all for it," he said. "The more of us there are, the better our chances."

"Alright," Maggie said. "I'll tell ye what I've told Dylan. 'Tis my fight. I must do this. I must be the one to defeat her. Ye can be there to support me, but please dinnae interfere."

"Agreed," Richard said, extending a hand to Maggie, who took it without hesitation. Dylan placed his hand on top of theirs to confirm their pact. "We should get some sleep. If you don't mind, I'll make my bed here by the fire." Richard got up and grabbed a blanket from his saddlebags, placing it on the floor.

Dylan pulled Maggie up from her spot on the floor and they made their way across the small room to the bed. They climbed in fully dressed, Maggie curling up with her head on Dylan's chest. Her mind returned to thoughts of the previous night spent in this same bed and despite the fact that she was happy to have Richard here with them, a little privacy would certainly have been nice. Dylan seemed to be reading her mind when he gently kissed the top of her head and wrapped her a little more tightly in his arms.

Chapter 18

The morning sun had begun its climb into the sky, but the usual sounds of the world awakening were missing. Maggie knew something was wrong immediately, when she awoke to total silence. Where were the birds, who were never deterred from their cheerful chirping each morning? There was no breeze rustling the leaves in the trees. Even the sound of the river was gone. It was as if the world stood still, watching and waiting. Maggie climbed from the bed, careful not to disturb Dylan, who slept soundly at her side. She crept past Richard, who was also still sleeping soundly on the floor. Opening the door, she stepped outside into a world that had morphed overnight in an otherworldly way. Everything around her appeared to have been frozen in place. Birds hung in the sky, paralyzed in midflight; Maggie's horse, seeming for all the world as if she'd been enjoying a good buck, had stopped mid-motion, with her hind legs in the air. The other horses stood still as could be in the grassy field, heads down and motionless, as if they had been captured by an artist in the middle of grazing. The eerie silence was abruptly broken by cackling laugher coming from one of the trees by the river's edge. There, sitting amid the branches of a giant pine tree she spied Brielle, looking quite comfortable in her lofty perch.

"Good morn to ye, lassie," Brielle greeted her brightly, with a sarcastic sneer curving her lips.

Maggie didn't answer, her mind whirling with thoughts about what Brielle had planned and how best to approach the situation. She suffered a moment of sheer panic, but forced herself to take a deep breath and grounded herself.

"Would ye care to join me?" Brielle asked. Before Maggie could consider what Brielle was suggesting, she found herself being pulled up into the air, as if she was being hoisted on invisible strings, high above the cottage until she was at eye level with Brielle. "That's better," Brielle announced. She was surrounded by dozens of birds, and not one of them was moving a single feather or even blinking.

Breathe! Breathe! Maggie continued to fight against the panic, which threatened to overtake her. She had always been afraid of heights and usually avoided them at all costs, but now she found herself hovering, fifty feet in the air, and she was completely terrified.

"Are ye afraid of heights, Maggie? If ye are, I could always send ye back down to the ground." Brielle laughed evilly and Maggie suddenly found herself freefalling towards the hard ground below. She squeezed her eyes shut in terror just as she was about to hit the ground, but instead, she was yanked back up to Brielle's level again. "Wasn't that fun? Would ye like to do it again?" Brielle tipped her head, waiting for an answer.

Maggie couldn't speak. She was nauseous and shaking violently, from the rush of adrenaline coursing through her bloodstream.

"Cat got yer tongue? Answer me, Maggie! 'Tis no fun at all if ye dinnae plead with me to let ye go."

Maggie did her best to relax. If she were going to succeed here, she needed a clear head. "I'll nae plead with ye. Drop me if ye wish, but then yer little game of cat and mouse will be over."

As Maggie watched Brielle contemplating her next move, she managed to calm herself enough to float gently back to earth and once her feet touched the ground, she made a run for the cottage. Bolts of lightning rained down on her from above, nearly striking her on more than one occasion. In a panic, she hit the ground and rolled behind a large boulder. Peeking over the top of the boulder, she could see Brielle had disappeared. She wasn't sitting in the tree anymore. Where had she gone? Maggie searched the vicinity, but she couldn't see anything out of the ordinary. The spell had been broken and to her relief, the birds were chirping and the horses were moving again. Everything was back to normal, or so it seemed.

Dylan and Richard both appeared in the doorway, concerned expressions upon their faces.

Maggie ran over to them, her hands still shaking from the ordeal. "Are you okay, Maggie?" Dylan gripped her arms, searching her face for an answer. "I had a really bad dream. I was paralyzed, and it didn't matter how much I tried, I couldn't move a muscle. You were falling from a tree and I couldn't do anything to save you."

"I had exactly the same dream," Richard said sharply, frowning heavily. "Perhaps it was not a dream at all."

"Yer right. 'Twas nae a dream. Brielle was here, sitting up in that tree over there," Maggie explained, pointing to the tall pine tree where Brielle had been perched. "Somehow, she was able to freeze time; everything was stopped in mid-motion, including the two of ye, I think. The only things that could move were Brielle and me." Maggie shook her head, still trying to come to terms with the events of the past few minutes.

"Where is she now?" Richard asked.

"I don't know, but I would imagine she hasnae gone far." Maggie shivered at the prospect. She'd been completely overwhelmed by Brielle's first attack - how on earth would she be able to stop her?

Dylan held Maggie close, rubbing her back to soothe her. "We've got to find her, Maggie. She could've killed you." His arms tightened around her protectively.

"But she didnae. She's playing with me and I'm nae sure why, but I need to be prepared for anything and everything. She caught me off guard this time, and I let my fear cloud my brain. Once I calmed my mind, I was able to float down to the ground unharmed. Keeping a clear head and not letting fear in, I believe that's what will help me defeat her."

"You'll need to draw her out. Make her come to you," Richard suggested. "If you can keep her occupied, I might be able to get a shot off at her with my bow."

Maggie shook her head firmly. "Nae. I told ye, I must do this myself. Nae matter what ye see, ye mustn't interfere."

The two men seemed ready to argue the point with her, but when they saw the determination on her face, they apparently thought better of it.

"Ye may stand with me in support, but that is all." Maggie wanted to make it clear to them, and tried to sound as confident as she could. "I can do this. Believe in me."

"I have faith in you, Maggie, but you have to understand how hard it is, to feel so utterly helpless in this situation." Dylan grumbled, obviously not enjoying the position Maggie had placed him in.

"Richard?" Maggie wanted his assurance as well.

"I believe in you, Maggie," he said.

"Okay. I have an idea. I'll need the amulet and a minute or two to gather my thoughts," Maggie entered the cottage, leaving Dylan and Richard standing outside, staring at her departing back in dismay.

* * *

"I don't like this," Dylan said to Richard. The two men had stepped away from the door of the cottage to avoid Maggie overhearing them, and they strolled towards where the horses were happily grazing. "I know Maggie is a powerful witch, but I think she's at a serious disadvantage here with Brielle."

"I agree. I think we need to have a plan in place, if things start looking bleak." Richard whistled to his horse, Arion. The great beast cantered right up to him and lowered his head for a rub. Richard obliged him and when he stopped, Arion almost knocked him off his feet as he butted him with his head, seeking more attention. "Arion, I cannot stand here all day patting you, will an apple be a reasonable recompense?" Richard pulled an apple out from his pocket and offered it to Arion, who happily gobbled it up. The other two horses stood nearby, waiting for treats of their own.

"I don't have anything for you," Dylan apologized. The horses both snorted impatiently at him and he chuckled. "Don't look at me like that."

Both horses ignored him, instead focusing on Richard, who had drawn another apple from a pocket. He halved it with his knife and gave one piece to each horse. They happily munched on them as Richard and Dylan worked on a backup plan, just in case Maggie found herself in trouble. As they headed back to the cottage, the wind began to pick up and the faint sound of Brielle's cackling laughter floated in on the breeze. The two men stopped dead in their tracks and spun around, trying to place the direction the laughter was coming from. Strangely, it seemed to be echoing at them from every angle. Striding purposefully back to the cottage, they found Maggie waiting for them in the doorway. She held up the amulet.

"I'm hoping this will do the trick," Maggie said, passing them on her way out the door.

"Wait, what are you going to do?" Dylan was desperately worried, but he hoped it wasn't being revealed in his voice.

"Lure her with the amulet," Maggie answered calmly.

Richard raised a questioning eyebrow and put a reassuring hand on Dylan's shoulder as they both turned and followed Maggie out into the open field.

* * *

"Oh, my," Edna whispered. She was back at her post, pacing next to the fire and she had a bird's eye view of everything that was happening. Edna had finally found a spell that would allow her to get around the barrier Brielle had put in place to prevent her communicating with Maggie. She could clearly see and hear Maggie, Dylan and Richard standing together outside of a small stone cottage. They were going to face down Brielle together. *The nightmares must have worked,* she thought with a satisfied smile. *Richard is there to help them, not to hurt them.* As for Brielle, Edna would keep watch and remain an unseen onlooker.

* * *

"Brielle!" Maggie called. She searched the treetops, expecting to see the witch perched up among the branches and birds, but she wasn't anywhere to be seen. "Brielle! I have something I think you might want." Maggie held the amulet up in the air, hoping that wherever Brielle was, she would be able to see it clearly.

"She's not here," Dylan said, standing right behind her.

"She is here. I can sense her." Maggie continued standing on the spot, the amulet suspended from her outstretched fingers. "We'll wait."

Richard took a stance to her left and Dylan to her right. Minutes passed and there was still no sign of Brielle.

A sudden movement from the trees had them turning in that direction, to discover three large, cat-like creatures running straight at them. They were enormous in size, all black in color with the exception of a single white spot on each animal's breast. Dylan and Richard pulled out their swords in preparation for being attacked.

"They're Cait Sith," Maggie shouted. She'd only heard of these creatures in folklore and hadn't believed that they truly existed until this moment, but perhaps they weren't real at all, merely something conjured up by Brielle to frighten them. If that was the case, it was working. The creatures were hurtling towards them with the clear intention of killing them, judging by their blazing eyes and the smoke emanating from their nostrils. Dylan used his sword to stab the first one, aiming directly into the white spot on its chest as it lunged at him. The Cait Sith dropped to the ground and vanished immediately. Richard wasn't quite as lucky. His sword hit, but only nicked the Cait Sith's shoulder, having no effect whatsoever on the great cat, other than to prevent it from reaching him. Maggie stood frozen in place as she watched the third Cait Sith draw closer and closer. She held on tightly to the amulet, not wanting to drop it. Dylan saw her dilemma and rushed to her aid, slashing desperately at the giant cat. He got between the Cait Sith and Maggie, effectively blocking it from reaching her as he continued to stab at its body. He finally managed a killing blow, once again to the single white spot on its chest and the cat flopped lifelessly to the ground and disappeared.

"Richard, aim for the white spot!" Dylan shouted. Richard was still fending off the assault, but hadn't been able to kill the beast. With Dylan's advice, he stopped for a moment and waited for the giant creature to come at him again. As it did, he saw his chance and ran his blade straight through, and watched as what had once been a massive cat, disappeared into thin air.

The Cait Sith were no sooner gone than the giant boulders, which lay strewn about the field began to rise, turning into stone behemoths before molding themselves into giant men. Maggie, Dylan and Richard started to back up as the ground beneath their feet began to shake with every step the giant stone men took. With each step, they tore enormous rocks from the ground and hurled them towards Maggie and the men, narrowly missing them as they sought shelter from the onslaught.

Maggie quickly recited a spell to try and stop them. She didn't know if it would work, but it was all she had to work with, in an effort to stop the magical creatures. These giants would be impenetrable to the weapons that Richard and Dylan carried. "Giant men made from stone, back to boulders you must go, fight no more with us this day, back you go to always stay." The giants had been closing in on them, but Maggie finished the incantation and they toppled to the ground, returning to harmless boulders before their very eyes.

The three of them remained on guard, waiting for the next assault to come and when it didn't, Maggie stepped forward. "Brielle! I guess you aren't interested in this amulet. Perhaps I should just smash it, then." Maggie made a show of pretending to drop the amulet onto the ground, but she merely concealed it within her closed fist. She lifted her foot as if to crush it, but a whirling sound began, growing louder and louder until Brielle appeared, standing nose to nose with Maggie.

Dylan and Richard lunged forward to protect her, but Maggie held up her hand to stop them.

"I'll take my amulet back." Brielle bent to retrieve it from the ground, but stopped in place, when she realized the amulet wasn't there. Slowly, she straightened back up and anger and rage showed on her face and in her posture at being fooled.

"I guess it is of value to you, after all," Maggie said sweetly. "If you want it back, you'll need to agree to my terms."

"Terms!" Brielle scoffed. "I'll nae agree to anything! You will give me my amulet, or I will turn your friends here to ash!"

"I wouldnae do that if I were you," Maggie warned.

"Do these men nae have voices of their own? Why do they nae speak? Perhaps they are not real men at all." It was obvious Brielle was trying to rile them and get a reaction. She eyed Richard curiously, with an impish twinkle in her eye. "Richard, I cannae believe you would betray me! Did ye nae tell me ye wanted yer revenge on the MacKenzies? Have ye changed yer mind?"

"Many things have changed since last we met, Brielle. I no longer seek revenge on the MacKenzie clan," Richard calmly replied. "In fact, I now stand with Maggie in her efforts to put an end to you and to protect the MacKenzie's."

"Then ye have made an enemy of me and for that ye will have to pay." Brielle vanished and almost instantly reappeared a short distance away. "I will teach ye a lesson ye'll never forget, *Sir* Richard!"

None of them noticed the fog rolling in from the edge of the woods. Maggie had focused all of her attention on Brielle, aware that she intended to harm Richard in some way. She would prevent it if she possibly could, but to her surprise, Richard inexplicably stepped *towards* Brielle.

"Richard. Stay where ye are!" Maggie shouted, but he didn't seem to hear her. Richard began to struggle, and it was apparent to Maggie that he was being drawn towards Brielle against his will. Maggie had to do something, before it was too late. Brielle could apparently read her thoughts, because in the instant that Maggie began an incantation to try and release Richard, Brielle let loose with a volley of flames, which roared directly towards Richard. Maggie quickly gathered her wits about her and without conscious thought, sent a wall of water rushing towards the flames. The water engulfed Richard and extinguished the flames at the same time, creating a mass of steam. Brielle was preoccupied with the backwash of water, giving Maggie enough time to search the area for Richard. He had disappeared.

"Where did he go?" Dylan demanded. He, too, was searching the immediate vicinity for Richard.

"How do I know? I'm new at this." Maggie was afraid she had inadvertently done something terrible. Had she harmed Richard? Was he dead? Maggie began to panic and as she surveyed the horizon, seeking some clue as to where Richard had gone, she noticed the wall of fog, creeping into the woods and dissipating. "Auntie, can ye hear me?" Maggie called to Edna with her mind.

"Aye, lass. It's all right, Maggie. Don't worry about Richard, I've taken care of him. He's safe."

Relief swept over Maggie, followed by a wave of anger directed at Brielle. The evil harridan had really meant to kill Richard! She needed to act fast, before Brielle could turn her attention to Dylan and hurt him. "Destroy the amulet," Edna's voice floated in the air to her ears.

"No!" Brielle shrieked, trying to get away from the water that now swirled around her legs. "No!"

Maggie looked over at Dylan who smiled warmly and said, "I love you, Maggie MacKinnon. You can do this. I know you can."

Maggie dropped the amulet to the ground and stomped on it. "It didnae break!" She tried again, anxiety beginning to build in her chest. "Am I doing something wrong?"

"Let me try," Dylan said.

"Nae. Dinnae ye remember, it burned ye when ye touched it." Maggie scanned the area around her. What would work? She ran towards the nearest large boulder and frantically searched the ground for a rock she could use to crush the amulet.

Dylan followed at her heels. "Maggie, what about your dirk? It's charmed. Maybe that will work."

"Yes, of course! That has to work." Maggie took out the dirk and set the amulet upon the stone. As soon as she raised the dirk above the amulet - the piece took on the shape and consistency of a human heart and began pulsing erratically. Maggie looked at Dylan and then over towards Brielle, who had managed to pull herself free from the cascades of water and was rushing straight towards them. The urgency of the situation pressed on Maggie and she used her magic to create a massive gust of wind to block Brielle's progress for a few seconds more.

"I'll hold her off," Dylan announced with determination. He took a fighting stance in front of Maggie.

"I'll kill him, if ye dinnae give me back my amulet!" Brielle raged, as she fought against Maggie's magick. "Give it to me!"

Maggie ignored her and swiftly lowered the tip of her dirk to the amulet, which now beat at a frantic pace. As Brielle drew closer, Maggie stabbed the beating amulet with the dirk, penetrating it easily. Black liquid oozed from it and dribbled down the sides of the boulder. She looked up from the heart to see Brielle silently screaming and clawing at the air around her as her body was reduced to the same black liquid and bled into the earth, disappearing from sight with only a slight puff of smoke marking the spot where she'd stood. The amulet had disappeared now too, not a trace remaining behind. Dylan and Maggie stood staring at one another in stunned disbelief at what had just happened.

"She's gone!" Maggie said. "We did it! She's gone!"

* * *

Dylan caught Maggie in his arms as she suddenly slumped to the ground. She had gone deathly pale and weak. The stress of her showdown with Brielle must have sapped Maggie of every last ounce of her strength, so he lifted her into his arms and carried her back to the cottage. She would need to rest, in order to regain her strength. Thank goodness she would now be able to do so, because the threat posed by Brielle was finally gone. He lay her carefully on the bed and covered her with a fur, noting that it was strangely peaceful inside the cottage after the battle they'd fought outside. The fire was dying out, so Dylan went to work building it back up again so that Maggie would be warm. Sitting quietly, staring into the flames, Dylan couldn't believe the things he'd witnessed since coming to Scotland with Jenna, but today had been the most unbelievable of all. His mighty little Maggie had singlehandedly defeated a very evil witch. The thought of it put a smile on his face and glancing back to the bed, a surge of warmth and pride ran through him. Rising to his feet, Dylan made his way to the bed and lay down next to Maggie, who immediately burrowed closer to him in her sleep. He held her like that until he too, fell asleep dreaming of the future they would share together.

Chapter 19

The first thing Maggie thought of upon waking was that Dylan had told her he loved her. Beaming with joy, she shook him awake. "Dylan, you told me you loved me. Do you really?" she asked.

Dylan rubbed the sleep from his eyes and opened them to look fully into hers. "Maggie. You're awake. Are you okay?"

"Yes. I feel amazing. Answer my question, please." Maggie waited expectantly for his reply. For his part, Dylan seemed confused. Maybe he hadn't heard her question. "You said you loved me. Did you mean it?"

A broad smile lit up Dylan's face. "Yes, I do mean it. I love you! I'll say it as many times as you want to hear it. I love you!"

"I love you, too! We're in love! It happened! I didn't think it was possible." Maggie was chattering on and on excitedly.

When she stopped babbling, she noticed Dylan had a strange expression on his face. "Why wouldn't it be possible, Maggie?"

"I thought you had to fall in love with someone in the sixteenth century. I didn't think it was possible for me to find love in our own time."

Dylan laughed. "We *are* in the sixteenth century, Maggie," he teased. "But I think I loved you from the minute I first saw you. I knew there was something special between us and I knew I was going to come back for you, but you beat me to it, by coming here."

Maggie dove on top of him, showering him with kisses. "I'm so happy! I can't wait to tell Uncle Angus and Auntie Edna."

"There'll be time enough for that, but right now, there's something a bit more pressing we need to take care of." Dylan waggled his eyebrows suggestively and propped himself up on his elbows, leaning in to kiss Maggie. One of his hands came up and cupped her head and the next thing she knew, Maggie found herself molded to Dylan's body. Not that she minded, it was right where she wanted to be.

Dylan covered her with kisses as he removed her clothing, sending goosebumps erupting across her skin. Turning the tables on him, Maggie explored every part of Dylan's body as she undressed him. All the handsome men she'd seen in the movies and in magazines had nothing on Dylan Sinclair. He was perfectly perfect in her eyes, and as she stroked her hands softly across his chest and belly, she took note of what he seemed to like, what caused him to moan, or to catch his breath, or to tighten his muscles in anticipation. She was swiftly learning. Her lack of experience was surely made up for by her sheer eagerness to please him. Dylan lay back on the bed and let her explore, seeming to get as much pleasure from her discoveries as she did, which made Maggie bolder with her touches and more forceful with her kisses. Did she dare take him into her mouth? How could she not? She wanted to, more than anything, but was unsure of her abilities. She tentatively kissed the hard length that presented itself to her and smiled when it jumped with her touch. That gave her the courage to put her mouth more fully on him and the moan of ecstasy that escaped Dylan's lips brought a smile to her lips and the knowledge that she was doing exactly as she should. She continued until Dylan pulled her up so he could kiss her lips. Breaking the kiss, she asked, "Was that okay?"

"It was more than okay. Now it's your turn." Dylan flipped her onto her back and began to lick and kiss his way down her body. Maggie tangled her fingers in his hair and raised her hips, letting him know she was eager for his attentions. She found herself writhing with pleasure as Dylan touched her core with his tongue and lips. Her brain focused on one thing only - the amazing things Dylan was doing to her. "Dylan, please, dinnae stop," she moaned. Fortunately, he didn't seem to have any intentions of stopping and she was glad of that fact. As the sensations she was experiencing began to peak, she moved in rhythm with his tongue, climbing and climbing towards her climax, until she reached the very top and her body was flooded with wave after wave of incredible spasms. Dylan immediately slid up her body, thrusting his rock hard shaft into her warm, womanly folds. She cried out at the feel of him inside of her, still sensitive from her own release. Dylan pumped into her, slowly at first and then his rhythm grew hard and fast. Maggie held onto him for dear life as she found a rhythm to match his. Dylan held tightly to her right breast with one hand, while the other kept her hands over her head. He nuzzled her neck, kissed her ear, and breathed her name in a quiet rhythm of pleasure. The rapturous feelings spread again and Maggie fell over the precipice for a second time as Dylan cried out her name and drove himself deeper inside of her, holding the position, a sheen of sweat covering his body. He rested atop her.

"Are you okay?" he asked. "Are those tears I see?"

"Good tears," Maggie reassured him. "Happy tears."

"Are you sure? I didn't hurt you, did I?"

"Verra sure. I've never felt such wonderful— I don't know what to call it, but it was verra, verra good." Maggie further reassured him by kissing him gently on the lips. Dylan moved off to lay by her side and she immediately tucked herself under his arm, resting her head on his chest. She could hear his heart beating and decided she'd never heard a more glorious sound.

* * *

They waited an extra day at the cottage, in hopes that Richard would return. It wasn't until Maggie was able to communicate with Edna again that she found he was not coming back. Edna had transported him safely to some point in the future and, as was usually the case when Edna was up to something, she kept the exact details to herself. No amount of questioning or prodding from Maggie was going to get the information out of Edna, so Maggie gave up trying. It was time for them to head back to Breaghacraig with the good news about Brielle. Maggie didn't want to delay any longer, knowing that Robert would be anxious to send word that it was safe for everyone to return. They'd take Arion back with them. The poor guy missed Richard terribly, pawing at the ground and whinnying for him throughout the day. In truth, Maggie appreciated the brief time she'd been able to share alone with Dylan, before returning to Breaghacraig.

"Dylan," Maggie said on their final morning at the cottage, "this has been the scariest and the most wonderful few days of my life." She kissed his nose and ran her fingers lovingly through his hair.

Dylan looked deeply into her eyes. "I can't think of anyplace I'd rather be than here with you right in this moment. This is a new experience for me. One I didn't know I wanted, until now." He glanced around the cottage one last time. "We'll have to come back here sometime. Maybe when the people who live here are back," he suggested. "I've grown quite fond of this little place."

"I'd like that," Maggie said. She mounted her horse and sat staring back at their temporary home. "Goodbye, little cottage. I won't forget you."

They turned their horses and headed for Breaghacraig. Dylan ponied Arion alongside his own horse and Maggie followed him as they entered the tree-lined path heading north. Their journey would be over in a few short hours and while Maggie was sad to leave the little cottage behind, she was anxious to begin the next chapter of her life, with Dylan.

Later that day, they were approaching the castle, when riders came rushing out to greet them.

"Maggie, Dylan, yer back! Did ye encounter Brielle?" Cormac was accompanied by Cailin and greeted them urgently, worry in their eyes.

"We did," Maggie said. "The good news is that she willnae be bothering anyone ever again."

"She's gone for good then?" Cailin asked.

"Maggie destroyed her. Brielle won't bother the MacKenzie's again," Dylan reassured the two brothers.

Cormac turned to Cailin. "Go on ahead and advise Robert that we can send riders out, we can bring the women and children back home safely now."

Cailin inclined his head in agreement and turned his horse, racing back towards the castle gates.

"How's Uncle Angus," Maggie asked anxiously.

"He's fine. We've practically had to tie him down since shortly after ye left. We had all we could do to keep him from following ye. We left him to Mary's care. She has chased him back to bed, every time he tries to get up. He'll be verra happy and relieved to have ye back." Cormac said.

"I cannae wait to see him," Maggie said wistfully.

"Neither of ye look worse for wear after your encounter with Brielle," Cormac commented, eyeing them up and down as they turned and travelled towards the castle. "And ye seem to have found yerself another horse."

"The horse belongs to Sir Richard," Dylan explained. "We met up with him when we stopped at a cottage for the night."

"You had to deal with the witch *and* Sir Richard?" Cormac questioned sharply. "Given that ye have his horse, can we assume he's dead?" Cormac glanced at Dylan and Maggie with a hopeful expression.

"Nae. Not dead, but we have no idea where he is."

"Well, good riddance to him," Cormac announced.

Maggie reached out and grabbed Cormac's sleeve, shaking her head violently. "No, you dinnae understand, Richard was helping us! He had experienced a change of heart regarding his past actions. We spent a few days with him and I truly believe he wanted to make amends with the MacKenzie clan. He seemed genuinely sorry for all the trouble he'd caused over the years. He was coming to Breaghacraig to apologize and beg for the clan's forgiveness."

"I find that verra hard to believe. Perhaps he was merely trying to fool ye," Cormac said skeptically.

"He was in truth, verra sincere. As I said, a changed man," Maggie looked to Dylan for confirmation.

"I agree with Maggie. I'd never met him before, so I'm not familiar with the man he was, but the Richard I met and spent time with had obviously experienced some sort of transformation. He told us about it and I'm certain he was telling the truth. He stood by our side during the fight with Brielle and it angered her. She really meant to kill him, she was forcing him to come towards her, and she was going to burn him to death with the magical flames she'd created, but Maggie was able to put out the fire." Dylan shook his head. "It all happened in a split-second, but when it was over, Richard had disappeared."

Cormac lifted his eyebrows. "It seems too strange to be true, but if ye and Maggie believe he had turned over a new leaf, I'll have to believe ye." He smiled softly. "T'would be verra good indeed, if it is true, for it'll mean one more thing we dinnae have to worry about in the future."

They travelled the last few feet and headed through the gates of Breaghacraig. "It's good to be back," Dylan said. "I wasn't sure we'd ever see this place again."

"What do ye mean, ye werenae sure," Maggie said indignantly, scowling at him.

"Maggie, you know what I mean. Even though I had every faith in your abilities, there were a few moments when I wasn't sure what was going to happen, especially after Richard disappeared." Dylan gave her his best puppy-dog-eyes.

"Well, when ye look at me like that, how can I stay mad at ye?" Maggie smiled, forgiving him instantly. They dismounted and handed their horses off to a couple of the stable lads. "I'd like to see Angus before I do another thing."

"He'll be happy to see ye," Cormac said. "He's upstairs in yer room, Dylan."

"Will ye join us, Cormac?" Maggie asked.

"I'll let ye visit with Angus on yer own. There's much to do in preparation for the women and children coming back." Cormac bid them goodbye and headed towards the great hall.

"Shall we?" Dylan asked, leading the way up the stairs.

Maggie followed behind, in a hurry to see Angus again. She had been so worried about him and now she had such good news to share. Their mission had been a success and they could go back home to Edna.

Dylan knocked on the door and Angus called out. "Come in." He sounded rather grumpy, but the expression on his face when he saw Maggie was that of a very happy man. "Maggie! Dylan! Yer back. All went well, I hope."

"It did Uncle Angus. Better than I could have hoped. How are you feeling?" Maggie sat by the bed and took hold of his hand.

"I'm fit as a fiddle," Angus replied. "Tell me all about it and dinnae leave out any details."

Maggie looked back at Dylan, who suddenly grew a shade paler.

"What's going on between the two of ye?" Suspicion tinged Angus' voice.

"Well, first I'll tell ye that Dylan and I are in love," Maggie blurted out. Angus' eyes darted from Maggie to Dylan, who had now gone from pale to very red in the face.

"What are yer intentions, lad?" Angus who had appeared so happy just moments before, now sounded distinctly grumpy.

"Well, Angus," Dylan stammered. "I haven't had a chance to ask Maggie yet because I wanted to get your blessing first. I'd like to marry your niece."

Maggie just about fainted dead away. "You want to marry me, Dylan?"

"I do. This wasn't the way I had intended on proposing, but I want to set your mind at ease, Angus. So, do I have your blessing?"

Maggie could hardly contain herself, practically jumping for joy. "Say yes, Uncle, please!"

Angus cleared his throat and a most serious expression settled on his face. Maggie thought for sure he was going to say no, and her heart sank, but then he burst out laughing. "Of course ye have me blessing, lad. I cannae think of anyone I'd rather have marry me niece. Ye were made fer each other."

"Thank you, sir," Dylan said, sounding relieved.

"Oh, thank you, Uncle!" Maggie looked expectantly at Dylan who got down on one knee in front of her.

"Maggie MacKinnon, I don't have a ring for you, and this may not be the romantic proposal you were hoping for, but will you marry me?" Dylan didn't have to wait long for her answer as Maggie threw herself at him, knocking him to the floor and landing on top of him.

"Yes! Yes! Yes! I will marry you!"

Angus had propped himself up on his pillows and was laughing and clapping as he watched. Dylan surrendered to Maggie's kisses and when she was finished, he stood up and helped Maggie to do the same. She couldn't seem to take her eyes off of him. Her dreams were all coming true. She felt like the luckiest girl in the world.

"Now that we have that out of the way, why dinnae ye tell me what happened with Brielle. I can hardly wait to find out."

"Well, Uncle 'tis a long story, but I'll be happy to recount it for you."

Maggie and Dylan filled Angus in on Brielle, Sir Richard, and the battles against the Cait Sith and the giant stone men. Between the two of them, they didn't leave out a single detail.

"So, ye say the amulet was like a tiny beating heart. Unbelievable!" Angus shook his head, seeming overwhelmed by what he was hearing.

"Aye, Uncle. It was," Maggie confirmed.

Angus appeared very content to hear that Maggie had done what she had set out to do. "I'm verra proud of ye, lass," he said, with tears of joy brimming in his eyes. "Now help me up out of this damn bed. I'd like to go downstairs and celebrate this momentous occasion with everyone. Check that passageway, to see if Mary is anywhere in sight. That woman willnae leave me be. I swear she appears out of nowhere, every time I try to get out of this damned bed."

Maggie and Dylan had a good laugh over that, but they humored him and checked for Mary, before they all headed downstairs, with Angus announcing very firmly that this time, he would fight tooth and nail to stay out of bed for the rest of the day.

* * *

Robert had sent riders off to Lena and Ewan's with word that Brielle would no longer be posing a threat to the MacKenzies and advising them, they should all return home as soon as possible. He also sug-gested that Lena and Ewan return with the others, so they could visit with Angus.

"As soon as I knew ye were back, I asked Mary to prepare the best feast she could manage, to celebrate yer safe return," Robert announced. "A toast to ye, Maggie and to ye, Dylan. Ye have returned victorious and spared us from ever having to deal with that witch again. I understand from yer uncle that the two of ye are to be married. We are all verra happy for ye. So, we drink to yer success and to yer future." They all raised their cups in a toast and drank heartily.

A few minutes later, Mary appeared in the great hall, followed by the stable lads, whom she had evidently put to work in the kitchen. They carried great platters of food, which they set at the head table and then hurried back to retrieve more. Mary kept a watchful eye on them as the food was being delivered to each table.

"Thank ye, Mary. Ye've done a verra good job on short notice." Robert bowed his head in her direction and Mary, who appeared quite flustered at the compliment, bobbed a quick curtsy and left the room, but not before giving Angus a stern look of disapproval. "Let's eat!" Robert dug into his food and the others followed suit.

The evening meal that night was filled with tales of Maggie and Dylan's adventures. Everyone was fascinated and full of questions regarding the battle.

"I've never seen a Cait Sith before," Robert said. "I didnae believe they really existed."

"I dinnae ken whether they exist or not, but Brielle somehow managed to conjure up three verra large ones," Maggie said, enjoying the way everyone was listening so intently to her retelling of the showdown with Brielle.

"And the giant stone men," Cailin said. "Ye must have been verra frightened."

"Maggie was amazingly brave," Dylan responded with a proud smile. "I don't think she was scared by anything Brielle sent our way."

"I didnae have time to be afraid," Maggie offered. "Everything was happening so fast. I had no time to think, only time to act."

"Well, we're all verra happy ye've returned safely to us. I dinnae believe Angus would have lasted another day, before he'd set off after ye." Robert winked at Angus, who leaned back in his chair and harrumphed loudly.

Maggie soothed him. "We would have welcomed his help, if things had gone on much longer." She patted Angus on the arm and smiled sweetly, mouthing the words, "I love you, Uncle." Angus returned her smile, grasping her hand and bringing it up to his lips.

"The feeling is mutual," he whispered back.

* * *

The room was filled with the happy voices of the men who had stayed behind to guard Breaghacraig. They ate, drank and toasted Maggie and Dylan, long into the night. The MacKenzie's even found it within their hearts to propose a toast to Sir Richard, after they all learned of his change of heart and how he had fought along with Maggie and Dylan to defeat Brielle.

When it was apparent that everyone was beginning to head off to bed, Angus spoke. "Dylan, ye'll be rooming with me tonight in the barracks. Maggie, ye can have Dylan's room upstairs."

Maggie tried to hide the disappointment she suffered at this pronouncement, but it seemed from Dylan's expression that he was equally unhappy about the situation. They kissed each other good night and before Maggie or Dylan was ready to be finished, Angus clapped Dylan on the back. "Come along, son. She'll still be here in the morn."

Maggie watched as a very dejected Dylan followed Angus out the door. Maggie didn't move until they were both out of sight, and then she slowly trudged up the stairs to bed.

As she climbed under the fur covers, she heard Edna's voice. It was so clear, Maggie could have believed Edna was in the room, althhough Maggie knew that was not the case.

"Maggie, 'tis me. I wanted to tell ye how verra proud I am of yer efforts. Ye were brave and strong and I can tell ye now - ye saved many a life by taking Brielle's."

"What do ye mean? I dinnae understand." Maggie was confused. She thought the only thing at stake had been the bridge.

"Maggie 'tis time ye knew the truth of it. Brielle made a bargain with me. One I didnae wish to honor, but she left me nae choice. She wanted the bridge, there's no doubt about it, but she also threatened to destroy the MacKenzies if I didnae send ye in me place. She thought that ye'd be much easier to defeat. What she didnae ken, but found out when it was too late, was that ye are a much more powerful witch than I am."

"Auntie, you've said that before, but I just don't believe that's possible. I've only just started to use my magick," Maggie protested.

"Ye may have just started, but that doesnae mean that the power hasnae been there all along, my dear. Believe me when I tell ye, that ye are the most powerful witch in the MacKinnon line," Edna stated proudly.

Maggie took a moment to digest that bit of information. "But I still dinnae see how I saved anyone's life."

"If ye hadnae stopped her, she would have been responsible for much death and destruction, as a result of what she intended to do with the bridge. She didnae care about what might happen in the future, she was only interested in gaining untold amounts of power from selling travel across the bridge to the highest bidders. There would be those who would have crossed with evil intention, to gain wealth and destroy their enemies. It could have changed the very course of history!

"Why didnae ye tell me, Auntie? I was so confused by yer secrecy." Maggie thought back to the anger she had suffered, being put in the position of dealing with Brielle so that Edna could have the bridge. She was relieved that it wasnae true, but she was having a hard time reconciling the fact that Edna hadn't told her the truth.

"I didnae tell ye, because I didnae wish ye to be carrying such a heavy burden into yer battle with Brielle. I knew ye would be under a great deal of pressure, and if ye knew that the world as we know it was on the line… well, I didnae want ye to be worried about failing."

"Does Uncle Angus know?" Maggie was concerned that Angus had only heard Brielle's side of the story.

"Yer Uncle doesnae ken all the details, but he kens that I love him and ye. I wouldnae have put ye both in harm's way for selfish reasons. I knew ye could defeat her, Maggie, but I didnae ken that Angus would end up in her clutches and that terrified me. I have thought many times that the bridge is a burden I wish was someone else's responsibility, but in reality, I'm happy to be the keeper of the bridge and I will never allow anyone to use it with evil intent. The bridge itself is not what's important here, it's what could have been done with it."

Maggie was finally beginning to understand how crucial it had been for her to destroy Brielle. "What about the MacKenzies? Do you think Brielle would have hurt them if she'd won?"

"First of all, she didnae win, but, yes, I was worried for the Mac-Kenzies. I am fond of them all and wouldnae wish to see any harm come to them. Brielle knew that and she used it against me and I believe she would have been intent on destroying them simply because of their relationship with me."

"And what of Richard, Auntie? I'm so worried about him." Maggie had thought of Richard often since the day he disappeared. She hoped that wherever he was, he was well and happy.

"As I've told ye, Richard is safe. I saw to it that he didnae come to any harm from Brielle. I could see that ye had yer hands full with her and I wanted to take that worry away from ye."

"But where is he?" Maggie asked.

"He is where he needs to be in order to find his happiness. We may see him again yet, dinnae worry."

"Auntie, I have some good news," Maggie said, relieved to know Richard was okay. "Dylan and I are to be married!"

"Oh, my dear girl, I am so verra happy. I knew he was the one for ye. I wish I was there to give ye both a big hug and to welcome Dylan to the family."

"Ye'll be able to soon enough. We'll be coming home soon." At least Maggie thought they'd be going back to Glendaloch together. She hadn't even thought to have that conversation with Dylan, just assuming that he'd want to leave Breaghacraig when she did.

"I'm happy to hear it and I cannae wait to congratulate ye both when ye get here. If ye need me, just call to me Maggie. I'm always here for ye."

"Good night, Auntie," Maggie said, as Edna's voice faded away. She was anxious to get back to Glendaloch as soon as possible. She didn't want her parents to worry unnecessarily about her absence and she felt she had a duty and a responsibility to return to The Thistle & Hive so that Edna could get away every once in a while. Edna had been tied to the inn for years and it was only recently - in fact, it was only when Maggie met Dylan for the first time - Edna had taken some time away from the inn with Angus.

Maggie was a bit chilly, so from her cocoon of furs on the bed, she stoked the fire with her magick and enjoyed the immediate increase in warmth that filled the room. She snuggled down, missing Dylan terribly. She had become accustomed to sleeping with him and it took her quite a long time to relax enough to fall asleep.

Chapter 20

Angus had been pacing nervously back and forth for hours each day, as he awaited the arrival of Lena, Ewan and the boys, Rowan and Ranald.

"Uncle, they'll be here soon enough," Maggie assured him. "It's been a few days since Robert sent word, so if they left right away, they should be arriving today."

"I ken that, Maggie, but I havnae seen my daughter in a verra long time."

"Well, I'm certain she hasnae forgotten ye, if that's what yer afraid of." Maggie hadn't seen Lena herself, since she had been about sixteen years old, but she remembered her clearly. She had always admired her older, more sophisticated cousin. She didn't get to see her verra often, since Maggie's family lived in another town where they ran a small tea-shop. She was looking forward to seeing Lena again and meeting her little cousins. She understood how Angus felt, because she was nervous and excited about Lena's arrival herself. "Yer going to wear a hole in the floor with all that pacing. Why dinnae ye come sit for a wee bit," Maggie suggested.

"Aye. Perhaps I should." Angus had hardly made it to the chair when cries came from the battlements and he shot through the door and out into the courtyard.

"They've arrived," Cailin shouted to Angus from his position at the gate. "They'll be here in a few moments."

Cailin and Cormac appeared to be as excited as Angus was. Of course, they would be thrilled - their much-loved wives were coming home. Robert came running outside as well. He headed straight to the gate and Angus followed. Dylan joined Maggie as they all waited expectantly, listening to the sounds of the horses and wagons as they drew closer. The approaching party was shouting greetings, and Maggie watched as Cormac and Cailin took off running, to greet their wives when they spied them amongst the group. The commotion got louder as horses began to come through the gates. Lena and Ewan were among the first to arrive and Maggie watched Angus, knowing he couldn't contain himself a second longer. As Lena stopped in front of him, he reached up and lifted her down from the saddle, hugging her tightly and crying with joy. Lena held on to her father just as tightly and shed her own tears. Ewan remained seated atop his horse, looking a little misty eyed himself. Two large highlanders were holding the little redheads, Rowan and Ranald, who were wrapped in furs to warm them on their journey. The men dismounted and set the boys down. Their feet no sooner hit the ground than they were circling Angus and Lena.

"Grandda! Grandda!" They tugged on his kilt and Angus finally let Lena go, so he could pick up one grandson in each arm. They threw their arms around his neck and each kissed a cheek. "Don't cry, Grandda," Rowan said, gently wiping the tears from Angus' cheek.

"I'm only crying because I'm so happy to finally hold ye in me arms," Angus said, kissing each boy on the forehead.

"Da, it's so good to see ye again," Lena said. "I've missed ye so much." Ewan had dismounted and joined her now and they both enfolded Angus and the boys in a warm embrace.

"Maggie," Angus called. "Come see yer cousin."

Lena threw her arms around Maggie and then held her away from herself, so she could take a good look. "Ye've grown into a beautiful woman, Maggie."

"Thank ye, cousin. It's been such a long time, but I'd know ye anywhere." They both laughed and hugged each other again. Maggie then turned to Angus, who still held his grandsons. "And who have we here?" she asked.

"'Tis me," Ranald said.

"And me," Rowan chimed in.

"Is that so, now?" Maggie chucked them both under the chin. "Well, I'm yer cousin, Maggie and I'm verra happy to make yer acquaintance." They obviously didn't want to leave their Grandda, so Maggie gave them each a kiss on the cheek, instead of trying to hold them.

"There's quite the family resemblance," Dylan observed. "You all have the same red hair and green eyes."

Across the courtyard, Maggie observed Cailin and Cormac each keeping a firm hold on their wives, who looked overjoyed to be home and in their husband's arms once again. Robert was kissing Irene and then bent to kiss and hug each of their children. Maggie brushed a tear from her cheek and leaned into Dylan for support.

"They're a very special group of people, wouldn't you say?" Dylan asked.

"Aye. Verra special indeed. 'Tis good to see people who love each other so much and who feel so much joy at being reunited. I only wish Auntie Edna were here. She should be here, too. She'd love to see Lena again and meet her grandbabes." Maggie felt a bit heartbroken that Edna hadn't been able to make this journey with Angus.

"Maybe she'll be able to come sometime soon," Dylan suggested. Maggie knew he was trying to make her feel better. He was so sweet and thoughtful that way. "Maybe when we go back to Glendaloch, she can take some time away from the inn to come visit."

"You mean you're really going to come back to Glendaloch with me," Maggie said, excited to hear this news.

"Of course, was there ever any question?" Dylan appeared surprised at Maggie's words. "We're going to be married, why wouldn't I be coming with you?"

"I don't know. I just thought... we'd never talked about it and... well, I wasn't sure you wanted to leave your cousin behind."

"As long as we can come back and visit every once in a while, I don't mind at all. You're my life now, Maggie. I can't imagine spending a moment of it without you."

Overjoyed and relieved, Maggie threw herself into Dylan's arms. "I love you so much," she said.

"And I love you," Dylan answered. "We'll make a good life in Glendaloch." He had a serious expression on his face now. "I have one question though."

Maggie wasn't sure what that question could be. "What is it?"

"Can I bring Chester?" Dylan asked.

"I wouldn't think of leaving him," Maggie answered.

Dylan looked deeply into her eyes. "You know, all these years, I've thought I was incapable of loving someone and now, I know that I'd only been waiting for you."

Epilogue

Maggie and Dylan approached the bridge at mid-afternoon and were pleased to see the fog was already there waiting for them. Dylan called to Chester, making sure that he stayed right by their side as they rode into the grey mass in front of them. As usual, they could see and hear nothing except for the small lightning strikes of color that flashed around them. Within moments, they found themselves in the clear. Maggie checked to make certain they were all accounted for and then smiled as she spotted Edna waiting for them.

"Auntie, it's so good to see you," Maggie said, beaming from ear to ear.

"I'm so happy yer back, my dear, but where is your uncle. Did ye lose him?" Edna anxiously searched the bridge. The fog had dissipated and Angus was not with them.

"Auntie, he wanted to stay and spend some more time with Lena and the children. He knew ye'd understand," Maggie explained.

"I see." Edna stopped speaking for a moment and her bottom lip trembled. "I was hoping…" Edna burst into tears.

Both Dylan and Maggie leaped down from their mounts and ran to her. Maggie gathered Edna into her arms. "I'm so sorry Auntie. I know you've missed him."

Edna sniffled and dabbed at her eyes with a hankie. "It's just that we've nae been apart since we first met. I thought he'd want to come home to me, but I do understand he wants more time with Lena and the babes. Do ye really believe he'll come back, Maggie?"

Maggie had never seen her aunt so distraught and she wanted to reassure her that Angus hadn't abandoned her. "He does want to come home to ye, but he didnae know whether he'd get another opportunity to enjoy the boys while they're still small." Maggie took Edna's arm and they started their walk back to the inn. Dylan and Chester followed along behind, leading the horses.

"Did he say when he will return?" Edna asked, appearing for all the world as if she might burst into tears again.

"I think he'd like to stay for Christmas and return soon after," Maggie said gently.

Edna wasn't saying anything and her silence had Maggie a bit worried. She peeked back over her shoulder at Dylan, sending him a pleading look.

"Edna, I wonder if maybe you'd like to join Angus? Maggie and I can take care of the inn. It would be no trouble and you'd get to spend the holiday with your family." Dylan winked at Maggie.

"But who would mind the bridge?" Edna sputtered. "I'm the bridge keeper."

"I would, Auntie. I believe it's time for a changing of the guard, so to speak. It's about time you had a life away from the responsibility of the bridge. I'm sure ye can trust me to guard it in yer absence. I'll be here when ye both return, which I hope will be for Hogmanay, as that's when Dylan and I plan to marry." Maggie stopped and turned to Edna. Searching her face, she could see Edna was obviously thinking carefully about what she and Dylan had suggested.

"Well, we've a lot to talk about then, and many plans to make," Edna finally said, regaining her composure.

Maggie smiled back at Dylan, happy to be on familiar ground once again. The path back to the inn was one she knew like the back of her hand, having spent much time exploring it alongside Edna and

Angus. Before she knew it, they were on the road heading for the inn. The ever-present Teddy was waiting for them.

"Teddy, please take the horses to Mrs. MacDougall's barn. Then come right back, I have some news to share with ye," Edna requested.

Teddy took the horses from Dylan and petted Chester on the head before leading them off towards Mrs. MacDougall's property. The big dog made his way to Edna's side, seeming to understand that she needed some comforting. She leaned over and rubbed his ears affectionately. "And how was your adventure, Chester?" she asked. He wagged his stubby little tail in answer. "Come, let's go inside. Have ye eaten?"

Maggie giggled at that. It was typical of Edna to worry about everyone else, even when she was dealing with her own sadness. They headed into the dining room, which was empty at this time of the day. Edna kept it closed until dinnertime, so they had the place to themselves. After they were seated, Edna hustled off to the kitchen while they made themselves at home.

"What do you think? Do you mind this being our new home?" Maggie asked Dylan with a questioning gaze.

"I'm very happy to be here. You might not believe this, but I've always wanted to live in a small town. I think it's the reason I loved Breaghacraig. Everyone knows everyone else. It's a tight knit community where friendships and unbreakable bonds are made to last a lifetime."

"True, but sometimes living in a small town is like living in a fish bowl," Maggie said.

"That's part of its charm," Dylan replied, in his usual laid-back style.

Edna returned a short while later, with a tray of food for Maggie and Dylan, along with a bowl of food for Chester. "Chester," Edna called. "I've brought ye a treat."

Chester, who had been napping in front of the fire, perked up immediately, cocking his head to the side and making Edna laugh.

"Here ye go, my sweet." Edna placed the bowl in front of him. Chester didn't hesitate for a second, diving right in and finishing up before Edna even got back to the table to sit with Maggie and Dylan. "So, ye wish to marry on Hogmanay," Edna said. "We've nae much time to plan."

"We don't need anything elaborate, Auntie. Just a small gathering of our families and some friends." Maggie glanced at Dylan who was nodding in agreement as she spoke.

"It will be lovely, Maggie. We'll have it right here at the inn. What do ye think?" Edna asked.

"That would be perfect. But what about you, Auntie? Will ye be crossing the bridge?" Maggie reached out to hold Edna's hand. "I believe I've proved myself capable. Do ye trust me to guard the bridge for ye?"

"I do, Maggie. I trust ye verra much. And ye Dylan. Ye will be here to help her and that eases my mind. I cannae tell ye how happy I am for the both of ye."

"And we're happy for you," Dylan said. "You've spent your whole life orchestrating the comings and goings across the bridge and now it's your turn. You get to go on an adventure."

"Aye. I do and I'm happy to go, but first I must be sure ye ken how the inn runs, so I willnae go right away."

"But ye will go soon. Uncle Angus will be missing ye as much as ye miss him. Ye cannae keep him waiting." Maggie new it was hard for Edna to give up control of the inn and the bridge, so she understood that it would probably take a few days, maybe even a week, before Edna could bear to pass the baton to her.

"Aye. Dinnae worry about me. Now, eat yer food and then ye can go get settled in upstairs for a rest."

"Auntie, Dylan and I will be sharing a room," Maggie stated firmly, although she was somewhat afraid of what Edna's reaction might be.

"Why would ye nae?" Edna asked, winking. "I'm not as old fashioned as ye may think, miss. And dinnae ye think that yer meeting was accidental. I may have had a wee bit to do with it."

"Well, I'm happy you did, Edna," Dylan said as he gave her a hug. "Very happy indeed.

About the Author

Jenna was born and raised a New England girl, just outside of Boston, Massachusetts, where her imagination was always bigger than she was. Surrounded by an abundance of nostalgic, historical landmarks her love of history and creative writing was formed. Her large extended Irish and Italian families were not only a great source of support and inspiration, but her home was always filled with laughter, love, lots of good food and amazing story telling.

After years of wearing many different career caps, Jennae was determined to do something she had always loved and her vivid imagination took over once again as she decided to follow her dream of writing stories that tapped into her love of magical people and places.

Jennae now lives in the San Francisco Bay Area with her husband, where they've raised two beautiful and talented children. Along the way they've gathered a menagerie of pets, including dogs, cats, chickens and horses to make their family complete.

Other books by Jennae Vale

The Thistle & Hive Series

Book One - A Bridge Through Time
Book Two - A Thistle Beyond Time

Coming in 2015

A Thistle & Hive Christmas
A Matter of Time - Book Four of The Thistle & Hive Series